AND SO IT BEGINS

A NOVEL

KATI KIRSTEN

This is a work of fiction. Names, characters, places, and incidents either are the product of the author's imagination or are used fictitiously, and any resemblance to actual persons, living or dead, business establishments, events, or locales is entirely coincidental.

No part of this book may be reproduced or transmitted in any form or by any means, electronic or mechanical, including photocopying, recording, or by any information storage and retrieval system without the written permission of the author, except for the use of brief quotations in a book review.

Copyright @ 2023 Kaitlyn Kirsten
Copyright @ 2023 Original Cover Art by GetCovers
Copyright @ 2023 Interior Design & Typesetting by Stephanie Kirsten
Editing Help By Clare Sloane, Stephanie Romano, and Annelle Snyder

The Story of Life and Death is the synopsis for Life & Death(A Love Story) by Double-TroubleWriting on Wattpad. The Story of Life and Death is not my idea and is simply used as its own story within this work.

All rights reserved.

Paperback: 979 – 8 – 9852274 – 4 – 4
Hardcover: 979 – 8 – 9852274 – 3 – 7
EBook: 979 – 8 – 9852274 – 5 – 1

To Kendra, the exceptional
You are the brightest young girl I know.

AND SO IT BEGINS

AMITY'S DIARY ○ JULY 26ᵀᴴ

THEY SAY ANNIVERSARIES ARE THE worst. I'm inclined to agree. The feeling pressing down on my chest is as dreadful as it was when it all happened. The nightmares are even worse. My own failure and guilt are twisted into a sickening concoction of painful memories and tethering fears.

In a few days it will be one year since I lost Zach, the kind soul that sacrificed his own life so that I could keep mine. That means Emma's one-year is right around the corner. My sweet, little sister gone for a year. It's almost too painful to believe.

Writing that out made my chest ache. I thought looking out the window would ease the pain, but my eyes found their way to yet another heartbreak, sending my mind into overdrive. As always, Sarge sensed my silent plea for help and pushed his warmth into me, giving me the strength to continue. What would I do without him?

Okay. I know I need to get this off my chest. Why? The trees on the edge of the property line are stripped of their bark. I've gone out every day to beat the shit out of them—the way Zach would want me to—but it doesn't help. So maybe this will. I need to work through my feelings, and something about writing drives my soul closer to my father's. I'm certain of it...

There'd been movement through the leaves and I took a moment to watch as Luke, the rogue A.L.F officer that helped get us into Force territory last year, made his way into the backyard amongst the tattered trunks. He's been a Godsend; hunting for food, finding water. Luke promised to stay with me. And, even though we were never meant to stay this long, he's kept his promise.

Mason and Abby, the brother sister duo that made our runaway group feel like a true family, needed medical attention as soon as possible. I'm hopeful that everything went well. Certainly they're wondering where we are, but I'm having a hard time leaving my mother and Emma behind. Anyhow, there's some solace in staying at my old house.

Zach once told me that it's okay to take a moment to try and hold on to my Humanity, but I think even he would agree that I've been hiding behind the comfort. Spending time in my own home with Luke and Sarge, living off the land, has given me a false sense of normality. It's kept me from fulfilling my promise: To kickstart a rebellion.

They say anniversaries are the worst, but maybe they serve as a reminder; stirring up old emotions and reigniting the fires that fuel the need to avenge. We must rise up and fight back. I've taken enough time. I won't let the Guardianship get away with it any longer…

CHAPTER ONE ○ LUKE

I'm staring at the yellowing ceiling, M cocooned in the crook of my arm, Sarge pressing her body closer to mine. The inevitable shift in her breath, when her nightmares take over and push her to new lows, will be here soon. So I'm waiting.

I've barely slept at all myself. How would I aid M with her night terrors if mine take me far away first? It's not like I need sleep to feel haunted these days, anyway. Instead, I stay awake, because exhaustion is the lesser of two evils.

It's probably four—maybe five—in the morning and she's only been asleep for an hour or so. Today is the one year anniversary of Emma's death.

I wish that M didn't have to know such pain. I would do anything if it meant I could consume her suffering, absorbing it as my own. My Force days plague my mind, but that's nothing compared to witnessing the agony in her eyes as everyone close to her is stolen. It's a wonder she still keeps me around.

An hour or two passes before M stirs next to me. It starts with a groan, then morphs into a series of incoherent shouts. My palm trails along her cheek; my fingers hook behind her head.

"M," I whisper.

"No," she cries, "no!" Her eyes pop open, and it takes a moment for the panic to subside. Once it does, her features soften. "Hi." Her voice is as small as her smile.

"Hi."

"I can't do this anymore." Her brow furrows while whatever is bothering her bounces around in her head. My brain doesn't comprehend what she means and, deep down, there's a part of me that's scared she's sending me away. Amity is an enigma that always keeps me guessing. "I can't stay here another night." Phew! At least it's not about me.

She wants to revolt. She says she wants to avenge Emma's death—Zach, M's friend, and other innocents like him, too. It's likely that a part of her yearns to see the people who did this to her suffer in the same way, even if she won't admit it to herself yet. But I completely understand.

What she doesn't know is that things have changed. The Force presence is heavier than ever in town. A Slum Trader explained that the Guardianship is condensing everyone into common areas and blocking the way out. They found an easier way to track us; control us. I think it's safe to say that Ren Keres is entering her endgame.

Far be it from me to walk away from a good brush with Death, but I'm tempted to keep M knocked out until I'm able to carry her out of this damn country. We should've left ages ago. She needed her time, I respect that. Hell, I'd live out the rest of my days here with her if I could, but it's only a matter of time before the Force comes busting down the door.

"Can we rebel from Canada?" I talk lightly. The softness of my voice never ceases to surprise me. I hadn't realized how sweet its timbre could be until dealing with M. Say goodbye to the hard and harsh officer I once was. I don't want to set her off, especially not today. I've been on the receiving end of M's wrath more times than I'd like to admit and it's not a fun place to be.

Her grey eyes tumble as they roll back into her skull. I'll take that as a no. She opens her mouth to reply, but the TV turns on, the

Guardianship's Update music blaring through the speakers. This is the only time that commoners get the luxury of television.

On the screen pops a video feed. A room. One from Omphalos. The camera is stationed in the upper corner, and the view shows the room at an angle. The only thing not visible is the door to the hallway.

I've got an inkling for what this is about. M's body tenses beside me, telling me she knows exactly what's going to happen. Sarge lifts his large frame up and crawls, wiggling his way onto M's lap. Any suspicion I have about the video is now confirmed.

A nurse enters the room. A young girl clings to one hand, a syringe is dangling from the other. This is the moment that Amity lost Emma. The slight trembles of M's muscles pierce my heart as she tries to keep herself calm.

I don't know exactly what happened that day, and I've never dared to ask. I only found her after; when Emma was already gone and Sarge was tearing the nurse apart. The information they had on Emma needed to be destroyed so that her tracker was useless, which left me hung up in the control room. I sure as hell wasn't expecting to find her the way I did.

"We don't have to watch this," I assure. "I'll bring you to another room."

"No," she answers. "I'm fine." There's no conviction in her voice to back up her claim. Stubborn as ever. There's nothing she needs to prove in watching this again, not to me at least. I'm sure she sees it every time she closes her eyes.

The audio kicks on, pulling my eyes back to the screen. The nurse is talking. "It will only be a pinch."

"And then I'll see Amity?" Emma's voice is hopeful, yet wary.

The nurse nods and motions for Emma to get into place. She crawls across the nurse's lap, laying diagonally. "Ready?"

"Will Sarge be there, too?" Emma questions with big, round eyes. "What about Daddy?"

The innocence of her voice is too much to bear, even for me. M's heart must be splintering into a million pieces right now. Her sniffles leave an ache in my chest as I pull her closer. She's not made a peep until now. I want to look at her, to make sure she's okay, but she doesn't like feeling pitied. So, I keep my eyes transfixed on the screen.

The nurse doesn't answer. Instead, he slowly inserts the needle. A loud crashing sound slams through the speakers. Then M is in the room. Emma's eyes widen as she strains to stand, but the nurse holds her tight before her head leans back and her body goes limp. M falls to her knees in front of them. The scream that exits her throat kills me as she looks up to the ceiling with an expression filled with anguish.

I hadn't realized she watched her pass; I was under the impression she found her that way. Poor M. Ren did this on purpose. There's no denying it now. She knew we were coming. The timing is too right to ignore.

The video cuts off before Sarge is shown tearing the limbs from the nurse, and long before I get there to pull M from the void she was sucked into. Instead, a picture of Ren fills the frame. Her evil eyes throw daggers through the glass. She's making an official address.

"People of Western America, you are now witness to a rebel getting their punishment. Rules and laws keep us safe. They keep us from breaking into war. Those that try to oppose the Guardianship *must* be punished." Her face tenses while she struggles to hold herself together. Ren gets worked up over law and order. Her superior sense of right and wrong has always been a driving force in her life, and I let her sweep me up into it, too. "Let this be a reminder to all citizens with rebellion on their minds. This could be you." Her voice is chilled and scratchy.

Ren Keres shoots a sharp glare into the camera before the screen goes black. M is no longer trembling. I turn to find a blank stare on her face. She sits quietly for some time before a look of determination settles in her eyes. Finally, she shifts to meet my gaze.

"I'm going to put a bullet between her eyes."

The way she's acting isn't like her. It sends me down the dark tunnels of my mind. Ren's voice is clear in my head. *Put a bullet between her eyes, Mr. Warin,* she orders me. *Make sure her family sees.*

I'm snapped out of the horror just as fast as I'd got sucked in. A shudder rips through me, but my body holds steady. M is not the first to be scorned by Ren; I've experienced all too well the pain that she inflicts. But I also know that she usually comes out on top. Unfortunately, there's no time to think of a reply before Sarge is upright and growling in the direction of the door.

A split second passes before he takes off, rushing through the frame into the living room. I speedily push myself out of bed. M scurries closely behind. It doesn't take long to find what Sarge had heard.

There's a rolling fog coming from underneath the front door. "Sarge, get back," I urge. He hesitates before returning to M's side as she motions him over.

"What is that?"

"We've got to leave now," I divulge. The door is smacked with a large object in the same second. I know I should explain to M what's going on, but I want her head clear.

Thankfully, we have every exit rigged to withstand a certain amount of pressure. At least that will buy us some time. The bad news is that I'm not sure which exit will be ours.

"Go, M!" I gently nudge her toward the back door. The fog is spreading throughout the place now, and if we get any closer, we'll be exposed.

I've had to use the fog in the Force. It's a gas that emulates fire. Standing in it would be like standing in open flames. Searing pain, blisters, lung damage. The officers can control its path, making it avoid certain people. If the goal is to kill us all, they could by sealing us in and unleashing it without constraint. But my guess is that they have a plan, and not everyone here is going to be left for dead.

CHAPTER TWO ○ AMITY

Luke hurries toward the front door. Whatever is flowing through the crack underneath is swirling in large waves at a faster pace than before. *Why couldn't you just tell me what it is, asshole,* I think to myself.

Sarge is leading me to the back. The kitchen and dining room area is safe from the fog, though it won't stay that way for long. I reach out to move the locks and barriers, but Sarge gently puts his mouth around my arm.

"What?" I whisper, though it's clear what he's trying to tell me. The same threat must be outside this door as well.

The thumping gets louder, more pressing, and the crack of splitting wood fills the air. Sarge jumps up, urging me to follow him to the living room again. I do. Just in time, too, because the fog is now rolling in from the back door as well.

"Luke," I call.

We round the corner to see that he's standing, gun in hand, ready to stave off whatever enemies come barreling through. He wants to buy me some time.

"Amity, go!" he says. The door busts open.

It takes my brain a few seconds to tell my feet to move, then Sarge and I bolt into my dad's old bedroom. I ignore the growing ache in my chest as I assess the surroundings. The windows have been boarded up for quite some time. Luke even reinforced them when we got here last year. The only window that wasn't reinforced is the skylight. That seems like our best bet.

How will I reach it? It's hard to imagine lifting myself out, let alone Sarge. Plus we're working on borrowed time. I should be working out ideas, but instead I'm focused on keeping the panic from weighing me down. Anxiety will get me nowhere.

"Where is she?" a voice I don't recognize booms from the other room. Luke retorts with his own set of curses.

I survey the area to form a quick plan. The skylight is in the middle of the room. This means I'll have to push the bed there first. Then, I'll need more height. *Ugh.*

"Come on, Sarge." I lead him to the king-sized frame. "Push."

He heaves his body against the side of the bed as I brace my elbows and lock my arms. It takes a few seconds to build the momentum we need, but we're able to shimmy the frame, positioning it directly under the skylight. I quickly grab an old box from the corner, making an effort to sturdy it in the middle of the mattress for the extra height.

Climbing up, I stretch my body, grabbing at the old boards that cover the glass. They splinter beneath my hands and it's like my fingers are going to bleed at any moment. "Come on." I push myself. "Come on!" The wood creaks and cracks as I pull, until finally they're torn from the surface. *Great. Now you'll have to break the glass and your hands are already busted up, Amity.*

The angle isn't ideal—well, really nothing about this situation is —but thankfully the window is already cracked. I rear back and jab my elbow upwards into the glass and it connects with a *thunk*. I do it again, and again, pushing harder, ignoring the pain, until the glass shatters and showers down around me in shimmering shards.

"Alright, Sarge, you first."

Sarge steps back from the bed. The exit is only so big and

lifting him isn't an option, so there's one shot to get this right. Lining myself up with the opening, I arch my back, bending as if I'm going to touch my toes. Sarge rips forward, leaping gracefully onto the mattress. Then he continues, connecting all four paws onto my back and I push up slightly as he angles himself through the broken glass.

He shoots past and claws his way onto the roof. As he steadies himself on the ledge, Luke plows through the door with a trail of fog around him.

"Go," he coughs, sputtering. "Hurry!"

Luke's body is red, raw, and blistery. His muscles are tensing and contracting as the fog swirls around him. I hesitate, but pull myself up through the opening, ignoring the pain in my elbow and gritting my teeth as the broken shards of glass rip across my stomach. Sarge grabs onto my shirt to help me the rest of the way. An intense, searing pain spreads along my ankles before my feet exit the room. A howl bellows from deep within my chest, unexpectedly.

Luke is right behind me now and he shoulders me up and out. My pant legs are singed and my skin is burned. *What the hell?* I quickly turn to grab Luke, ignoring the blazing my arms receive while reaching them back into the fog.

Fumbling through the haze, I finally connect with Luke's bicep, completely sticky from the sweat and scarring. I guide his hand up, and Sarge and I work tirelessly to yank him out. The expression on his face unnerves me, but he's still half in control of his body as he stands.

"Woods," he wheezes, "now."

The drop from the roof isn't so bad. I land, tumbling behind Sarge. It's Luke who grunts and contorts as he falls. It won't be long before the officers along the front and back notice us taking off toward the tree line, but for now we have a slight head start.

We flee to the forest surrounding my house and a strong sense of déjà vu takes over me. Only now, instead of leaving my father behind, I'm leaving my mother and Emma. No goodbye, no closure. Sarge keeps his pace with me just as easily as always, but Luke is stumbling ruggedly, the pain from his wounds clearly too much for him.

The fog must have been modified somehow. My ankles throb with burns, like I stuck them in a fire. Same with my arms. Luke seems to be dealing with severe second degree burns almost all over his body. Who knows what damage there is on the inside from the inhalation. I shudder, suddenly hyper aware and fearful that he won't make it.

The thud of pounding footsteps and angered shouts ricochet through the woods, the echo chasing us. I don't allow myself to panic too much, though it's tough to manage. Right now, I have to focus on our escape.

We run for a while, my lungs burning. Luke's breath is a raspy wheeze somewhere behind me. I think we've outrun—and outsmarted—the officers, but something doesn't feel right. Fear creeps up under my skin and pokes into every nerve ending as we continue.

It's not long before Sarge does a quick turn, stopping suddenly. I match his actions and turn to find Luke heaving, his face red as can be.

"Are you okay?" My heart thumps in my chest. It's a stupid question, really. Clearly, he's not.

And yet: "Fine," he spits, barely recognizable. It's like it takes too much energy to fully enunciate the word.

"You look…" I start, but then I'm interrupted as Luke's hazel eyes roll into the back of his head. He slams to the ground with a loud thud. "Shit!"

Sarge and I double back, rushing to get to Luke. When my hand reaches his arm, my palm burns from the heat. *Holy smokes! He's scorching!*

What am I going to do? These types of wounds are probably too much for even a medically advanced salve such as Regrowth, and all we'll be lucky enough to find is normal medicine, if any. *Damn it, Luke, hang in there! You told me you weren't going anywhere.*

"Can you hold him on your back, Sarge?" Luke's weight might be too much for Sarge to handle, but if I can drape him over his back, we'd at least be able to search for help. If not, it would kill me to struggle and drag him. Or worse...leave him here to die.

Sarge answers by standing tall, bracing his legs for the extra pounds. Carefully wrapping my arms around Luke, I strain and stretch to shimmy his motionless body up and over Sarge's back. Luke's feet and arms are scraping along either side, but Sarge is holding him up pretty well.

"Can you walk?"

Sarge steps forward, his legs wobbling as he gets used to the added weight. Then he steps again more confidently. By the third and fourth steps, he's keeping the momentum, so I start walking alongside of him, pressing my palm against Luke's back to steady him. *You still with me, Luke? Don't you die on me!*

Eventually we make it to a small cluster of houses. Seeing them in the distance causes my heart to flutter with both hope and fear. My instincts tell me to run away, but my brain says to push on. Ransacking them is the only way we'll find something to help Luke with.

Sarge and I close the distance, carefully coming to the first house of the group. "You wait out here." My voice quivers as I step onto the rickety porch of splintering beams. It creaks under my slight weight while I cross toward the door. *Please be empty of people, please be empty of people.*

I push through the dilapidated door into a shoddy living room. The sun is creeping up higher now and just barely lights the room through the boarded windows. The first thing I notice is the giant hole in the middle of the floor. It's an open abyss funneling down into a deep, dirt pit.

Everything is covered with dust, and cobwebs fill every corner, even draping from the broken ceiling fan like vines. The house looks like a backdrop to the horror stories my father used to tell me. I glide along the floor, praying my weight isn't enough to send me plummeting through.

Hastening around the house, I locate the bathrooms and rummage through cabinets in hopes to get lucky with finding a stack of medicine or painkillers; something, anything to help Luke hold on until a better plan presents itself in my mind. Unfortunately, nothing can be found, so I exit the first house, moving onto the next one a few hundred feet away.

As I step outside, a quick once-over of Luke is done subconsciously; a few seconds' halt to check if his chest is still rising and falling. It is, but subtly.

The next house is as useless as the first, and as I finish rummaging, Sarge barks from outside. I bolt through the rooms, blasting through the door to find Sarge pointing his snout in the direction of the house after the next one in line. My heart crashes down into my stomach, my instinct to survive taking over.

Grabbing Luke's gun from his waistband, I lower myself as Sarge and I ease our way to the house. "What is it, Sarge?"

His body language is somewhat rigid while closing the distance. *Maybe he just saw an animal?* But as we get closer, the door squeaks, and two beady eyes recede back into the shadows. The gun trembles in my palms. Suddenly I feel like running. Gathering up all of my courage, I muster up a harshness into my tone; one that demands an answer.

"Show yourself."

Sarge is alert next to me, but he's not in a defensive stance. It's unclear if this is due to the fact that Luke's weight is pressing him down, or if the stranger isn't a threat. Either way, the gun stays trained on the person through the door. This may not be the idiot-proof one from the Force I used a year ago, but Luke taught me how to shoot. There's no way they'll be getting out alive if that's what it comes to.

A few grueling seconds pass before the door creaks open and a tiny, old lady hobbles onto the porch. The gun lowers in its position, my subconscious telling me not to pull the trigger. I side-eye Sarge and, after confirming his body is completely relaxed, I lower the gun the rest of the way.

The old woman has a full head of grey hair that trails down her back in a long braid. Her skin is a deep shade, indicative of a long life lived in the sun. Her wrinkles settle on her face in symmetrically asymmetric patterns, and her eyes are a deep blue that remind me of Mason's. Her body is short and plump as she shuffles.

"Can you help him?" My voice breaks when my head tilts toward Luke. The woman's face shows no worry as she looks over his body draped across Sarge's back.

"Come," her voice rasps.

CHAPTER THREE ○ AMITY

Sarge and I carefully follow the old lady into her crumbling home. Once we enter, my nose is bombarded with all types of fragrances. The house is cleaner than I anticipated, and much brighter. None of the windows are boarded. Instead, deep black curtains cover the ones in the front. The ones in the back are wide open, letting air and sunlight cascade through the kitchen.

"Help your friend get him up the stairs, into the first room. I'll be there shortly."

The lady continues forward toward the kitchen and I tilt my head, studying the steep staircase to my left. How in the hell are we going to get Luke up there? Sarge maneuvers his body, positioning himself at the base of the stairs. I decide standing behind him to keep Luke from sliding off his back is the best option. We move as one up the incline, but it definitely isn't graceful. At one point, I almost slip, causing havoc for Sarge.

We finally make it to the top and into the first room after struggling for what feels like a century. The room is bare except for a large, flat table-bed in the middle of the floor. Sarge steers me toward the center, and I shimmy Luke's limp body onto the platform, carefully. He groans as I slide him against the cloth and wood. *Don't give up yet, jackass.*

A few silent minutes pass before the shuffling sound of unsteady feet filters up from the base of the steps. Dishes clink as the old woman shakes, carrying her tray into the room and setting it beside Luke.

"Would you be a dear and help me remove his garments?"

My face flushes red, but I nod, positioning myself on the opposite side of her. Her expression remains impassive while we peel the fabric from Luke's sticky, blistering skin. Mine, on the other hand, is showing something along the lines of horror mixed with embarrassment. *Poor Luke.* His flesh is covered in burns. There's barely any healthy skin on him. I've not seen him without clothes on in over a year, and it feels wrong to see him like this. Considering we've never officially had a conversation about what our relationship is these days, it's like I'm crossing a boundary.

The old woman reaches for her tray, fiddling with some greenery, pushing it out of her way. *Can I trust this woman I've just met?* I'm eyeing her cautiously. She must notice, because she gives an explanation for everything she's doing.

"Treating burns is fairly simple," she starts. "A cool compress, some aloe and calendula extract, maybe some honey and leaves." She's dipping old strips of cloth into a deep bowl, then wringing them out with her crooked fingers. "How long ago?"

It takes me a moment to register that she's asked a question, and another to think. Two hours, at the very least, had to have passed. The sun is higher in the sky, and it was barely a sliver over the horizon when the officers stormed the house. "Maybe two hours?"

"Hmmm," groans the old woman. She lays the first piece of cloth over Luke's left ankle and then systematically places them up his body. "The compress will alleviate the burning sensation and, hopefully, stop the wounds from burrowing deeper."

I'm hearing her words, but something within me won't let me be hopeful. A regular burn may be easy to treat, but what about the aftermath of an engineered fog? I've lost so many people in my life—felt so much heartache—that the thought of one more is threatening to send my teetering soul over the edge.

"What's your name, dear?" the woman asks with kind eyes and a gentle voice.

Snapping out of my rapid-fire thoughts, a whisper passes my lips. "Amity."

She smiles a toothy smile, revealing several missing teeth. "What a lovely name," she coos. "My name is Josephine, but please, call me Nan."

I allow myself to break into a small smile for a second before my brow furrows. "Do you really believe he'll make it?" My voice cracks at the last syllable, the weight of the question crashing down. I'm worried that something as simple as aloe vera or honey won't be enough to push through the severity of Luke's wounds.

"Trust in this old lady, will ya?" She smiles confidently, causing her face to gain wrinkles. "The Guardianship may know a thing or two about science, but nature is on our side, dear. Have faith."

It's an hour before Josephine is done with Luke. The first thing she had done was pour something into his mouth, clenching his jaw with her crooked fingers, forcing him to swallow. Luke groaned and grumbled as she cleaned him up, but for the most part he stayed knocked out. She rubbed aloe and calendula extract all over his body. The last thing she does is smear honey onto giant leaves and wrap them around the worst areas like bandages.

"There," she says. "The only thing we can do now is wait." She places her small hand on my shoulder and gently squeezes.

"Thank you, Nan." I fail to sound soft. Instead, my voice is clipped and stoic. I truly am grateful for what she's done—I could never repay her—but something inside of me doesn't allow my emotions to show.

"His body is doing most of the work now," she explains.

"Something tells me he's a fighter." Her wrinkled face lifts when her lips curl in a sweet smile. "Why don't you let him rest? There's another bedroom right next door." I know what she really means is that I should get some rest, myself.

I nod.

Josephine hobbles out of the room and out of sight. My gaze turns to Luke lying motionless on the platform. His body is rigid and the redness of his skin is hard to miss. It pokes out along the edges of the thick leaves. There's a tight expression on his face. *You could've lost him, Amity.* I shudder.

I get up and lean forward, kissing his cheek ever-so-lightly, before escorting Sarge on a search for Josephine. I need something to keep my mind off of Luke. We traipse to the now dingy-looking kitchen where Nan is fiddling with some cookware. She's raising herself to a normal stature as we enter. There's a teapot in her shaky hands. She smiles.

"Something told me you'd find me." She shuffles toward her water bucket to fill up the pot.

My body plops down into one of the rickety chairs and I sigh quietly to myself. Sarge immediately lays down at my feet, putting his head on his paws.

The kitchen is adorned with old fixtures and appliances. The paint on the walls is dulled and chipping, but the greenery hanging from nearly every available space has it appearing brighter than it actually is.

"What are all these plants?" I ask, attempting small talk. Curiosity has always gotten the best of me, anyway.

"My livelihood," answers Josephine. She flicks a match, lighting a small pile of sticks under the coils of the stove. She sets the teapot on top, then shuffles around, moving toward me. "These plants are the only reason I'm alive."

"What do they do?"

"All types of things!" Her face lights up, making her eyes appear younger. "My mother had been an herbalist, like her mother before her, and her mother before her." She floats around the kitchen gathering up different roots and plants before settling down in the chair next to me. "The aloe plant does wonders for burns and faint skin irritation. Feverfew helps with mild pain relief. Dandelions are high in vitamin K, C, and B6 among other things."

After each plant, she slides them into my view and encourages me to feel them, smell them, and—in the case of the dandelions—taste them. She even begins to rub the aloe on my arms, hoping to reduce the effects from the fog. Her enthusiasm makes my heart lighter. I think Emma would have clung to Josephine like a vine.

"What was it that you gave Luke?" The mystery liquid in the beginning had left me apprehensive, but now it's piqued my curiosity.

"It's a recipe I concocted," she shares. "It's chamomile, valerian, Dreamroot, and Silvershade. Brewed sweet and hot."

"What's it do?"

"Chamomile and valerian have been used for centuries for calming anxiety and stress. My great grandmother used to use this around the tribe when her people were dealing with mild pain." I listen closely as she explains. There's something exuberant about Josephine, something that makes me want to listen. "When morphine was discovered, my grandmother started making an herbal sedative tea for more severe pain."

"Morphine came from plants?" I never realized how important plants were before. Not like we would've been taught this in school, anyway. Morphine has been eradicated for a while now.

"Papaver somniferum is the scientific name. More commonly known as the Opium Poppy. The isolated morphine was an excellent painkiller, but it was highly addictive. That's why some of the best scientists came around and genetically mutated the poppy into a purer form. My mother was one of the original creators of the synthetically designed Dreamroot."

"Really?" Surprisingly, I'd heard of Dreamroot, but I've never seen it; never knew where it came from. Whatever wildlife wasn't affected by the Undoing, the war certainly took care of, and whatever happened to be left, the Guardianship wreaked havoc on. The plants here are the most green I've seen, maybe ever.

"Mhm. Dreamroot extract is non-addictive, but it puts the recipient in a dream-like state in which they feel no pain. It was kept in tight hands for a while so that demand would never surpass supply."

"So how do you have it?"

Josephine's wrinkled face lifts with a playful smile. "My mother was a crafty little devil. She snuck seeds home and cultivated her own supply. Here." She hands me a small plant with purple petals dangling from the stem.

I twirl the Dreamroot in between my fingers, studying it mildly. All that from such a tiny plant. "What about the Silvershade?"

"Similar origins. My mother was tasked with breeding a plant that could kickstart the body's healing process. Thus, Silvershade was born."

"So you gave Luke Dreamroot to keep him pain-free, and Silvershade to send his body into overdrive." It's not a question. I think I'm truly starting to realize how powerful these plants can be. *Maybe Luke* will *make it.*

"Right," she says, winking at me. "He should come to in a few days' time. I'd project about a week before he'll be up and walking."

I release a sigh of relief, attempting to keep my heart steady. He's going to recover; he has to. *I can't lose anyone else...*

The teapot starts to hiss and Josephine leaps from the chair with as much enthusiasm as her old bones will allow her, mildly startling Sarge who must've fallen asleep. He flicks his golden irises to my grey ones and snorts. A quiet chuckle breaks free from my lips at him as Josephine sets a rattling cup of tea in front of me.

"No Dreamroot in this one," she jokes.

I offer up a small smile, snaking my long, thin fingers around the ceramic. It's warm on my skin, instantly comforting me. As I sit, relaxed, thoughts of time spent in my own grandmother's house filter through. Tiny snippets are what flash in my mind because I was young, but the feeling is bittersweet. Emma never experienced Grandma's company. *She never experienced a lot of things.*

"What's the frown for?" Josephine questions, snapping me out of my intrusive thoughts.

"I was thinking I should go check on Luke." My brow furrows as I slide the chair back.

"Ah, yes. Young love." She sends a knowing smile in my direction.

My face burns red. This is something I haven't thought about... for good reason. *Do I love Luke?* "I just want to make sure he's okay."

"It's a beautiful thing to find love in a world like this," Nan muses before I leave. "Love is the sunlight that brings flowers to break from the earth."

I nod, returning her smile with an uncomfortable one of my own.

Sarge and I hike our way through the hall and up the stairs, quietly entering the room where Luke is still motionless. His breathing is slow and steady, but his face holds a pained expression. I drag the chair from the back corner of the room until it's positioned beside Luke's head. Then I sit, leaving room for Sarge to place himself at my feet. The redness of Luke's skin already looks better in some spots, giving me a slight bit of hope. I know how dangerous hope can be, so I don't allow it to carry me away.

He looks so peaceful lying here that I almost can't stop my hand from lifting out of my lap to feel his skin beneath my fingertips. Just as I'm about to make contact, the Guardianship Update music fills the air, startling me, causing me to yank my hand away.

Luke must have made sure to grab the Relay, the hi-tech communication device that commoners have to sell their soul in Slum Trading for. Last year, he stole a few batteries from the control room so that way we didn't have to worry about electricity. I thought we'd left everything behind when we ran, but I should've known Luke would pull something off.

I grab the Relay from Luke's pants pocket on the floor in time to see the Reaver pop onto the screen.

"My fellow citizens," she starts, her eyes daggers as she speaks. "For those of you that think breaking rules does not result in chaos and destruction, I'm here to remind you that this is not the case. Order and laws keep us from staggering into war, and keeps us, as humans, in check. Being a rebel runaway leads to deadly consequences for not only yourself, but everyone around you. So please remember; trust in the Guardianship, for we vow to protect those that cannot protect themselves."

The screen goes black after a few seconds. My initial reaction is to roll my eyes and scoff. Then, an image of a mother and father being killed for a crime they didn't commit shoots its way into my brain. Last year, the Reaver had punished the innocent to get to us, and it would've worked had Luke not been there to explain. Unfortunately, he's not able to talk me through this one. The panic hits me full force, leaving me winded and red eyed when I come to. What's her plan this time?

○   ○   ○

It's only been a few days, but Luke should be awake any minute. His wounds are much better, and Josephine decided to lessen his dosage of Dreamroot. She told me he shouldn't be moving around yet, but getting to have a conversation with him is enough. These past few days have been torturous seeing him like this.

"What happened?" His voice breaks me out of my thoughts, sending my heart rate sky high.

Sarge leaps up and immediately starts licking his face. I'm forced to yell at him to stop for fear of making Luke's recovery harder. "You've been out for a couple of days. How do you feel?"

"Like Hell." He closes his eyes. "But I'll be fine." His eyelids open slowly, and his hazels settle on my greys. *Oh, how I've missed seeing them.*

We're both silent for a long time before the emotion is too much for me to hold in anymore. "I thought I lost you." A single tear escapes, but my face remains smooth.

"You can't get rid of me that easy." A small smirk finds its place on his lips. "I told you I'm not going anywhere."

CHAPTER FOUR ○ LUKE

M AND SARGE ARE SITTING SOMEWHERE OUTSIDE WITH Josephine. I'm almost back to my old self, but the limitations on my breathing are still present. M filled me in on what happened while I was unconscious, and I gave Josephine as much gratitude as I could.

Today we're headed on our way. I'm not quite sure where we're going, all I know is that we have to keep moving. M has tried to convince Josephine to come along, but she says her place is here with all her plants and herbs.

I've been wracking my brain about the Update that M mentioned in passing. There has to be some sort of hint in Ren's address. She savors mind games too much for her words to mean nothing, and her zest for order and punishment tells me that there are no empty threats. Ren has something up her sleeve. It's driving me nuts trying to figure it out. I've no doubt in my mind she's got plan after plan laid out to investigate our weaknesses. That's always been her tactic.

The small bowl of water in the bathroom is warm as I dip my slightly scarred hands in it. Splashing the liquid onto my face, I hope to wash away the exhaustion and negative thoughts. M had been worried about losing me, but I'm worried of losing her to Ren's bullshit. I meet my own gaze in the cracking mirror. My skin holds a pinkish hue, leftover from the redness of the burns.

M would never admit it, but the scarring along my body makes her avert her eyes. Maybe it's all in my head, but it's easy to catch her irises bouncing back and forth as we talk. Josephine says that the tissues will hopefully correct themselves with the help of the Silvershade, but that's not a guarantee.

I'm finishing up my daily clean when Sarge's wild barking interrupts the calm. Peering through the small, cracking window, I scan the surroundings. Nothing immediately jumps out at me, but then, off in the trees to the west, I see it. A Force car racing to our location.

"Shit," I curse to myself, sprinting from the tiny restroom down the flight of rickety steps. "M!"

"Luke?" There's a small bit of terror in her voice. As I round the corner, I notice Sarge pressed against her side as if he's trying to merge his body with hers.

"They're coming."

Josephine is hobbling her way inside now, her old bones struggling to carry her the speed she's aiming for. She turns to fiddle with her greenery, but I'm too focused on M to zero in on what she's doing with them. The look in M's eyes tells me this is going to be rough for her. She wants to convince Josephine to join us, but deep down M knows she won't leave.

At the same time the thought pops in my head, M turns away from me to reason with her. "Will you come with us, Nan?"

"I'm sorry, dear, but my place is here." Josephine smiles a sad, toothy smile. "Please, take this." She hands M an old pill organization container.

"Is this...?" M's voice fades as Josephine nods her head.

"Yes, dear. Take care of them, would ya?" It must be seeds and herbs, or something.

M returns the nod, reaches her arms out for the old woman, and gently pulls her in for a soft hug. The moment is only quiet for a second or two before a deep growl tumbles from Sarge's throat.

"Come on." I step toward them, resting my hand on M's back. The tension of her muscles is tangible through the fabric of her shirt. "We need to leave."

"Nan," she sniffles, pulling herself away.

"It's okay," Josephine assures. "Go. Take care of yourself."

As she finishes her sentence, the front door flies open with a loud smack, my gun in my hand shooting faster than I thought possible. Three bullets exit the chamber in under a few seconds, and two officers fall to the floor. The rest of the soldiers back out, taking cover on the other side of the wall.

I keep myself facing the door, gun pointed at any potential targets while I back everyone toward the door in the rear. "Nan, it won't be safe here," I start, but her soft, wise voice stops me.

"Stop worrying about this little old lady, will ya?" she chides. "Now get out of here!" She steps in front of me, attempting to shove us out the door. It's at this moment that I realize two things: One, Josephine is a badass rebel. Two, she is willing to die for us.

The backyard is covered by a large, wooden privacy fence with sporadic holes in it. We'll have to bust through. Hopefully the officers don't have the property surrounded. I've still got one hand on my gun, but I reach out to put the other on M's wrist to guide her. We bolt to the back edge of the fence and my shoulder slams into one of the boards, splintering the wood.

"Go back where you came from, you filthy Alfies!" M and I turn to see Josephine standing fiercely against a few officers, only to be backhanded across her delicate face and collapse to the floor.

"Nan!" M cries, pulling against my grasp.

"Get 'em," shouts the officer standing over Josephine's shaking body.

"M, let's go!" I pull her as she fights against me. Sarge is torn, wanting to appease his owner but knowing that it's not safe. Eventually, I give up and wrap my arm around her body, carrying her away, all while shooting at the officers closing in on us.

"No!" she cries. Her arms and legs flail wildly, like an animal stuck in a trap. "Let me go!"

My lungs burn during our race through the woods. I'm afraid that this amount of exertion will prohibit my healing, but I'm terrified that the aftermath of Josephine may be enough to lose M forever. I run until I can't possibly go any further with M's weight. There's another house in view. Slowing a bit, my voice is raspy as I speak.

"I'm going to set you down now," I warn, "you're not going to run back, are you?"

M scoffs. It's not far off to assume she's rolling her eyes. "No." The word is clipped.

When I release her, she shoves herself away from me angrily. Sarge's excitement is cut short once he picks up on her attitude. "Are you seriously mad at me for pulling us to safety?" I'm trying not to make things worse, but honestly, the agitation growing in my own chest is hard to ignore. The burning of my lungs is still ever-present, and that only serves to make my irritability multiply.

"We shouldn't have left her like that." Her voice is harsh.

"She's a grown woman, Amity," I sigh, "she wanted us to go on without her." The words come out of my mouth, but they don't help the situation any.

M stares at me, standing immobile, with a blank look in her eyes. Actually, she's not looking at me, she's looking *through* me. She's trying not to breakdown; she's trying to keep herself numb. It's a feeling I'm all too familiar with, and I'm sent spiraling back into a memory I've spent countless hours trying to forget: The day of the Undoing.

The ground shook all the way in Arizona. Nine year old Lucas Warin runs to his father in the night, too scared to be alone. "What's happening?"

"I don't know, buddy," his dad answers. "Come here."

His stepmom, Janet, rushes into the room cradling his baby sister, Lily. She's only one. She must be really scared, thinks Lucas.

Tiny Lucas doesn't know how long his family holds onto each other, but eventually the shaking stops and the TV pops on. The man on the screen tells them that a freak natural phenomenon has destroyed more than half of North America. They don't believe there are any survivors.

Lucas feels a pit in his stomach. His mother—his *real* mother—lives out there. He doesn't remember her much, but his father said she lived there. He said she'd never come back, but Lucas held out hope.

"What about mommy?" Lucas sniffles at the TV. "We need to help her."

"No, son," his father cuts him short.

"Yes!" Lucas is adamant. "She needs help!"

"No, Lucas!" his father booms, causing Lucas to cower. "She's a grown woman. She didn't want us, and now she's gone! There's nothing we can do."

This cuts deep into Lucas. His father was a fighter. So why wouldn't he fight to save Lucas's mother?

Approaching the house returns me to reality. I do a quick sweep to make sure it's empty. It is. M is off in a faraway place as she and Sarge meander into the quiet living room. The only thing that breaks her from the trance is the Update music blaring from my back pocket. I slide the Relay from between the fabric, and M shuffles slowly over to me, still keeping some distance. It's hard to ignore the ache this causes in my chest.

The screen lights up. M's heart smacks the ground when Josephine's face fills the frame. She's gagged with black cloth, her eyes watering. It's dark around her, like they are in a of bunker, or enclosed room, with no windows. I resist the urge to reach my arm out to pull M closer to me.

"This message is for a certain rebel." Ren's sickening voice floats over Josephine's sweet face. "My final warning to you, Miss Thorne: Turn yourself in before anyone else gets hurt."

A hand reaches into the shot, aggressively removing the cloth from Josephine's mouth. "Be strong, dear! Don't let them...!" she cries before a bullet is lodged between her eyes. Her body slumps forward. M's hand shoots up to smother the cries that are fighting their way up and out of her throat. Her legs lose their strength, and I catch her before she collapses to the ground.

"Only a selfish, ignorant human being would allow this much Death. Do the right thing." The Relay shuts down. M's trembles are strong as she clings to me.

"You know that's bullshit, right?" It's a bit harsh, but it's the truth and it needs to be said. M is smart, she has to see that Ren is playing a game. It's no different than the killing of that innocent couple on the Update last year. "She's the one who's hurting people. Not you."

M doesn't say anything. Pushing her any further is out of the question, so instead, I clench her body tighter. When her tremors finally stop, I turn to face her. All I see is disconnect.

"You can't actually be considering this." I watch her expression. She'd opened her mouth to speak, but I stopped her before she could. The look in her eyes told me all I needed to know; I didn't like what I saw. "How could you actually be considering this?" I don't want to speak ill of her, but she's acting rather dumb right now.

"What other choice do I have?" Her expression clues me in on the fact that she's already tired of arguing with me.

"Well, for starters, you could not go. How about that choice?"

"You're overreacting." She rolls those beautiful grey eyes at me. Overreacting? Me? Pfft. I've always tried to stand by her, but this is insane. We should be on our way to Creyke Point right now, not discussing whether or not she's going to walk straight into the enemy's arms. *Here, Mr. Officer. You're out of bullets so take my last one and you can shoot me instead.* The sarcastic tone of my intrusive thought takes over my brain.

"It's a trap. Do you not get that? She'll kill you the second she can." It's astonishing that I even have to explain this to her. M is one of the smartest people I know.

"That's not really her style," she says, nonchalantly. "If she wanted me dead, she could've killed me at any point. Instead she just...let me go." Her expression grows despondent as memories of her sister's death plague her mind along with everything that's happened to her in the last year, up to and including the brutal murder of Josephine.

If only I could see what was going through her head. If only I could take it all away—the nightmares, the memories, the pain. Maybe then she wouldn't be thinking about this. But she has a point; once again seeing right through me. It's clear Ren wants her alive, otherwise she would've been dead long before ever making it to Omphalos. Even after, there should have been more guards on the way out, but we ran through those halls without interruption.

I found the situation odd back then, and I've thought about it a lot since. Ren had signed off on me killing my father, but it was much more than that; she wanted Janet and Lily to watch. It's like getting into people's heads and torturing them from the inside out is what gets her off. I'm convinced that was her plan for M all along.

M snaps out of her memory. "She wants people to live with the pain," she continues. Drawing a breath from deep within her lungs, she mentally prepares herself to say the next words. "Which is why it's important that you and Sarge stay as far away as possible."

"What? No." My voice is stern. How ridiculous of a request is that? If I can't convince her to turn a blind eye to Ren's games, then at the very least I'm going with her. And Sarge? He would never leave her side.

"Yes!" She slams her hands down on the dusty coffee table, looking me square in the eye. Damn, this woman is the most beautiful creature I've ever laid my eyes on. Sarge jumps from the noise and positions himself directly at her side. "I don't think she'll kill anyone if I go alone, but if she sees Sarge? He'll be the next pawn in her game with me." Her tone is resigned and distant. "I need you to stay and take care of him." She reaches her delicate hand out, placing it on Sarge's head to gently stroke her fingers between his fur.

I want to tell her how ridiculous she sounds, but there's no denying she's right. Ren Keres would relentlessly torture Sarge in front of M to break her already shattering spirit. There's a small part of me, deep within my chest, that is hurt that M doesn't fear the same fate for me. She's only concerned that I take care of Sarge, so *he* can be safe.

"What if I go in your place?" I hadn't thought about stepping in for her until the words come flying from my mouth. I don't want to die, but it sure as hell beats having her be tortured.

"And how would that work?" Her grey eyes tumble as an exasperated sigh falls from her lips.

"I could tell her you're dead?" I'm grasping here. I know M won't go for it, so maybe what I'm really searching for is the same amount of worry that she has for Sarge. I immediately feel shitty about it. It's stupid of me to be jealous of a dog.

"She's not dumb, Luke," M scoffs, lightly. "If it's me she truly wants, then she'd use you to get me there." She huffs, blowing the strands of her hair that have fallen into her face. "She must know I'm still alive. I'm just trying to do whatever leads to the least amount of collateral damage."

Collateral damage. Ha! I almost laugh out loud. I never believed for one second that I could stop this woman. Describing her as headstrong would be putting it mildly. And although she didn't exactly say she doesn't want me getting hurt, it was implied, so I'll take it.

"Besides," she starts again after a few minutes of silence. "Someone I know once told me to walk toward Death and come out holding it by the neck." She smiles suggestively at me.

She's smart to use my own words against me. That's not exactly what I had said, though. I never wanted her to do it, I only shared what I was taught to do. And suddenly I can't stop the words flowing from my mouth. "Could you at least act like you're not in a rush to get out of here?" I'm trying not to yell at her, but the frustration running through my veins is rough on me.

Her brows pull together, and her hands curl into themselves, folding together in her lap. "I'm sorry," she whispers. Her eyes hold a hurt expression in them. "I just don't want anyone else to get hurt."

Anger boils in my chest. I recognize it's because I'm upset she could leave so easily knowing how bad it feels on the other side. And I'm furious that Ren has found a way to take the little piece of Heaven I've uncovered after losing my family. But M doesn't need to know that, so I count down from five, and when I get to *one*, I push a smirk onto my face and say, "I don't think you ever let yourself live in the present."

M's lip twitches in a struggle to hide her growing smile. Then it fades, her eyes dulling. Whatever's crossed her mind has soiled the sliver of happiness I've presented her with. "You make it all feel so normal...effortless." There's despondency in her voice.

"You don't have to leave," I point out. She sighs.

"Yes, I do. And you know it."

My jaw tenses and I swallow hard, pushing myself off the couch. I decide not to say anything more for fear of making M feel worse. Today very well could be one of our last days together, and ruining it is the furthest thing on my mind. I slap on another smirk and say, "At least you have my mundane personality to look forward to when you get back."

M studies me, her mouth turned up in a sad smile. She's looking at me as if we both know it's a lie. She's already resigned herself to the fact that she'll never get out of there. M is willing to sacrifice herself so that no one else has to hurt. But what she doesn't realize is that she's hurting me in the process.

M doesn't say anything more, though. Instead, an unfamiliar look settles in her eyes as she steps around the coffee table and closer to me.

Every cell in my body stands to attention. She leans in, pressing her soft lips to mine. It's the first kiss we've shared in over a year, but it feels more like a goodbye than a hello. M backs me into a wall and pushes her body against mine, indicating what she wants.

"M," I say into her mouth, "why are you doing this?" This is painful. Knowing, in the back of my mind, that M and I may never get to share in a moment like this again is too much for me.

The scrunch of her face against mine, along with the wetness of her tears, takes me by surprise. "I just want to be normal for one more moment," she sniffs, gripping my t-shirt in her clenched fists; her forehead pressed against my chest.

My hands find their way up to her face, and I press my palms against her cheeks, gently lifting her lips back to mine. Her body melts so I pick her up, letting her wrap her legs around my waist as I walk her through the house. Once I locate a bedroom, I lay her down, her hair flopping into her face, partially blocking her eyes. Reaching out, I tuck the strands behind her tiny ear. I stop for a moment to scan her features, my fingers lingering on her skin.

"I'd do anything for you, M," I start. "You know that?" I wish I could get down on my hands and knees to beg for her to stay, but I know she could never live with herself if she did. I can only go along for the ride and start thinking of ways to get her out and take down Ren. I'd go to Hell and back for her if she asked me to, and I'm starting to think that's exactly what's going to happen while she's gone. Even though I don't want this to be soiled with goodbyes, I can't deny her what she's asked for.

She nods, her big, grey eyes wide. I lift her shirt above her head, tracing my fingers along her skin. Her tiny, appreciative breaths are fuel to my fire. But it doesn't last long before she flips me onto my back, straddling me, taking the lead herself.

M yanks my shirt off. "Let me do it," she says.

I chuckle. I guess I wasn't doing it fast enough.

She slides her palms along my chest causing a shiver to tear through my body. She's determined to get lost in the moment—I see it in her eyes. M is still working through how to handle saying goodbye, so I'll be here in any way that she needs. I once told her I wasn't going anywhere...and I meant it.

CHAPTER FIVE ○ LUKE

I WAKE UP TO FIND M ASLEEP NEXT TO ME. HER FACE IS CRUNched together, and her lips are stuck in a hard frown which means it won't be long before her nightmares tear her from slumber. I'm not sure what time it is—probably noon by the looks of the sun outside.

When M comes to, she's going to insist on hiking back to her hometown of Burns, Oregon with her hands above her head in surrender. The Force is going to cart her off to Omphalos, and I'll probably never see her again. There's an unexplainable feeling that spreads through my chest, and Sarge lifts his head, putting his chin over M's body to look me in the eyes. They hold the same expression as mine.

I'm idly hoping that when M wakes up, she'll see how awful her plan is and decide to finally head to Creyke Point. Unfortunately, it's painfully clear that her big heart won't let her walk away if it will cause people to die. And if she can somehow get passed those feelings, she's too stubborn to say I'm right.

Therefore, I've been going over things in my head. Is there enough time to tell M everything she needs to know? I'll give her my code, along with my keycard. I doubt any of it will work, and it will most likely be confiscated immediately, but it would at least give me some peace of mind; a small sliver of possibility. Though, I know more than anyone that Ren isn't the type to give third chances.

I'll tell M about the Brain. It's the core for all of the Guardianship's operations. The computers aren't hard to use despite the fact that they are complex. The Force has everything basically idiot-proof. But these are still top notch systems, and M will need to get into at least one of them in order to delete her records. If she doesn't, they'll always have her location at the touch of a button.

The Brain is interlaced throughout every computer. It's smart. It has the ability to pick up oddities in pattern and adjust accordingly. So not only will M be up against the countless Force officers and Ren Keres herself, she'll also have to deal with the Brain at some point.

And speaking of Ren, her deranged psyche leads me to the millions of different ways she'll torture. How am I going to warn and prepare M about it all? The only reason I know about most of them is because I was once a part of it. Will she think me a monster?

"What's on your mind?" a tiny voice asks from beside me. I've been so lost in thought that I didn't realize M had woken up. I turn my face toward her. "I'd know that worried expression anywhere."

I take a deep breath, sighing. "You sure there's nothing I could say to convince you to go to Canada?"

"Not this again." She rolls her eyes, but her small smile remains.

"A man's gotta try, right?" My voice sounds sad. I'm not used to this. I'm starting to truly understand M's want for keeping everyone at arm's length.

My body is sluggish as we leave. M doesn't seem to have a care in the world. This observation puts me in a sour mood. Then the guilt makes itself a home in my chest about an hour into our trek because I realize I'm wasting my last day with M by being a piece of shit. Sarge is glued to her side, and her hand hasn't left the soft fur of his head. Does he know he's about to say goodbye, too?

Once I get over my moodiness, I use the time we have left to explain everything to M. The torture techniques, the Brain, the filth that is rooted in Ren's demented cranium. The worst part is that I'm not exactly sure of Ren's plans. I'd always been on the other side, always the torturer. Now I have to recount, in detail, the things that I've done; the things that M may have to survive.

Memory Actualization Processing, or MAP for short, is her first stop. They'll make her relive her worst memories to learn her patterns, and wear her out. They want to change her from the inside. Ren knows that a human is more compliant if they feel they've made the decision to change themselves. She calls it the Organic Approach.

It's hard to forget the desolate look in the patients' eyes at Omphalos. They say the mind is your greatest weapon, and it wasn't until studying the aftermath of the MAP that I truly understood how twisted Ren had taken that sentiment. Picturing M like that is like taking a harpoon to the chest.

There are elemental pods to simulate different, yet equally brutal, deaths. Like everything, the MAP isn't foolproof. If M proves too strong to break, she'll be sent there. If the patients after the MAP were hard to look at, these ones are damn near unbearable to witness. It's a good thing the pods are soundproof, because the screams that exit their throats are enough to haunt you for a thousand lifetimes. I don't want M to get to this level, but that means she'd have to be lost forever. I'm not exactly sure what's worse.

There are white rooms. They are devoid of any color, noise, stimuli. You spend a few days in there and you're almost always ready to talk because you're terrified of being put back in. These are only used in severe cases, for people that don't have someone—or something—to use as leverage. Ren may resort to this if she can't break M, but knowing how big of a heart she has, I don't think Ren would ever have to use this on her. At least I can thank the stars for that.

There's Limbo, which I can't even recount without a shudder. It's brutal torture personally tailored to an individual that is too tainted to keep, but too valuable with information to let die. I'm afraid with M's stubbornness and Ren's zest for punishment, this is exactly where she'll find herself.

I don't look at M. She doesn't talk, she lets me get everything out. I'm sure it's all too much, too overwhelming. She must think I'm a monster. Who wouldn't? When I feel I've warned, or prepared, her sufficiently, I leave her to process everything. I decided against mentioning the birthing rooms or the sterilization chambers. I don't tell her of the direction Ren is heading with Humanity. I should. But I don't. I'm already spiraling down a train-wreck of horror-filled memories from my Force days. It causes my throat to close.

A few more apprehension-filled hours pass with nothing but silence between us. It isn't until we get closer to goodbye that I open my mouth again. "Things are…different in town."

"I know," she says immediately. There's confusion plastered all over my face as I study her. "You think you're the only one who's snuck there?"

Suddenly I realize just how far into the back of her mind Creyke Point had been. She probably never planned on going. I chuckle to myself because of how dumbfounded I am. If I don't force myself to laugh, I might yell.

We're almost into town when we stop to say our goodbyes. We discussed a meeting point, and I tell her I'll go every day, twice a day, in hopes to meet her again. We spent the last year getting her directional capacity above rock status. I hope it's enough. She won't have Sarge or a Relay to rely on this time.

"Hey, bud," M whispers softly as she bends to say goodbye to her best friend. "I have to go away for a while, but you're going to stay with Luke. Doesn't that sound fun?" Her voice lacks all conviction for what she's saying. Her eyes water, causing Sarge to fidget in an attempt to get closer to her. He licks her face and M smiles the most beautifully sad smile, the kind I've come to know since meeting her. She pulls him in for a long hug, her hands gripping into his fur to hold him close. Somewhere, a faraway voice in my mind says that I crave the same treatment. I tell it to shut up.

A few minutes pass before M is finally able to tear herself away from Sarge. Damn, she's a mess. Still stunning, though. She wipes the tears from her cheeks. "Get out of this place. Camp out, keep moving," she says, reminding me of the lifeless officer I used to be. "I really think you should head to Can…" Not this again. She's not the only stubborn one.

"I told you I'm not leaving without you," I state, sternly. She nods.

"Thank you." Her voice is a whisper as she rests her hand on my arm. I know she's not talking about the *staying here* part.

"I'll protect him with my life. The same way you would."

Tears prick her eyes once more, and I pull her into my chest. She grips me tightly, her little body wracking with uncontrollable, yet quiet, sobs. I'm going to miss her. Sarge wiggles his way in between us, pressing his snout straight up against her stomach.

"Okay." She pulls away, straightens herself, and turns halfway. "I'm off." She smiles warily, trying to lighten the mood. It doesn't work. I watch her with furrowed brow as she tells Sarge to stay. Then, she trudges away from us.

"M!" I call to her one last time. I know I shouldn't have waited so long to say this, but here it goes. "I love you."

I should've told her the first night we kissed, and every day after that, but I didn't. I couldn't. So this is my last ditch effort to get her to stay, or at the very least, let her know in case I never see her again. She stops and looks toward me, her grey eyes sparkling in the light.

"Doesn't love just suck?" She smiles at me, but it doesn't quite reach her eyes. Still, though, I'd like to think it's her own way of saying it back. She hesitates for a moment before continuing on her way.

At a certain threshold point, Sarge attempts to catch up to M, but I grab him, using all of my strength to keep him back. "Let her go, it's okay." He's thrashing and biting and jerking and clawing. "You have to let her go."

My heart constricts at my own words because I realize I'm saying them more for myself than for Sarge. I'm struggling as he nips and barks and cries. I hope for M's sake she doesn't look back. A single tear drips from my eye for the first time in years as I watch my whole world walk away, getting smaller with every step she takes.

CHAPTER SIX ○ AMITY

I walk toward burns, my legs shaking like gelatin in an earthquake. Sarge's incessant whines coming from somewhere behind me are breaking my heart. The tears flow down my cheeks as I walk away from my whole world. *Poor Sarge.*

My hands tremble once I'm close to the edge of town. Why did I decide to do this again? Oh right, because Madame Keres, the literal Reaver of our Humanity, would kill more innocent people. And why did Luke have to admit his love for me now? It's not like I haven't had an inkling over the last year, but that's precisely why I have to leave him behind. I can't let the Reaver maximize my suffering by using the ones close to me.

As least if she kills me, then I'm deserving of it. Luke will carry on the rebellion. I've no doubt he'd burn the whole world to avenge me. It's disheartening that everything has barely even started with me and now it's about to die with me, too. But, my death would be the best thing for the Resistance. Though, maybe I could take a page from the Guardianship's book and start the riots from the inside out before they kill me.

The blinding white of the A.L.F's signature uniform blasts through the trees, and my heart thumps in my chest—the sound reverberating through my skull. *You can do this, Amity.*

It takes my brain an eternity to tell my body to move. Maybe deep down I know I should've stayed with Luke and Sarge. I'm far enough away now that the squealing whines from my best friend are nonexistent to me. At least, not in reality. I don't know if that makes me feel better or worse.

The truth is, I have no clue if this will be worth it. The Reaver will still kill innocent people—just as many as she would if I don't place myself perfectly at her doorstep—but perhaps, by turning myself in, it takes Luke and Sarge out of harm's way.

So, here I am. One foot out of the forest, then the next. Then my body is out of the brush, and I'm exposed. There's a split second where I'm suspended in time; where the officers haven't noticed me yet, and I'm still a free woman. But then, it all comes crashing down. Before I could even think to run back, I've got four guns pointed on me. The sun is glaring, and I'm squinting into the light with my hands held high above my head. There are voices shouting at me.

"Get down!" growls one.

"Put your face on the ground!" orders a second.

"Do it, or we'll shoot!" screams a third.

I slowly lower myself until my chest is against the earth, pushing my cheek into the dirt. It's not long before there's a knee in my back and a gun barrel pressed to my temple. The panic starts to rise in my chest, but I take a deep breath. *Just relax, Amity.*

"Madame Keres asked for me," I choke out.

"Did I say you could talk?" the first guard spits from above me, the metal pushing harder into my skull.

My teeth clench as the pain spreads, making it easier to keep my mouth shut. I want to tell him to step off. I want him to just kill me now and end it, Reaver be damned. But innocent people are dying, and I need to do something. So, for now, I'll stay quiet.

"Who are you?" asks the officer pinning me. He knows who I am. He wants me to tell him what a stupid commoner I am.

There's no strength in my body to answer since he's pressing his weight into my lungs, but it doesn't matter anyway. Someone else speaks first.

"Get off of her," says a new voice. It's deep and dignified. The soldier on my back pulls away immediately. "The Headmistress wants her delivered in one piece."

I'm yanked off the ground by a large hand and brought face to face with a tall, broad-shouldered man in a black version of the A.L.F uniform I've come to know. His hair is slicked back into a thick wave, and his eyes crinkle around the edges. He turns his lip into a lopsided smile.

"Hello, Miss Thorne." There are two guns hanging at either side of him, but his hands are free of a weapon. Instead, they're clasped together in front of his waist, causing his chest to puff out. The officers around me are standing at attention. This man must be a leader of some kind. He reaches out his tough hand, grasping onto my arm. "Come with me," he says before addressing the soldiers. "At ease."

The other officers relax, returning to their original posts while the man in the dark uniform leads me further into town. There are other commoners here. They're frail-looking, but they watch me as I'm being tugged through the street with a hunger I'm not familiar with. Who knows the last time they've been treated like human beings.

The worst part is the look in their eyes. It's something I'm struggling to comprehend. It's like they're happy that someone is below them at this moment, and it makes them feel better about themselves, if only for a second; like I'm the dirt, the scum, the filth of this earth and the reason for their suffering. *How sick is that?*

"I'm First Sergeant Marcus Giles. I'll be overseeing your trip."

"Where am I going?" Not that it matters since I'm most likely never getting out anyway. But the meeting point with Luke is on the outskirts of an old city in Washington, called Aberdeen. Luke assumed the Reaver has ordered me to where it all started in California: Omphalos. Once I'm out, I can follow the main interstate road all the way North. Either that, or I could follow the ocean. But if she's sending me anywhere else, I may not be able to find my way back despite Luke's survival training.

"Main facility like the rest of the traitors," he answers. "You'll put in the same three months as everyone else." He chuckles to himself, the eerie sound of his tone cutting deep into my bones. "And then some."

His grip on my arm is tight as he leads me into the center of town where a black Force car is waiting. He opens one of the rear doors and pushes me in. There's no driver in the car, which is why I'm surprised when Giles walks around the vehicle and gets in next to me. He slaps the back of the driver's seat twice, and the engine roars to life as we start moving.

The tires spin on the rock and crumbled asphalt. I study the buildings in passing as we head off on the Central Oregon Highway. They look even worse than I remember. Any of the structures that remain are fragmented and dull. Most are just piles of brick and stone. There are old tattered tents taking up the spaces that the buildings used to. Officers guard the entrances. These are the community houses that the Guardianship is demanding everyone stay in.

Here's a list of the horrid things I've seen in just a few minutes' ride: a child being ripped away from her mother, a large pile of dead, rotting corpses, a man having his eyes gouged out, and an officer raping a young girl. Then I stop looking out the window. It takes everything in me to keep the bile from rising into my throat. I even try counting down from five, but that reminds me too much of Luke. So instead, I physically try to shake the thoughts from my head.

As we make it to the edge of town, I'm already exhausted. I'm afraid to remove my eyes from the road ahead, but something catches my gaze. It's a building. I don't recognize it, though it does look new. There's electricity, and fresh, vibrant paint. The Guardianship symbol is adorned on the front with the A.L.F seal on the door. This must be where the officers stay. God forbid they have to live like the rest of us. God forbid they see what it's like.

I guess that's the best way to keep us and them separated. It's harder to identify with the commoners if you aren't living like one; being treated like one.

"Why'd you join the Force?" I question, keeping my eyes forward. My rational side is questioning why I've asked. Maybe it's because I want to show him that I'm not afraid, even if I am. Maybe it's because I've allowed myself to get comfortable in the company of others, and now I want to feel less alone. It doesn't matter either way.

"Because I want to make the world a better place," answers Giles. Clearly he's delusional. Marcus Giles is one of those officers that actually believes the Guardianship's cause is worthy of supporting. He's a blind follower.

"You think treating your fellow human beings like garbage is making the world a better place?" I feel as though Giles is someone you can't reason with. I mean, he's not just any old A.L.F officer, so he's got to be tough. He's the type that's so deep in their fantasy that he physically cannot see the true reality. But it's a long drive from Burns to Omphalos—almost nine hours—and it would feel even longer if I didn't at least attempt conversation.

"Doing what's necessary to keep people in check is making the world a better place. Those of you unable to see the bigger picture would end up sending us into war again."

"Well I think doing what's necessary to stop the Guardianship is helping to make the world a better place. So why am I the traitor?" His features are hard and his brow is pulled in, creating a dark hood over his crinkled eyes. Even if Giles doesn't have a complete one-eighty transformation of his thinking, hopefully I've just planted the seed.

CHAPTER SEVEN ○ AMITY

I OPEN MY EYES WHILE DRIVING DOWN THE LONG DIRT ROAD toward the mountain. The two tower guards atop the main door are visible in the distance, suspended above the trees. Giles is sitting, stoic, next to me.

During the trip, he shared something that I wasn't expecting to learn: Luke had been a Master Sergeant. In fact, he was one of the best and most efficient in his rank. He'd quickly climbed the ladder and held the title by the time he was nineteen, just a year after the start of the Force. By twenty-two, he was a First Sergeant, the one in charge of Master Sergeants; what Giles is now.

Luke was well on his way to becoming Sergeant Major—the highest rank of the A.L.F—the one who calls the shots, the Reaver's right hand man when it comes to Force operations. But then he deserted his post.

This news had surprised me, but not by much. It wasn't hard to learn that Luke was a natural leader from the start. A real hard-ass if he wanted to be. The initial shock was realizing how close he was to the top. The four stars embossed on his ID must signify his rank.

I've idly been wondering if part of the requirements to being dubbed Sergeant Major is killing your own father to show an unwavering loyalty to the Guardianship. That's my theory as to why Luke never made it.

Giles had talked about Luke as if he were a celebrity throughout the Force; the best of the best. Yet, his disdain for him was clear. How has the Reaver explained his absence? Does she use him as an example to the Force like she had used me for the commoners? A small thought whispers in the back of my mind; something I hadn't considered until now. Was getting me here never truly about me, but always about Luke?

The car pulls in front of the glass doors. The two guards point their guns in my direction. "Don't move," Giles plays, exiting the car and circling around to free me. He nods to the guards. They nod back, keeping their weapons trained on me.

The door is opened, and I hop out of the back. Giles returns his hand to my arm, leading me toward the glass. I glance up at the tower guards to see their guns following me until I'm under the roof and out of their view. *Jeez, if they're so ready to kill you, Amity, why don't they just do it?*

Giles opens the first set of doors to shuffle me into the glass cubicle before the next. He pulls out a keycard from his pocket, tapping it against a small screen on the wall. *That's new. Before it was a swipe.*

The screen animates while a picture of Giles appears. "Giles comma Marcus," says the mechanized female voice. "Please enter your PIN." The image of Giles is replaced by a number pad, and he quickly taps in his six-digit code. The light above the door turns green as the lock clicks open.

Deep down I knew having Luke's keycard and code meant nothing. I figured it'd be confiscated immediately, but it's becoming clear how much their process has changed in just this short introduction.

Giles drags me through the doors, into a lobby of sorts. There's a desk with a computer screen on it, and doors on either side of the desk along the back wall, both with red lights above them. I'm pulled to the computer for Giles to position me directly in front of the screen. My reflection stares back at me. The exhaustion in my expression is all I notice, but then Giles says *hello* and the face lights up, awaiting the next words, causing my reflection to disappear.

"What would you like to do, Giles comma Marcus?" asks a robotic-like man's voice. Something gives me the feeling deep in my chest that this is the voice of the Brain.

"Check in patient Amity Thorne," Giles replies beside me.

"Gladly," answers the Brain, and my name scrolls across the top of the screen. A light pops on around the rim of the glass, followed by a flash click. Instantaneously, I'm staring at a picture of myself. "Patient Thorne comma Amity check-in successful."

The light above the right door changes to green, and Giles nudges me. "It's time for the next phase. I'll be catching up with you once you've finished."

I hesitantly move toward the door, my feet carrying me despite telling them not to. My hand reaches out for the handle. It's cold in my palm as I turn it, pushing through the opening. The lock clicks behind me while I take in my surroundings.

The light in this room is dim with purple and orange glows. It's stark white like the rest of the facility, but it's long and narrow. Compartments line the walls every ten feet or so, yet from where I'm standing, it's impossible to make out what's hidden in them. A conveyor belt with white metal railings extends directly down the middle.

The mechanized female voice surrounds me. "Welcome Thorne comma Amity. Please take off your clothes and place them into the basket on your left."

The floor opens up beside me, a white basket rising from below the surface. This is surely an ironic symbol of Hell. *Throw your past to me, and I'll descend once more.* My fingers tremble as they lift my shirt above my head, and continue to shake as I slide my jeans down my legs. Luke's ID is in one pocket. I left the photo of Emma with Sarge, but the one from my attacker's bag is still with me. Maybe I should've left them all with Luke, but knowing that I carried them as long as I could gives me a small semblance of peace.

Now my undergarments and socks are all that's left. I'm not sure if I'm supposed to get completely naked, but after a few minutes of silence, I slip off the rest and place them in the basket with the others.

The voice cuts in again as the basket lowers out of sight. "Step forward." I put my feet to the conveyor belt in front of me, hesitating. Once my feet are fully on, it starts to move. "Washing will now commence."

The belt is smooth in its transport. I'm heading toward the first compartment. The voice tells me to put my hair up and lift my arms, so I do. Then, large robotic beams jut out from the walls, circling around me, covering every inch of my skin in white suds. The spray stops just below my chin. My skin tingles as the soap does whatever deep clean it's supposed to do.

I'm told to keep my arms out as the conveyor belt brings me to the next compartment for the rinse. The water is the perfect temperature. When I glance down, I notice there's no hair anywhere on my body. *Now I know why it stopped at my neck.* Clearly they want us to look less disheveled, more clean. Apparently that means getting rid of all body hair and anything that makes me look like a poor commoner.

The next compartment is a hyper-dryer, and every drop of liquid is blown from my skin in mere seconds. The final compartment sends out a smaller, thinner robotic beam. I'm instructed to stand still as it shoots something into my arm, just below my shoulder. The pain is only there for a millisecond, and I tilt my head to see a scar about a quarter of an inch long. This must be the tracker. Luke told me that I'd have to delete my records if I wanted to escape, but now I'm worried that too much has changed. *What if deletion is no longer an option?*

At the end of the conveyor belt is a new set of clothes. They're a light grey. A plain t-shirt with simple pull-string pants—the same clothes Emma was wearing when she died. I shudder as I pull them over my body, but they're soft against my freshly cleaned skin. By the door, there's a pair of matching grey sneakers, perfectly and conveniently my size. I slip them on, waiting for the voice to tell me what's next.

"Thank you, Thorne comma Amity. Proceed through the door."

The light turns green and the lock clicks. I don't need to reach out for this one, though, because it opens on its own. There's a chair in the middle of the next room with a woman standing beside a bunch of tools. She motions for me to sit. I do. She doesn't say anything as she washes my face and hair.

This whole experience so far seems uncharacteristically nice. For a lot of commoners, this is probably their first truly warm shower. A real spa experience for some. I guess this is how the Reaver gets her patients to trust the process and let their guard down.

My face glows and my hair is perfectly styled as I exit the tiny room into the next one. Gone is the fizzy mop. All that remains is a smooth curtain draping down my back, not a single strand out of place. Giles is waiting for me; his smile is wide and inviting like the rest of the last half hour. It's all very oxymoronic. Giles had called me a traitor not too long ago. Now I'm being treated with nothing but kindness since stepping through the door. It's confusing. *Is it all to get into your head?*

"You look much better now," he says, returning his hand to the normal spot on my arm. "The Headmistress isn't so bad, you see?"

Giles thinks I look *better* now. What he really means is, I no longer look like an impoverished commoner caked with dirt. It's unclear to me how Giles is blind to the wickedness here. Just because she gave me the first decent shower I've had in a long time, doesn't mean she wasn't the cause of my filth in the first place. It doesn't change the fact that she killed my sister. Even though she hasn't immediately ordered my death, it's clear she's taken so many pieces of me away that I can barely say I'm alive.

But I guess, for Giles, it's easier to accept that his *Headmistress* is on the right side of Humanity, because at least in that narrative he's a hero. If he chooses to see anything else, then suddenly he has to admit he's a monster.

He leads me through the hall and down the stairs, into a room with a table in the middle. He sits me roughly, handcuffing me to a link on the table. The handcuffs are unlike anything I've ever seen. There isn't a keyhole anywhere on them. Instead, there's a tiny screen on each of the circles. They click and blink red as Giles tightens them around my wrist and the table.

"The Headmistress will be in to see you shortly," he says, before turning and leaving me alone.

I use this time to glance around, surveying my surroundings. The room is completely white, sticking to the theme from the rest of the building. The table is black, standing out with its *out of place* darkness. The walls are bare except for a large mirror that takes up almost all of one wall. I stare at my reflection, but can't seem to recognize myself. My hair looks silky, and there aren't any bags under my eyes. I look healthy, well-rested. It seems they've tried to wipe every instance of possible trauma away without actually removing it.

I'm interrupted when the door clicks. My heart rate spikes as I meet the Reaver, Ren Keres, face to face.

CHAPTER EIGHT ○ LUKE

SARGE TRUDGES BESIDE ME WHILE WALKING ALONG THE SOUTH Fork John Day River. We've been going almost nonstop since this morning. I'd say we've travelled over thirty six miles. Sarge looks like crap. I probably do, too. It's already after midnight, but I'm not ready to stop. We could've gotten further by now, but it took damn near an hour to finally get Sarge to cooperate with me. Poor guy.

I had to tether him with a rope, which is sitting tightly around my waist as we walk. Sarge's loyalty lies with M, and it's hard for him to believe that she would ever leave, despite her final words. He's smart, but he's hurting. I don't want to stop because he'll definitely find a way to break free.

It shouldn't take longer than a month to get to Aberdeen, as long as nothing goes wrong. Hopefully Sarge can pull himself together long enough to wait it out. M would never forgive me if I let Sarge get away.

The water running beside us breaks up the silence of the night. It's hard to keep my mind from picturing what M is going through. If I dwell on it though, it will only serve to make me angry. But the more I try to push it all away, the harder it tries to shove its way in.

What game is Ren playing? I've been struggling to figure that out since we somehow made it through the patrols *mostly* unscathed last year. There has to be something more to this. Ren's goal has always been to advance Humanity, and M holds an important role to her, but why? Weed out the Tainted, breed the Exceptional. Find the kinks and beat them out. So where does M fall?

My thoughts distract me while we walk, and I'm idly keeping track of the miles we put behind us. I'm not pulled from the torrent until Sarge acts up.

For the most part, he's resigned to the fact that he's stuck with me, but now he's yelping and pulling and tensing. At first I'm confused, and the sudden unruly behavior irks me. The anger instantly shoots through my veins as he tugs at the rope. But then I catch his golden eyes and the rage bubbles away. He turns his head. I follow his gaze down the river to notice a young boy gripping onto a rock, looking lifeless in the moonlight. If it weren't for the clear tensing of his tiny arms, I'd assume he *was* lifeless.

I know what M would want me to do. It's the same thing Sarge is alluding to. But deep in the back of my mind, an image of a girl with pale blue eyes crashes into view, stealing my breath away. This boy is most likely tainted, and the risk isn't worth it to check for the slight chance that he's not. I don't want to have to do the same thing to him that I had to do with Trixie a year ago. The guilt buried deep within me—and I've tried to lose it forever—but the sight of the boy has it rushing full force at me again.

M would never forgive me if I leave this boy, but I could never forgive myself if I have to kill him. I made a promise to M, and that was to keep Sarge safe. That means having to walk away from this poor kid and never looking back. "Come on, Sarge," I order with a tug of the rope. My heart splinters as he whines and pulls and struggles against my grip.

I've almost completely turned away when a small voice calls for help behind me. The noise takes me off guard, allowing Sarge the opportunity to snap the rope with his teeth. He takes off in the direction of the boy, and I'm left dumbfounded.

"Shit," I whisper, cursing myself. "Sarge!"

Sarge bolts toward the river, and the little boy's eyes grow wide. His movements become more frantic the closer Sarge gets. I want to yell, to tell him not to move; he's weak enough already, and I'm sure the rock he's clinging to is slippery. Unfortunately, that may set a Force tracker off. Hell, I'm not even completely sure if Sarge won't set it off himself.

I race after Sarge, hoping to catch him before he gets to the child. M would be devastated if I broke my promise, and I'm not about to lead the Guardianship to our location. I'm pushing my body to its limit which, on its own, isn't faster than a dog. Leftover tar from the fog inhalation makes it ten times worse. I'm struggling to get the air I need into my lungs. It feels as if I'll pass out at the drop of a dime.

Before Sarge gets to the edge, the boy slips away with the current, his face dipping below the waterline. Sarge leaps into the water after him, the speed sweeping them both away at a faster pace than I can match. But then, adrenaline hits as I watch Sarge bob beneath the surface and I speed up, heat coursing through my veins.

I throw my body into the water after them, gagging as the rippling current finds its way down my throat. The rope is still around my waist, so thankfully I can use that to tie the boy to me with hope it will entice Sarge to follow. I'm getting closer to them, enough to see that the child is gripping Sarge, but Sarge is struggling to stay afloat.

It's a few minutes before I get to them, but once I do, I quickly tie the rope around Sarge's body and the boy's. Then the adrenaline takes over, pushing me the rest of the way. I'm successful in pulling them both to the side of the river and out of the rapid waters.

My chest struggles to expand and contract; breathing is almost impossible as I hyperventilate. The boy and Sarge are doing the same. When I get my breathing under control, all of my remaining energy is used to focus on the boy's limb. There's a small scar on his arm, right below the shoulder. Damn it.

I raise my finger to my lips, looking into Sarge's golden eyes so he understands the seriousness of the situation. Then, the Relay is in my hands and I'm typing my message to the boy as fast as possible. He's probably eleven or twelve, and if he came from the facilities then he should be able to read. He looks malnourished, like he hasn't eaten in days and his body is sucking whatever it can out of him. His eyes are sunken in and dark.

> **Hello, my name is Luke. I can't talk out loud because the Guardianship will hear me. You can talk, though. What's your name?**

I slowly make my way toward the boy, hoping not to startle him. His lids are closed. He's lying flat on his back, breathing heavily. I reach out my hand and gently tap him, causing his eyes to pop open with panic. The natural urge to shush him and tell him it's okay is hard to break, and I almost set the tracker off immediately. I hand the Relay to him. He reads the words carefully.

"Sam," he whispers. A smile works its way onto my face.

I take the Relay back and type out another message:

> **Are you hungry?**

As if on cue, Sam's stomach rumbles. My head nods in understanding while typing my response. I want him to stay put while Sarge and I find food. But as I walk away, I realize quickly that Sarge is not following me. I use M's hand signal for "come", but Sarge's ass stays firmly planted next to Sam.

What am I supposed to do? What would M do? On one hand, the boy would be much safer if Sarge stays. But on the other hand, if Sarge decides to run away, there's a chance he would set off the tracker and I'd break my promise to M.

I swap tactics and give Sarge the hand signal for "stay". Hopefully he'll listen to that. Obviously my plan to leave the boy in the water was ruined, and now maybe Sarge somehow knew that I planned on leaving him again. Am I a monster? Yes.

I trudge through the woods on the lookout for something to eat. I'm pissed I don't have my bow. Actually, I'm pissed about a lot of things, and I'd like to shoot something. That won't truly help anything, though.

So instead I punch the nearest tree until my knuckles bleed. M had spent the better part of the year outside, beating the trees with a stick, screaming at the top of her lungs. Zach had been the one to show her the technique and I figure now is as good of a time as any to give it a shot. A loud, grotesque scream exits my throat as my fists slam the rough bark.

It's several minutes before I pull away. I've effectively scared every animal within a two mile radius so I'm not sure what I'm going to do for food. How could I be so stupid? Sarge and I should be deep in the woods by now, far away from the dangers of a tainted child, and closer to the rendezvous point for M. Instead, there was a momentary lapse in my focus, allowing risk to slam into our lives, jeopardizing our chance at getting to Aberdeen safely.

After an aimless walk of a mile or two, and constant anger flare-ups thinking about my own stupidity, I happen on a small doe. You don't see many deer these days, but the proximity to the river must be what entices this one to stay. I've never once felt bad for pulling the trigger on an animal, but something about shooting this one causes my gut to do flips. What is wrong with you, Warin?

The doe is unsuspecting, as if it's never had someone hunting it. A part of me—the part M has touched—tells me to move on and find something else. M knows that survival comes first, and never once has she told me to stop killing for food, but she has a regard for all life that I never really understood until today. Before this, it was me, and me alone. Now I'm realizing how much I've changed.

But then the rage takes over. The part of me that I've never quite been able to control. The part that reminds me nothing has really changed at all. Fuck this deer for not knowing what it's like to be hunted. I've been running for almost two years now and I've been hunted every step of the way.

The anger is what pulls the gun from my waistband. The anger is what drives my finger to the trigger. And the anger is what will always send me back to what Ren Keres made me into: Lucas Warin, cold-blooded killer.

CHAPTER NINE ○ AMITY

The reaver slinks toward me. She dons a tight suit in a darker grey than the clothes I'm forced to wear. Her face is clear of any and all marks; not a wrinkle in sight. Her lips are a deep plum maroon, and she gives me a wicked smile, revealing her perfect, white teeth. Her hair slants toward her face in a long bob that sits at her shoulders.

Her eyes are piercing me as she closes the distance between us. "Miss Thorne," she starts, "I assumed you'd have your flea-riddled mutt with you. And Mr. Warin." Her smile is tight-lipped.

I stay quiet for a second. *What's her game?* "You asked for me, right?" It takes everything to keep my voice steady. Of course she'd want me to bring her some leverage. She must think I truly am a stupid commoner to walk in here and willingly hand her another loved one to use against me.

"It's a pleasure to finally meet you, regardless." Her voice cuts straight to my bones.

"Wish I could say the same." I fight the urge to tear my eyes from hers and roll them. I imagine this encounter like a standoff in the wild: The second I show any sign of weakness is the second I'm defeated.

She cackles, dignified and harsh, placing her snake fingers on my shoulder. "I speculated you'd be the quiet type."

I resist my body's signal telling me to shudder, and instead keep my head tall, staring at our reflection in the mirror. "That was before you killed my sister."

The Reaver turns, meeting my eyes in the glass. "I did no such thing," she proclaims. There's no remorse in her voice, no sorry look in her eye. I hate this woman.

"You may not have put that syringe in her arm, but it's your fault she's dead."

She leans forward now, placing her palms on the table next to me. Her face is smug as she studies my image. "With that logic, you hold as much blame as I do."

Goosebumps instantly appear on my skin and my mouth pops open slightly. I silently curse my body's subconscious reaction. *Damn it, Amity! You've shown your weakness.*

"All I did was love her. I wanted her to have a normal life. You took that from her." My voice is shakier than I'd intended, but my eyes stay fixed on hers.

"Miss Thorne," she says. "You have it all wrong. Her death was a waste; she was a star pupil. The perfect example of the Exceptional." The Reaver leans back, straightening her spine. "I had great plans for her." For a second, her eyes soften, and the expression in them is sad. It's gone in a millisecond as she says, "But such is the cost."

Cost? *Cost for what?* I don't say anything back, allowing her to study me for a few seconds. There isn't much silence before she starts again.

"Do you know why you're here?" She walks around the table, sitting in the chair directly across from me.

"You were killing innocents. Did I really have a choice?" I grit.

The Reaver chuckles once more. "Oh, Miss Thorne. People are hardly as innocent as they appear."

"That family you murdered last year over the Update was

innocent. Josephine was innocent. Emma." My eyes bore into her with every bit of hatred I have. We stare at each other for a few minutes before she slowly slides the chair back and circles the table once more.

"The human brain is a remarkable machine. It controls thoughts, memory, speech. It sends signals to the rest of your body to make your hair stand on end when you sense something is off."

I'm attempting to keep myself calm, trying not to let my thoughts take over while wondering where she's going with this.

"Isn't that how you felt the day your sister died?" Her hand is a snake, slithering over my shoulder, behind my neck. She bends low again and, as if on cue, my hair stands. Her breath is ice cold on my ear. "Have you considered that my men let you get by that day?"

Fear smashes into my chest, causing my heart rate to spike. *Where are you Sarge? I need you.* The thought had crossed my mind multiple times, but hearing it straight from the devil's mouth is something too sinister to explain. The thing I never understood was the why, but now it's all slamming into me at once.

"You knew I was coming," I say, my voice fading at the realization. "You made it so I'd have to witness it."

Her eyes darken as her lips turn up in a sadistic smile. Memories shoot in my head from a year ago. The lack of inside patrols, the poor shooting from the guards, Luke's credentials working. It was all a part of her plan; it was all to get me there at the right moment.

The Reaver walks away from me again, sitting back down, blocking my view of the reflection. "I thought the death would set you straight, that maybe you'd lose yourself enough to back off. I wanted to use your story as a warning. But somehow it's being used as a beacon for rebellion." She folds her boney fingers together, interlocking them on the table in front of her. "Believe it or not, Miss Thorne, I'm a big advocate for second chances." She leans forward, bringing her face closer to mine. "But I rarely give a third."

Her eyes are menacing as she squints, scrutinizing me. I scoff. "I have no idea what you're talking about." There's no need to feign confusion; I've spent the last year hiding out in my old house. But it doesn't take much thought to settle on a reasonable explanation: Mason. He must be using the story as a way to rally the people. Of course he would. His politician brain is always looking for an angle to play.

I was the one who wanted to start the rebellion, but I got too comfortable in hiding. I let too much time pass. I was hurting. As far as I know, Mason thinks Luke and I are long dead by now, so why wouldn't he try to use my story?

"If it's not you that's using her as a martyr for revenge…" My eyes widen slightly, but I keep my face plain as she speaks, "Then something tells me you know who is." Her evil smile returns.

"Even if I did," I deride, "I wouldn't tell you." I'm not very good at lying—she definitely sees through me.

"Fighting me is futile, Miss Thorne. I'm going to break you one way or another." She gets up from the table and walks away. Something in me wants to get her talking, keep her fighting. I won't let her leave while she still has the upper hand.

"Is that why I'm here? To appease your need for a sadistic game?"

She stops in her tracks, slowly turning on her heel. Her lips are downturned, causing her perfect face to wrinkle slightly. "Rules are put in place for a reason. People who break those rules must be punished." A vein pokes out in her forehead as she continues. "Order is the most important thing; resistance causes destruction. We don't need chaos, Miss Thorne, we need stability."

The Reaver is completely beside herself. Luke had been right; this is clearly a sore topic for her. I decide rather quickly that I'm going to push some buttons. "If you're worried about a few measly commoners, then perhaps the Guardianship isn't as solid as I once thought."

She takes a deep breath, smoothing out her features. "This is much bigger than the Guardianship, Miss Thorne. I thought maybe you'd understand the sacrifice I'm making for everyone, but not many people do." Her voice is dripping with sorrow, like she actually believes what she's saying. "Don't worry, though. You will." The harsh tone returns and she twists around, slithering out without another word.

I take a moment to gather my thoughts, then look up and stare at myself in the mirror. My eyes are glazed over, my skin is pale. I could barely recognize myself before, but this is a complete stranger staring back. There's a thumping in my chest and a growing ache in my gut. I don't know what I was expecting our first tête-à-tête to be like, but my head is pounding.

Her sacrifice? What about everyone else's? None of this makes any sense. The Reaver implied that she had already offered up a second chance for me in the form of child murder, so why bring me here at all? Why waste this time on me? There's something to it, my brain just can't connect the dots yet.

With the killer headache and the silence of the room, I miss Sarge even more. If only we were together. He always knows what to do to make me feel more secure. But hopefully Luke has led him far away by now.

I'd say it's probably been twelve hours since I left them. Luke would never break his promise to me, so they should be on their way to Aberdeen. If the Reaver finds them, then we're all screwed. I'll be used to toy with Luke if they find out how he feels. Luke would be used against me.

And Sarge? He's the only true victim, because torturing me wouldn't really get them anywhere with him; he can't give up any information. This means the most effective strategy would be to torture Sarge relentlessly, hurting me in the process, and hurting Luke because of my pain. Sarge doesn't deserve that. He's the only true innocent one among us.

I never explicitly asked, but I'd hope that if all else fails, then Luke would kill Sarge so the Guardianship wouldn't be able to hurt him. This thought breaks my heart, and a deep ache spreads throughout my chest. No one should have such a gruesome back-up plan.

This is just another reason why the Guardianship must fall.

CHAPTER TEN ○ AMITY

Giles enters the room after an amount of time I couldn't even guess. My mind is cloudy, my eyes are heavy, my hand is numb from dangling in the handcuffs for so long. My gaze is fixed forward as he marches in. He waves his ID over the cuff around my wrist, and the little screen turns yellow. Next, he presses his thumb to the screen and it blinks green, clicking open after a few seconds, releasing me.

"The Headmistress has tasked me with showing you to your room."

"It would've been easier if she tasked you with killing me," I groan out into the open space. Being left alone with my thoughts must have been the first part of my torture, because in the time I've been sitting here, I've done a real number on myself.

"She's not a killer, Miss Thorne." Giles fails in his attempt to convince me. His fingers clasp the familiar spot on my arm. "She's making the world a better place. You should be honored that she's chosen you for the help."

Giles's face appears saggy with exhaustion, but his eyes are alive with admiration as he talks about the Reaver. It makes me want to punch him square in the nose. He's going to need a lot of convincing to see the evil that dances in her eyes—and even then—he may not ever be enlightened.

If there are enough people like Giles, then reasoning alone will never work. They're too far gone, their empty brains filled with the Reaver's lies disguised as a morally-just vision. I knew that resistance wouldn't be easy, but I was hoping that it wouldn't have to be violent. I realize how stupid of a thought that is. *But how would we be any better than the Reaver?*

I'm lead down the white halls with the grey stripe on the wall, idly trying to figure out where we are. Every hallway, corner, turn looks exactly the same as the last, until eventually we're at an elevator. Giles taps his ID against the scanner, and the UP arrow flashes after a few seconds. We must be on the lowest level because down isn't an option.

It's not long before the doors slide open and Giles gently pushes me inside. I'm staring at myself no matter what way I turn my head. The walls are mirrors that fill the entire space. Giles steps in behind me, touching the number two illuminated on one section of a mirror.

Suddenly my gut is screaming at me, telling me that something is wrong. I used to tell Emma that she should never ignore this type of feeling. But this time, I have to.

The lift moves at a faster pace than I thought possible. Barely any time passes before Giles is pulling me out of the doors and onto the second floor. I'm left with no time to quell the growing panic.

As I'm dragged through the halls, recognition settles in my brain. The dread in my chest makes it hard for me to breathe. My body goes into autopilot. The sound of my feet slapping on the ground fills my ears, the surroundings change as I walk, but none of it is happening consciously.

"Here we are," Giles says, stopping in front of room 204. My heart is beating so fast I fear it may rip out of my chest. Of course she'd make sure I was assigned this room. The room they murdered Emma in. There's a guard standing by the opening.

"Welcome to your new home for the next three months."

Giles pushes me into the space, causing me to trip over my own feet and stumble slightly. The first thing I notice that's different besides the guard is the fact that there's no door. Instead, once I'm inside, a clear force field separates me from those on the other side.

The second thing I notice is the colorful desk on the side wall. It stands out amongst the whites and greys. I don't remember much from this room before—nothing much except for Emma—but something is drawing me to the desk. A strange feeling settles over me.

I slowly walk toward it, allowing myself to focus on the scene. There are pictures of Emma, smiling happily in various settings. Her standing next to a small man with a thick beard. His ID says Richard Mire on it. There's another one of her concentrating on whatever project is in front of her. Then my eyes move to a drawing. It has Emma's large printed signature at the bottom. It's of me, her, and Sarge. A tear glides down my cheek as I run my fingers over the paper.

There's a final photo after the drawing. Emma is in the middle of all her classmates, smile as bright as ever. I look at the other children, wondering if they've all shared a similar fate.

For a second, I'm scared that the Reaver is right. Maybe Emma *would* still be alive if I had just let her go. But then I shake my head, trying to physically rid it of the thoughts. *You can't think like that, Amity.*

As I go over the photo again, one of the other students catches my eye. There's no immediate recognition from this angle, just a small girl hiding behind her classmate with a thumb popped in her mouth. But it only takes a few seconds for me to locate those dark curls in my memories. It's Trixie—the tainted child I had found in the woods last year; the child that Luke had killed.

Emma knew Trixie. My body shudders.

Losing the strength in my legs, I drop to the floor and cover my mouth to stifle the sobs that beg to claw their way out of my throat. I should've never come here. I should've let Luke carry me away. *Stop it, Amity! You're here now, so get your shit together and be strong.* Rage takes over and my fingers pull at the photos, ripping them from the wall, shredding them apart like my heart is.

It takes a moment for me to calm myself, but then I turn away from the desk and wreckage toward the bed with plain sheets along the opposite wall. It's gotta be after midnight by now and sleep is calling to me. It's been a long time since I've slept by myself, so I doubt this will be successful. Definitely not now, not after seeing those images on the wall. I'm sure the scenes will get twisted in my head somehow. If the Reaver wants to torture me, she could leave me alone. Eventually my own twisted mind will kill me.

I glance in the direction of the door to see that Giles is nowhere to be found. There's that guard standing tall with her back toward me now. It makes me wonder if she's here to keep me from escaping, or to keep others from getting to me. I'm not sure it matters either way.

The camera is in the top left corner above the door. The same place from the video. Luke told me it has a hard time picking up whispers, but if they think I'm up to something, they'll enhance the sound. I was going to look for a wire to loosen, or place something on it to muffle the sound, but I didn't account for a live guard playing babysitter.

I walk in the direction of the woman standing rigidly outside the clear wall. "What's your name?" I ask, getting closer.

She doesn't answer. She doesn't even turn her head. I don't know what pushed me to ask. Even if she wanted to talk to me,

I doubt she would be allowed. But I decide to ask again, this time a bit more forceful. I'm left with the same result.

Perhaps the force field is sound proof? *Only one way to find out.* I open my mouth, screaming at the top of my lungs. It feels good to let everything out. But it also confirms my suspicions. No one can hear me. Well, except the people listening in on my live feed. A few more of those and it might get them to tune me out. But for now, it's time to crawl into bed and slowly drive myself mad.

The sheets are stiff and cold against my skin. It's as if Emma's cold, dead arms are wrapped around my body. What a morbid feeling. What a hopeless existence.

o o o

My eyes are crusted over as the hustle and bustle from the hallway picks up. I guess the force field only works one way. The weight of exhaustion is keeping my body pressed against the mattress.

I don't know what time it is, but it's as though I've been away from Sarge and Luke for years already. Leaving Emma's body behind feels like a lifetime ago—her death like a century. Is it too late to say I've had enough? *Is it too early?*

The hours pass by and I'm still stuck in bed. My head is pounding because I've been laying down too long, but the only other option is to get up and pace around; to see the remnants of the photos. Somehow that seems worse. When I finally have enough energy, I let out a few loud screams for good measure.

Eventually the swishing sound of the force field fills the air, the thumping of heavy footsteps following. I don't move my head, instead I keep staring at the ceiling. The sensation of being watched burns into me as a shadow casts across my body.

"Rise and shine, Miss Thorne." Giles's voice breaks through the silence. It bothers me that he's so chipper. "Come on, now."

He steps into my view. My eyes flick to his. Is there sadness behind his pupils? *No. It's pity. Oh, woe is me, Amity Thorne, the troubled girl who needs Guardianship intervention.* I slowly slide my legs across the stiff mattress and pull myself to a stand.

"That's the spirit," cheers Giles, a grin spreading across his face.

He takes my arm, leading me out of the room. My feet drag across the tile because it's too hard to find the energy to lift my legs high enough. I wonder what the Reaver has in store for me today?

We walk through the halls, into the elevator, down to where my first face to face meeting had been the night before. It's odd to me that the *Headmistress* has time for such meetings, considering she has so much else to do according to Giles. He's going on about how I should've been ready, and we need to be punctual because she's taking time out of her busy schedule to meet with me. I honestly don't know why she doesn't just kill me. From everything I've heard so far, it would cause a lot less trouble.

The Reaver is waiting in the room—arms crossed, lips pursed— when we arrive. Her perfectly ironed bodycon dress is the same deep grey as her outfit from last night, and her plum lipstick accentuates her frown of disapproval.

"A little more prompt next time, yes?" Her eyebrows raise, and the grip on my arm tightens slightly as Giles gulps beside me.

"Of course." Giles nods.

"Shall we?" The Reaver reaches her hand out as Giles nudges me in her direction. Her eyes bore into me while I stumble toward her.

"I'd rather not." My voice is monotone in my answer. Surprisingly, I refrain from rolling my eyes.

The Reaver's lips twitch, and her cold hand grasps my hot,

sticky skin. "Always with the attitude, Miss Thorne."

She leads me out the door into the bright white hallway. We go through a few doors before coming to a room with a large machine in it. *Is this my first chamber of torture?* "What are we doing?" I struggle to keep the nonchalance of my tone. The truth is, I'm terrified. But the Reaver can't know that or I'll be dead in the water.

"Getting your examination done." Her words are clipped and formal, as if answering is the most inconvenient thing she could ever do.

A nurse interrupts us when she comes into the room through a different door. She's a bit top-heavy, her face is young and smooth. Her hair is perfectly silky in a tight brunette updo, and her eyes hold a slight sparkle in them—a sign that her life hasn't lost all meaning yet. She's surprised to see the Reaver here. "Madame, so nice to see you." Her tone is drenched with nervousness.

"Good morning, Miss Haddler. I'm here to watch over Miss Thorne's examination."

"Oh!" The young girl jumps into action. The Reaver steps toward the big screen to get out of the nurse's way. Once she's close enough, I clock her name tag. Nicole. "Sit please, Miss Thorne." She pushes me to the table. I sit. "Okay, now lay flat."

Nicole is sweet. She reminds me of Abby, Mason's younger sister and the kindest person I've ever met. The thought sours my mood even more, if that's possible. I actually miss my friends. Nicole explains the procedure, and I nod slowly, barely paying attention. Then, she presses a button that causes the table to recede into the tight white tube. The closed space makes it hard to breathe, makes it hard to stay calm. The only thing that gives me even the slightest bit of comfort is knowing that I'm experiencing what Emma had, and now she's not alone.

There are dim orange and purple lights that circle around me in quick succession. Then the table slowly rolls out again and Nicole's smiling face is hovering above me. "Not so bad, yeah?" Her eyes glow.

"Interesting," the Reaver says as she stares at the screen. "Where did you get those types of wounds?" She takes her bony fingers and turns the screen for me to see.

There's a body outline with my whole profile. My name, blood type, blood pressure, heart rate, are all listed. On the body, there's a slight red mark on the triceps, and deep gouging pools of maroon on my shoulder, arm, and ankle. There are red speckles over both my hands and up my forearms with barely any markings on my legs.

"These." The Reaver points at the deep maroon after a few minutes of silence; the markings of the wolf attack.

The thought of that day makes my throat close up. "Here, Madame. Click on the details button." Nicole comes to the rescue.

The Reaver clicks on a bright blue button in the bottom right. Then the body lights up like an interactive anatomy lesson. She presses her finger to the wound on my shoulder and the screen splits. On one side, it zooms in on the body, showing the exact shape of the bite mark. On the other side, a virtual model of a wolf is rendered based on the measurements taken from the bite. Even the approximate dates of the attack are listed. *Damn, they have everything.*

"Wolves," she says with slight amusement in her tone. "Interesting. Show me a simulation."

Nicole types something into the screen so a modeled simulation plays. For what it's worth, the scenario it's showing is pretty damn close. I'm simultaneously amazed and appalled at having to witness it. The wolf grips an ankle, then pulls back, gripping my arm before launching at the shoulder. It thrashes back and forth to match the tearing that my tissue had at the time.

She turns to me with engrossed regard. "Just one?"

The simulation doesn't show me fighting back. The simulation has no idea that Sarge was fighting two more only a few feet from me. I shake my head. "Three." My voice is raspy.

"Fascinating." The Reaver flicks her gaze back to the screen. "Let's start the stress test."

"Of course, Madame." Nicole makes her way to where I am and pulls out restraints from the side of the bed. A look of fear creeps into my eyes. I'm not ready to be tortured, but I have to be strong. "It's okay," Nicole whispers as she tightens the straps across my chest, "you won't be conscious for it."

"What do you mean?" I question.

"Miss Haddler?" the Reaver interrupts.

"Yes, Madame?" Nicole nervously turns away from me.

"Please hurry it along." She's impatient. Nicole steps away, readying a syringe. To keep my heartrate low, I distract myself with conversation.

"Do you normally accompany all of your patients to their exams?"

What is it about me that gets under the Reaver's skin? Luke never wanted to talk much about it, but I had a theory that somehow I was an important key in all of this.

Nicole comes over to stick the syringe into the back of my neck, at the base of my skull. The last thing I hear is the Reaver's answer. "Only the ones I'm curious about."

CHAPTER ELEVEN ◦ AMITY

I'M SURROUNDED BY NOTHINGNESS. IT'S BRIGHT WHITE ALL around. The Reaver is standing next to me, perfectly still. Then, all of sudden, everything pixelates and I'm in a long open hallway.

The Reaver clears her throat once she's animated. "Welcome to your test," she starts. "Let's begin."

"What am I supposed to do?"

Luke had explained that the simulation reacts like reality, so I won't have super human strength or anything. But every stimuli appears real even though this is an implanted construct in my own consciousness. So much so, that if I die in here, I die in real life because my brain won't know how to process it. Anything less than death and they can "save" me.

"Your goal is to get to the end of this hallway as fast as possible." There's a smug expression on her face. I wish I could knock it off of her.

"What if I refuse?" I ask. Surely there can't be serious consequences for not participating. They can break my bones, torture me, but it's not real—even if it feels that way. So what if I die? I doubt she'd go through all of this trouble to kill me. Then again, who knows...

I'm better off than most; I was warned about the test. The Reaver wants to dissect me, figure out what my strengths and weaknesses are. So what happens if I don't play along? Is that how

I finally meet my demise?

"Stubborn as ever, Miss Thorne. Your body will naturally fight to preserve itself, and in the process it reveals its greatest strengths and its deepest weaknesses. We'll get you one way or another. Now run." Her voice grows dark.

So that's how it works. I twist my neck to study the long hallway in front of me. When I look back, the Reaver is no longer standing close by. Scanning the area, I realize that there's now a wall closing in behind me. Then, a thick fog rolls in. It's the same kind from my house. *She thinks I'm going to run from some imaginary smoke?*

But the fog tumbles into my legs, surrounds my ankles, causes a sharp scream to tear its way from my throat. "You should run, my dear, or you'll be in a world of pain." The Reaver's voice envelops me like the fog, mixing with the sweet tone of Nan as she says the words *my dear*. But I have to be stronger than this.

"No," I grit, the fog circling up my body, licking at my neck. The pain is practically unbearable. *This is how Luke must have felt.* "I won't."

The Reaver doesn't reply. Instead, the fog totally encases me, traveling into my nostrils, down my throat, into my lungs. The searing pain covers every inch of my body, inside and out. Still, I refuse to move. My muscles contract and tense, my chest burns, my eyes are clenched shut. But I won't let the Reaver win. Even if it means I die.

After a few minutes of agonizing pain, the fog pulls away from me. "Very well," the Reaver speaks, and for a moment I believe I've won. But then she continues. "Will you run to save your friend?"

Down the long hallway is Luke's structured frame. He's chained to the floor and he's cursing, pulling at the restraints. The fog creeps up behind him. *This isn't real. It can't be.* Where is Sarge? He's supposed to be keeping him safe.

"You don't have Luke!" I shout. "I know this is a trick!"

"Is it, though?" the Reaver taunts me. "You don't think we found him and your mutt yet?" My face turns stark white as the blood drains from it. *It's not possible.* "You've got the key. Go ask him yourself."

When I unclench my fist, I find a key in my palm. *This has to be some sort of game. Right?* There's no way she has Sarge. Luke would've killed him. But then the fog nips at Luke's heels and his agonizing cries send my body hurling down the hallway before I can even think to stop myself.

The fog curls up around his back, and he howls with an intensity I've never heard before. My legs carry me even faster as I race to save him. Deep down I know that there has to be some type of angle she's playing, but the anxiety pushing up through my chest can't be stopped. It's as if I have no control.

The hair on his body starts to singe, and his cries become more desperate as he begs for relief. I race through the long corridor, picking up my pace, struggling to keep my heart from pounding out of my chest. I need to get to him. This ache in my chest will go away once I do. It has to.

I finally reach the last stretch of hallway, realizing that the haze has extended past Luke. There's no hesitation as I delve into the wall of fog. My skin instantly blisters and boils, and my muscles tense and seize. The pain is nothing with adrenaline pumping through my veins. *Luke needs you, Amity; you can't give up or give in.*

My arms wrap around Luke's body. His skin burns against my raw blisters, but it feels good to hold him. There's no time to waste, though. "Where's Sarge?" I pull away, searching his face for answers.

He replies with a series of thick coughs as he gags on the fog.

I give up on my questioning to get back to the task. My hands fumble around the chains, but the keyhole isn't in plain sight. Luke continues to hack and sputter. I shift to his legs to look there.

When the lock is finally cradled in my fingers, I slide the key into the hole. Once I do, everything turns to sand and the grains slip from my hands. The chains, the key, Luke, everything. The fog dissipates. I shudder as the Reaver's voice blasts into my skull.

"Very good, Miss Thorne," she praises. "Now we'll start the next round."

In the same second her voice fades out, a new landscape is constructed around my gangly frame and I find myself on a cliff. I instantly press my back against the rock, aiming my face toward the sky while the wind whips around me.

"What do you want from me?" My teeth are clenched together as I spit my words. There looks to be a path of rocks to climb above me. I could shuffle to my right or left and get to a more wide open area of rock than I'm standing on now. I can only imagine what she's going to instruct me to do this time.

"You don't have to do anything," the Reaver states. There's no doubting the confusion I feel. But in the same second, a tiny voice screaming bloody murder comes from somewhere above me. The child must be on the next cliff up. I'm left in the dark about everything else. Panic starts to form in my chest.

"Nothing. Are you sure?" I don't understand the test here, and for a moment the same stubbornness as earlier comes back. Is this a trick to get me to move, or a test to see how long I will stay?

"The choice is yours, Miss Thorne." What is the angle? There has to be one. The screaming is thrusting a wedge into my heart, and the drive to save whoever from their pain is getting harder to fight.

I take a moment, thinking to myself, *what would happen if I don't play along?* It's crazy to me how easily my brain was fooled, and deep down I'm aware of her having the upper hand. If I don't play along, will I reveal more about myself...or less?

Luke, and Sarge by proxy, had been used as a way to get me to move. But if I had moved on my own, would she have come to the same conclusion? Maybe it's time to see if I could lead her down a rabbit hole—a path of misdirection.

Looking to the left, then the right, I try to gauge which direction is shorter. After some careful examination, I head right. The screaming is getting worse, but I'm trying my best to tune it out. It would have taken me two seconds flat to try and help in the real world, so hopefully this throws the Reaver off. *But is it going to be enough?*

An amount of time passes that I can't even begin to guess. It seems like an eternity, but I know it's more than likely only been several minutes. Their shrieking is eating away at my soul. The longer I sit here, the worse I feel. Then, fear hits me all at once, crippling me, and sending away any drive I have to resist. Is it possible that this person could die, too, if I don't save them?

Luke had been constructed in my head, or at least I hope so. I don't believe he was real. But is it possible that whoever is up there is *not* a construct? Is it possible that I'm letting someone else die?

Immediately I spring into action. I've already wasted too much time. "Who is up there?" I ask out into the open air, shuffling across the dirt and rock ledge to where I first started. Hopefully the Reaver is honest with me.

"Does it matter?" Her cackling voice floats to me through the wind. I'm under the climbing rock path now, and the screams are insufferable. The Reaver is goading me; playing her sick mind games to get inside my head. But if there's even a small chance that this person will die, then it matters.

"Yes," I state, matter-of-factly.

There's a pause, a split second in which the Reaver is calculating her next move. Then, she speaks. "You are hearing the screams of a Tainted getting their final punishment."

Not if I can help it. My hands instantly shoot up over my head, searching for the right placement. I scramble along the mountainside, trying to keep myself calm. One hand, one foot, next hand, last foot. Over and over. It's almost as if the distance is growing the further I go.

My arms ache, my shoulders are sore. As I'm about to reach the top, my foot slips and I have to clutch the rough rocks with all of my strength to keep myself from falling. *Is this potentially fake human being worth the risk of death, Amity?* I mentally slap myself. Of course they are. I've made too many decisions in the past that have led to the death of others. I will no longer choose to stand back when I'm capable of helping.

The frustration and anger bubbling through my veins help push me the rest of the way. It takes all of my energy to pull my body off of the rocky ledge and onto the flat ground above. That's when I see her.

A young girl is slowly sinking into some kind of quicksand. She's crying and screaming. The pit must be modified in some way. Steam billows out of the grits. I wonder if it's something similar to the fog.

The girl is almost completely submerged. Her arms are stuck somewhere in the sand, and I'm struggling to plan how I'll help her. I scurry over as fast as I can. "It's okay," I say, "I'm here now."

My knees are on the edge of the sand. The heat bubbles up while I lean over in an attempt to reach the girl. It's no use, though. She's too far away. This is going to take some quick thinking. I look around for a branch, or maybe some rocks, anything to create a temporary bridge to get to her, but there's nothing. Her screams are getting louder as her body burns away in a literal pit of Hell.

"Let her go!" I shout angrily into the sky. What is the point of this?

When I look at the girl again, she no longer appears the same. This time it's Trixie's small face staring back at me. *What's going on?* I shake my head and look again, only to see Emma's terrified eyes instead. "Are you giving up that easily?" The Reaver's voice plays. "I control how you perceive her, but the fact is that she's still a young girl getting punished. I didn't see you giving up so quickly." The evil in her voice only enhances my aggravation. She's taunting me. This means Luke was most likely a tainted soul being projected differently to me and I never even knew.

Does the Reaver have a point, though? Do I work harder for those I love? For those that I feel I must protect? Do I give up if it's someone I don't know? *Maybe I'm learning things about myself, too...*

I decide on one more attempt to stretch and reach the girl. She looks like her normal self, and she's begging me with those sad eyes to save her. *No. It doesn't matter who is in need of help.* I'm going to give my all.

This time, I extend my arms, edging into the burning sand. The fabric of my pants burns into my skin, but I ignore the heat. The extension of my arm is hurting my shoulder, and the muscles of my stomach are tense as I struggle to keep myself upright. Just as I'm about to reach her, I lose my balance, falling into the pit which instantly becomes the consistency of water. I'm suspended in the shadowy wetness.

The Reaver laughs a dark and heartless cackle. It completely encases me. "The Tainted can't be saved," she says.

Suddenly, I materialize in an opening of a jungle. Thick dense trees surround me. There's a gun in the middle of the dirt. It's equidistant from a young woman about my age standing across from me along the opposite tree line. She seems scared, yet determined. I strain to catch my breath and slow my heartrate.

"As you now know, we can connect the constructed planes of different individuals. This is another patient taking her stress test. Kill her," the Reaver instructs. *What?*

"Why would I do that?" I'm not going to kill someone. Especially knowing that if they die in here, they die in real life, too. This young woman hasn't even been deemed tainted yet, has she?

"Because if you don't, she'll kill you instead."

Suddenly the jungle starts to shake around us and the ground widens, making it a further distance for each of us to cross. It is no longer open. There are vines, stumps, trees, and other hazards obstructing my path. The other woman can barely be seen through it all now.

"So what?" I scoff, feeling my usual stubbornness. I'm questioning everything. Could I have saved that child if I didn't try to throw off the direction of my test? Would saving her really be worth it if she would be forced into another day of torture? I'm wondering if I should race to the gun and kill this woman here and now so that she doesn't ever have to suffer from the Reaver's games again. My mind travels to Trixie and the mercy that Luke felt he was showing her. *Should I do the same here?*

"Go," the Reaver's voice orders.

The woman sprints toward the gun and I can't stop my brain from telling me to do the same. It's a race against time as we cross from opposite sides of the forest. I duck and weave and jump and push myself long past when the beating of my heart becomes irregular.

Once the gun is in view, my mind starts to panic. *Am I really going to kill this person to save her from a life of torture?* How could I? Before I can think any further, the woman jumps out from behind the trees, sending my legs into overdrive. Adrenaline pumps through my veins, pushing me.

As we near the last stretch, the young woman's foot gets caught in a root along the tree line and she slams to the ground. I don't falter as I break through the trees, launching myself toward the gun. The look in the woman's eyes is enough to haunt me for the rest of my life. Her face is etched with terror.

Something in me sends my body to a sliding halt. My fingertips are about to touch the cold metal of the weapon, yet they stop short. I can't kill this person. This is a scared, living, breathing human being. A human being that doesn't deserve death. She deserves a chance to live and see a new world. She deserves the chance that was ripped away from Emma.

The young woman's forehead is pressed against the dirt as I walk calmly over to her. She's resigned to the fact that she lost. But then the clunky sound of the metal hitting the ground causes her to jump.

She lifts her face, her gaze meeting mine with a shocked expression. "What's this?" she whispers.

"Go ahead. Kill me."

At first she hesitates, thinking this is something of a trick. Then she slowly helps herself off the ground with gun in hand. The metal clinks as she shakes, and I drop down to my knees, shuffling forward. The cold barrel of the gun presses against my forehead as I lean into her uncertain hold. My eyes close.

This is it. This is how my life ends. I try not to think about the fact that I'll never see Sarge again, that I'll never talk to Luke after this point. But I will get to be with Emma and my mom. Zach, too. There will be no more pain, or guilt, or anger.

A minute passes and nothing happens. Still, though, I keep

my eyes clenched shut. It isn't until the metal is removed from my forehead that I open them.

"No," the girl says. "Please!" She looks scared again, and for a moment I think she's talking to me. Then she turns the gun on herself. "I don't want to die! Stop!"

Suddenly I'm panicking again, confused with what's unfolding in front of me. She presses the gun to her temple, tears cascading down her cheeks. I will my brain to move, to get the gun back on me, but I have no control over my body anymore. It's clear it wants to move, to help, to save the girl. But it doesn't.

"No! Please, stop!" The girl gets more frantic and I watch on in horror, unable to turn my gaze away. "I don't want to die. Please! Plea..." The gunshot rings in my ears, and my eyes close again as the sickly smell of the gunpowder permeates my nose.

I open them to find myself in the testing lab at Omphalos. Nicole's eyes are wide, like she's seen a ghost. The Reaver looks slightly agitated and mildly winded.

"You don't speak a word of this to anyone." The Reaver's voice is low and menacing. I barely hear it over the ringing in my ears. She walks over to me, forcing Nicole to spring into action, working on removing my restraints as the Reaver takes hold of my arm.

"What was that?" I choke out. My throat burns as if I've been screaming for ages, and my body is tired and hot. Nicole averts her eyes, focusing on the task at hand...or trying to. Whatever she just witnessed wasn't normal, and it's shaken her to the core as well. But maybe I can get the Reaver talking. "Come on. That wasn't a test at all, and you know it." My voice is muted and ominous to match the Reaver's, and the waves of apprehension flowing from Nicole tell me I've portrayed it well.

"Miss Thorne," the Reaver starts, "when under severe stress, you learn the most about who a person is. Do they run and hide?

Does their body completely shut down?" She's in her element. The inner workings of people's minds must be her holy grail. My mouth stays shut as I await her point. She's good at derailing my thoughts. "You are brave, smart, courageous, stubborn. Your vitals are good. All around, you're a healthy young woman. But we do these tests to find your level of resistance and the best way to navigate your brain. Do you want to know what yours revealed?" Her smile is evil, yet her voice is playful. She's completely ignoring the bug from the test; the death of that innocent woman. *I want to lunge out of the bed and poke your snake eyes out.*

"I want to be taken back to my room," I say. She never loses the smirk.

"Very well."

I'm begrudgingly led back to room 204 without a word. Giles trails behind us to protect Madame Keres. Nicole had warned me that it might be difficult to differentiate fake from reality moving forward.

The thing I'm realizing is that it doesn't matter what I do; every choice I make has a consequence. The truth is that I feel like a shell of the person I once was. The Reaver knows my strengths, my weaknesses. She knows exactly how to break me now, and I don't want to be broken. I want to somehow become whole again. I realize with all of my missing pieces—Emma, Zach, Sarge, Luke—it's almost impossible, but still something I want nonetheless. Maybe that's my greatest weakness of all.

The guard in front of my door is no longer the tense woman from earlier. Now it's an older man with a kind face and gentle eyes. He catches my gaze for a few seconds before ashamedly turning away. My gut tells me I may have just found an ally; something I desperately need. Although, I'm not sure how trustworthy my judgement is these days.

The man steps aside, standing tall as the Reaver nods to him. She puts me in the room, but before she presses the button to shut me out, I ask, "What was my weakness?" I turn around to look her in the eyes. They're dancing with a familiar playful mischief. "What did my test reveal?"

I shouldn't have let my curiosity win this time. I should've kicked it into the dirt and not let it up again. But the truth is, I want to know so that maybe I could try and get stronger. Whatever happened at the end of my test is eating away at me and I need to make sure that something like that never happens again.

She presses the button for the force field. "Guilt."

CHAPTER TWELVE ○ LUKE

SAM AND SARGE ARE CHASING EACH OTHER THROUGH A FIELD of tall grass. It's dangerous in the open, but it makes them happy so, who cares. Well, you do, Warin, but whatever. Sam has only been with us for a week, but Sarge has glued himself to that boy as if it were his job. I admit, he's grown on me as well, but I'd never say it out loud. Having Sam here isn't all that bad. The thing that weighs me down the most is not being able to talk.

The added risk that comes to us with having him near still eats at me sometimes, but I was trained for the unexpected. Ren thought she was making it impossible for me to survive without the Force, but the truth is, she made it easier for me to adapt.

I raise my hand above my head and circle my arm like a tornado until I catch either Sam's or Sarge's attention. Once they stop to look at me, I thump my palm to my chest twice—the signal to come. The boys run at me with an excited energy surrounding them.

It's been interesting working with Sam to develop a way to communicate. At first it was mostly him speaking and me typing on the Relay. Then, we started creating signs for quicker communication.

As I child, my father taught me sign language. It soon died out as doctors found a way to combat deafness, but my father always thought it would help with survival. Having the background has definitely helped in teaching Sam what I now call TC, or Tainted Communication.

I lay out the meal I've cooked on some leaves, presented as nicely as possible for Sam and Sarge. They both run up and immediately gobble the contents. Sam's body hasn't taken well to the slim pickings of the outdoors compared to the steady feedings at Omphalos. Even the most tainted of children are fed three meals a day. It may not be gourmet food, but it's a consistency—unlike out here.

Sarge, on the other hand, is loving it. I was afraid he'd never eat again once M left, but Sam has given him a new purpose. He's not a healthy looking dog in the slightest. He's big, he's powerful, but his ribs poke out where there should be more meat. Looking at him now, I realize he's taking on a wolf's appearance even more these days. Lean; scraggly.

The boys finish up their meals, casually looking on what's left with hungry eyes. *More?* I sign. *Still hungry?*

Sam says, "You've got to eat, too," and shakes his head slightly. His eyes stay wide with hunger, though.

It's okay, I sign back, trying to reassure him. I slide the rest of the meat toward them. It's all that's left of the deer. It's not a lot, but hopefully it will satiate a bit of his hunger. Sam takes the food and splits it into three piles. One for him, one for Sarge, and one for me. It actually sends a twinge of unexplainable emotion deep into my chest. Sam is a thoughtful, caring, sweet kid. The exact opposite of everything that I am. I wish M were here. She would love Sam, and Sam would love her back.

"What happened to you?" Sam asks out of nowhere. My first guess is that he's talking about my scarring. It's less noticeable now, but it's there, nonetheless. I'm glad Josephine did as good a job taking care of me as she did, though. Soon it should be completely gone.

I type my reply on the Relay and let Sam read it. His eyes grow wide as he processes what I've written. He knows how bad the

Guardianship can be, and I think when we found him in the river, he was ready to give up. I hope he sees my scars as a reminder to never give up on the important things.

Sam opens his mouth to speak, but promptly shuts it as Sarge lets out a deep growl.

I'm instantly on alert, pushing away any worries that rise in my chest over the noise. The tracker doesn't appear to be set off by growls or barking, but I can't be entirely too sure.

Sarge is doing his best at telling me what's coming. It's not like I can ask him to be more specific, anyway. Even if Sam wasn't with us and I could talk, Sarge would only be able to share so much. His body language and savage growls suggest it's a rather pressing and dangerous issue, though.

He gets up and circles his large body around Sam's tiny frame. Sarge nudges Sam, hoping he'll move. This leads me to believe that the threat is human; something, or someone, that could set off the tracker. I give them the hand signal to go, ignoring the growing pressure in my gut. If I can't find them again, then I'll break my promise to M. But if we set off the tracker, I risk losing Sarge in a different way entirely.

There's not much time to think before footsteps approach from in the distance. I hold my breath to count how many sets. More than one or two. Probably four or five. I've got three guns, but all of them are running low on ammo, so this is about to get interesting.

I keep myself calm, sitting around the fire I'd used to warm our food. I've no doubt the smoke had been a signal; a beacon to lead every sorry miscreant right to us. I was dumb to do it, especially in an open field, but Sam's growling stomach was tearing at me.

"Well, well, well," a shitbag wielding a bat says as he taps it into his grimy palm from off to my left. "Looks like dinner is served!"

He steps out of the tree line with four other dirty individuals. They are scraggly, weak-looking, but each holds some kind of blunt weapon, and the confidence in their eyes speaks for something. After all, there is merit for strength in numbers.

But whoever these people are, and whatever gang they think they've created, means nothing if they're up against me. They see an easy kill, and an even easier loot. But they're wrong.

It's no surprise that gangs of rotten human beings would form amongst all the ruin. Ren never really cared too much about them because they did a lot of her dirty work. The Force often turned a blind eye to such groups as long as their hate was directed toward other commoners. It's clear this gang hasn't been humbled in a while, and my lip twitches into a smirk as I revel in the knowledge that I get to do the honors.

"Sorry, guys," I joke, keeping my smirk tame. "I wasn't expecting this many. I'm fresh out." I stay seated, keeping my head forward, but watching every move out of my peripheral.

Laughter spreads throughout the group as the leader says, "You think you're funny, huh?" with a stupidly condescending smile. His lazy face bothers me, and I stop myself from immediately jumping at him and ending this. I need to play it smart. I'm sure if I pulled my gun out right here and now, they'd all run away. But where's the fun in that?

"I'd like to think so, yeah," I shrug. There was a part of me growing up that felt humor was a coping mechanism I'd picked up to avoid the shit I had to deal with. But in the heat of the moment, I know it's my confidence that helps the humor flow. "You'll have to find some other host," I insist.

There are general murmurs of non-agreeance filtering among the crowd until one voice sneaks through. "Who said you could camp out in our territory without paying the fee?" a woman asks, her thick eyebrows raised with assertiveness.

"Who said it was your territory?" At this I stand up, feeling the rage bubble through my veins. It's been a while since I've given a good ass kicking, and my knuckles are already tingling at the thought. It's clear this group doesn't feel good about my cockiness. It makes them angry.

"You're about to meet Death," the leader smiles, all of his lackeys showing a similar hunger for blood.

I chuckle a laugh from deep within my gut. "I've walked toward Death, and came out holding it by the neck. Which of you pansies will share a similar fate?"

The taunts only serve to make the leader angry. But I thrive in chaos and he's about to pour gasoline on my fire. They aren't the only ones with bloodlust.

The leader sends the other four to attack me. Stupid move because now I know what kind of fighter he is. I'm trying to keep an eye on everyone's movements, though, so he'll have to wait. From the looks of it, the tall young man with a broom handle will get to me first, and he seems dumb enough to immediately swing it, so he's my first target. Two other members break off on either side, most likely going around my back.

As the group closes in on me, the tall one gets ready to strike. I'm patient in waiting for the perfect moment. Right as the shaft is mid swing, I circle around, ducking, and grab the other member sneaking behind me on my right.

The leader doesn't react fast enough, and the wood smashes into his friend as I push him closer, knocking him out. There. One down. Three to go.

The fact that I've already outsmarted them seems to piss the leader and the group off further. This time the member to my left grabs one arm, and another grabs my right, trying to hold me back.

But rage is one volatile element, and I'm so full of it I'm about to blow. I use all of my force to bring my hands together, causing the two members to stumble into each other and smack their heads.

In the split second that one of them releases my arm, I use my free hand and grab their scrawny neck, delivering them right to another member about to slam a stone into me. Once that one is down, I swirl my body so the momentum of the stranger still attached to my arm is enough to knock the rock thrower off his feet.

Then, I take the scrawny kid hanging off my limb and lead him toward the fire. As we get close, hes panics. When he tries to pull away, I grip his arm tightly and jam his head close to the flames. So close it's like his eyebrows singe. "You wanted to hold on so tight before, what happened?" I play.

His loud sobs don't cover the footsteps of the guy with the rock. He must have gotten his bearings and is coming back for more. I quickly slam the sorry sap into the fire, his scream music to my ears as the heat burns his flesh. Then, I swiftly turn on my toes, spinning into an uppercut that leaves the rock thrower reeling.

The leader is standing back in awe at this point, whether in self-preservation or shock, I'm not sure. He's the type that makes others do his bidding. He's selfish. And after the last of his members are brought to a sleepy halt with a few uppercuts and jabs, I finally catch the fear in his eyes.

There's a small pile of unconscious bodies around me, but I don't feel bad at all. Their quiet whimpers are the calm to my storm. These are the worst kinds of people. The ones that prey on the weak. I can say this because I used to be the same in the Force.

The leader hesitates for a second before deciding to run, but it doesn't matter anyway. The gun is pulled from my waistband and there's a bullet in his leg faster than he can turn. He's shouting in agony, swinging his bat violently with one hand. Funny he thinks it will keep me away. His other hand grips his thigh. The bat is ripped away from him in no time and the panic in his eyes gives me a feeling of power that I've missed since leaving the Force.

"You're a coward." I hold him by the throat, pulling his face close to mine with a menacing grip. "So I guess you're the lucky one." I smile an evil grin.

Our little group of runaways tried to help others. M, Lacy, Abby, Zach, and Mason. Even me. We used our number strength to do the right thing rather than the wrong because all—well most—of us aren't monsters. So screw this guy and his goonies for choosing the evil path.

"You're...a...psycho," he chokes and rasps. His eyes have that sorry look about them. But I don't feel sorry. This man was ready to run away and leave behind those that trusted him. He deserves to be punished.

"You're damn right," I seethe, "and I hope you see these psycho eyes every time you close yours." The anger pulls from deep within, and I fear I'm stumbling too far into the rage. Woah, Warin, calm down. Take a step back. I drop the man to the ground, his body basically lifeless. "Don't terrorize anyone ever again."

I rear back my leg, kicking him in the gut once for good measure. He curls over in pain and wretches. Good. *Serves you right,* I think to myself. Working quickly, I gather up the small amount of stuff we have. Once the rage settles back into its place like a rabid bear to its den, I take off in the direction that Sarge and Sam had. There are subtle tracks for about a thousand feet, but then the trail goes cold.

I hate that I can't call out. How am I supposed to find them? I slam my palm into my chest twice in hopes that Sarge will hear it. In hopes he'll come find me. If anything happened to him, or Sam, I wouldn't be able to forgive myself.

After searching the area for an hour, I begin to lose hope. My fists ball at my sides and I desperately search for a tree to teach a lesson to. But as I'm about to throw my knuckles into the bark, sharp teeth clamp onto my arm.

I turn to find Sarge and stop myself from screaming as I yank him to my chest, remembering the need to stay quiet. Then, I glance around looking for Sam. I don't see him. "Where is he?" I whisper, suddenly worried that something might have happened.

Sarge's golden eyes peer into my hazels, and deep down I know Sam is safe—in the relative sense.

"Take me to him."

I follow quickly behind as Sarge bolts through the woods. I didn't expect them to go this far, but at least they're alright. It's nearing dark by the time Sarge slows. He leads me to a small burrow in the ground.

Sam is curled up as much as he can manage to hide himself away. Sarge gives a small whine to alert Sam of our presence. He peeks his head out of the hole, but looks at me as if he's seen a ghost. He cowers back down.

I glance at Sarge for some answers, but I get nothing. So I quickly pull the Relay from my pocket and type out a message.

Is everything okay? What happened?

I nudge Sam and realize he's shaking. *Please,* I will to him mentally. As if a miracle is granted, he lifts his head and slowly reads my message. It takes him a while to formulate a sentence.

"I saw you," he finally says in a small voice. "I watched you hurt those people." Sam's eyes cut into my soul. Not only do I look like a monster with my charred skin, but now he's seen me act like one. I know I'm the bad guy sometimes; it's the way you have to be in a world like ours. But I've scared this child and made him feel even more unsafe. I know M would be upset with me. She would also know how to fix it.

> **I'm sorry you saw that. It had to be done. I wanted to keep you safe. Will you please come out?**

Hesitantly, Sam climbs out of the hollow spot in the ground a few seconds after reading my message. I type out another.

> **I'm sorry, Sam. I hope it never happens again.**

A tear is streaming down my face. I never once thought I'd feel like this, but someone as good as Sam deserves to keep their innocence. He doesn't know anything about my past, and I know nothing of his. These actions may be somewhat justified, but they are still murky. To a young kid who feels there is no one to trust—that a monster lurks behind every corner—I've certainly driven it home. I hold my arms out for a hug, and it's not long before he dives into my chest. He starts crying on his own. Sarge joins in and we sit, nuzzled like this, long after dark.

My father was an honorable man, but he never wanted me to be soft. My real mother left us before I could remember, and my stepmom, Janet, never wanted to overstep. But M has taught me that softness might not be a bad thing. So if I can give that to Sam, I'm going to. I wish I could promise him that I'm trying to contain my rage; that I'm trying to be a better man. He needs to know that not everyone is an enemy capable of doing terrible things.

CHAPTER THIRTEEN ○ AMITY

Madame Keres has left me to my own devices. I've been in this room for about a week and, quite frankly, I feel like Death. Nothing has been accomplished on my end except that I've managed to loosen the wires in the camera. I still put in my daily shouts for good measure, though. I believe the day guard, Charlie, saw me, but he never said anything.

There's something about Charlie that I connect to. Maybe he's as lonely as I am. Maybe it's because he actually treats me like a human being. He's always kind and gentle when delivering my food to me. I've not eaten since being here and my stomach growls at the thought. I look at the bland grey clock on the wall to check the time. It's almost lunch.

Charlie is standing with his back to the force field, but he occasionally turns his head to make sure I'm okay. It's endearing, really. I glance at the clock again. Barely any time has passed since I last time I checked. *Ugh, this is the worst torture of all.*

Any minute now and I'll have the only human contact I'm allowed. It lasts a total of ten seconds, but it's the only thing that gets me through my days lately. I know it's only been a week or so, but it already feels like I've been a prisoner for centuries.

The big hand of the clock rests on the twelve and, just like that, the cart with my food rounds the corner. Everyone else has the freedom to retrieve their own meals from the cart. But me?

I have Charlie.

The force field disappears and Charlie turns his back to the hallway. "Here's your lunch, Miss Thorne," he says, sliding the tray across the ground to me. I've been choosing to sit on the floor in the middle of the room for about three days now. At first Charlie seemed worried, but it took him almost no time to get used to it. *Why would he even care, Amity?*

This has been a normal part of our day for the better half of the week and admittedly the only thing I look forward to. So it doesn't surprise me when Charlie nods and turns away, lifting his hand to hit the button for the force field. However, what does surprise me is the fact that, this time, I speak up.

"Oh, come on. Can't you leave the force field open?" Charlie hesitates. "It would be nice to talk to someone." Maybe it's the constant loneliness, or a desperate attempt to find an ally, but whatever it is, it gets Charlie's attention.

His face is etched with sorrow. "Miss Thorne," he sighs, tilting his head to the side in order to scan the hallway. "I really shouldn't."

A die hard Reaverite (that's what I'm calling dipshits like Giles) wouldn't even entertain the idea. The fact that Charlie responded shows me that my inclination of him had been correct. So I push a bit. "Please," I beg.

His eyes grow wide. "If I get caught..."

"It's completely invisible. Just stand with your back to the door. No one will know." Charlie subconsciously glances in the direction of the camera. Can I trust him with my secret? Something tells me the answer is yes. Besides, I think he already knows. "They can't hear you if you speak in a hushed tone. The wires are loose." At least, that's what Luke told me the outcome would be. I have no idea how true it is since everything here has changed.

"Would it help you eat?" Charlie whispers. His eyes hold a

concerned expression. It reminds me of my dad. Something about Charlie's voice leads me to believe he's also a father.

I nod.

"Okay." He turns around, keeping to his normal positioning. I hesitantly reach forward and pull the tray toward me. My stomach growls again. The thought of eating makes me feel simultaneously sick and starved.

There's a thin slice of slimy ham in between two flat slabs of bread. Nothing else. No mayo; no cheese. You'd think with all the advanced technology they have here, they could, at the very least, provide a decent selection of food and some damn cheese! *Jeez, Amity, maybe you're hungrier than you thought.*

I take a bite of the blandwich, chewing it slowly. Questions to pick Charlie's brain are swirling around in my head as I swallow. Surprisingly, though, he speaks first. "I'm sorry about your sister," he whispers.

Whatever little bit of appetite I'd gained from finally putting food in my stomach is lost with those five little words. I don't know why I thought Charlie would have no knowledge of my past, but that was my understanding up until now. I guess he'd have to know everything in order to guard me. Perhaps if I was a crazy con artist with the gift of persuasion they'd have to be warned. But what exactly was he told? Was he given the truth, or the Reaver's version of it?

"Why'd you join?" I ask as I set the sandwich down. *One bite is enough for now.* A Reaverite wouldn't feel sorry for me, so I know Charlie didn't join for the cause. Unless, of course, he had a change of heart. But either way, his answer may give me some insight into the way the Reaver works.

Charlie doesn't say anything for a long time, and I begin to think that he hadn't heard the question. Then, my mind takes me down a darker tunnel, leaving me to wonder if someone is watching him. But soon his hushed whisper carries into the room as he tilts his head to the side. "My daughter."

Ah. So he *is* a father. Last year, Luke shared with me that one of the reasons he had joined was to protect his family. Is this the case for Charlie as well? "To protect her?"

"To save her."

"Wh..." I start, but don't get to finish. Charlie smoothly glides his hand to the button and slyly double presses it, giving the illusion that it's only just been opened.

"Good afternoon, sir," Charlie stands at attention and steps aside, leaving room for Giles to pass. I meet Charlie's eyes. There's a sorry look settled over them.

"Miss Thorne." Giles nods to me, holding out his hand; a silent command telling me it's time to get up. He doesn't help me, though, because apparently that would make him too decent of a human being.

I let Giles place his hand in its normal spot on my arm and he drags me into the hallway. As we pass Charlie, my eyes plead with his. Yet, I feign excitement to Giles. "What do we have on the agenda today?"

"MAP." *Map?* Oh, right. Memory Actualization Processing.

The Reaver had told me my weakness. Now I'm preparing myself for the rough road of memories ahead. There are certain ones that will no doubt show up. But will any others? Will long forgotten, deeply buried memories come back from their graves to haunt me?

The hallways bleed together like usual as I'm tugged through them. It still amazes me how these people are able to find their way. I'm doing my best to ignore the worry that's circling my brain, but as we step in front of a grey door that reads "MAP Lab", I can't get my mind out of overdrive. I'm tearing open every door of my memories, trying to burn away the guilt and preserve my sanity.

Giles uses his ID to scan us in, and suddenly I feel woozy. This room is large—not like the physical examination and testing lab that was not much bigger than the machine it holds. There are many tiny spaces in this one, divided by curtains like a hospital room. Though, instead of two or three beds, there are dozens. My eyes catch a glance through the crack of a covered one. It's a kid, probably slightly younger than me. His eyes are staring off at nothing, but the pain in his frown is apparent. Whatever is going on in his head must be terrible.

Each section has a bed with scratchy grey sheets and a screen hooked up to a control panel. As Giles leads me deeper into the lab, I feel as though my legs will give out.

About halfway to the end, there's a split in the room. On one side, there's a door left unlabeled. On the other side, there's one marked with "Private MAP Viewing". This is the door Giles brings me to. A similar bed to the ones in the common area is set up in the middle of the room. There are two monitors in here, though. A small personal one connected to the control panel, and a larger one overhead like a movie theatre screen. The ceiling holds a large mirror. Nicole and the Reaver are here, waiting for me.

"Thank you, Marcus." The Reaver nods as Giles hands me over to Nicole. She gently nudges me toward the bed. I don't say a thing as I lay down on the hard mattress.

It stays silent while Nicole does her thing. She sticks something to my temple, and the screen turns on. This must be how they see into my brain. I struggle to keep my mind blank in case they're watching it now. But it's no use.

This is what Luke had prepped me for and my thoughts are erratic, taking me back to his words in between Nicole's actions.

The first few times, you'll be forced to relive it, he said.

She hooks me up to the IV and I sit, strapped to the bed, awaiting whatever torture is about to ensue. "What percentage, Headmistress?" Nicole asks, finally breaking the silence.

Once they pick up on patterns, they'll start to manipulate it, he warned. "Hm," the Reaver thinks aloud, scrunching her perfect lips up. "Start with ten percent. Her medical showed no signs of resistance, ironically."

"Very good, Madame."

It'll be sort of like a dream, but it will feel so real that you'll have a hard time distinguishing it from reality.

She taps on the small screen, and a blue solution from one bag drips alongside clear solution from another. They meet in a singular bag before traveling down the tube and directly into my bloodstream. Whatever this concoction is, it makes me heavy, instantly.

Pick up on the inconsistencies and you can shut them out, Luke had said; his final bit of advice.

"What's...target...for...day?" Nicole asks as I fade in and out of consciousness.

"Mem...of...guilt." The Reaver answers, and I'm out.

When I open my eyes, I'm in a room with my mother. She's in the beginning stages of her sickness, but I didn't know it at the time. She's telling me I can't go hang out with Jeremy since Grace won't be there and I'm yelling at her because I'm young and stupid. "Why can't you let me have a normal life?" I scream at her.

"Amity Belle Thorne," my mother grinds. "Quiet your voice. Your sister is upstairs."

"Ugh!" The exasperated feeling is strong, but my head is battling it. "I hate you!"

Next thing I know, I'm in my room. Emma runs in, her tiny feet thumping along the ground. She leaps into my bed and snuggles against me. "What's the matter?" I ask as I hug her to my chest. She sniffles.

"I want to be with momma, but I don't want to be a gift!"

My heart splinters. "Oh, sweetie," I soothe. "You won't be a gift," I say, and mentally curse myself for telling her something that might not be true.

"I want to stay here with you."

"I'll always be with you, little M. I promise."

Guilt instantly floods through me, and I clench my eyes shut, trying to block out the drowning sensation in my chest. When I open them again, I'm in the woods behind my house. My father is tugging against my wrist and the pain in my chest is unstoppable as Sarge digs his teeth into his ankle. "I'm sorry," I whisper, and deep down inside I'm crying because I know this is the last time I'll see him.

A few seconds pass, and the grip on my wrist travels while dirty hands creep onto my neck. I'm gasping for air. The struggle to get them off is painful, but once I finally do, the scene around me morphs into a small lakeside one. I'm shoving the guilt as far away as possible as I pull a faded photograph of a young girl out of a dirty bag. I don't know who she is, but somehow I know I've left someone important to her to die.

Turning away from the photo, I come face to face with Trixie. She's shivering, her eyes begging me to help her. But then Luke materializes and I watch in horror as he puts the cold metal of a gun to her forehead. It's her or Emma. It's her or the runaways.

I blanche as Luke pulls the trigger and suddenly I'm exiting a tent. There's a war scene around it, and Mason is yelling. "Him?" He's angry. "You chose him?"

I fall to my knees, bring my palms up to my face, and when I look out again, Sarge's eyes hold desperation as two wolves pin him to the ground. He's left in pain, unable to save me.

When I crawl toward him, a wolf grabs at my ankle and I'm forced to look away from my best friend. Turning around, it's no longer Sarge laying there, but Zach. His body is cold and motionless, and I nestle myself into his chest.

I'm not sure how long we sit like this, but when I pull away, it's Emma's lifeless body that's now in my arms and the guilt is overtaking me, drowning me. I stare out blankly, unable to tell my brain to function normally, and Luke waves a hand in front of my face.

"What are we?" He seems unsettled. I snap out of my trance and realize we're in my living room. Normally he doesn't push me about my feelings, but today something is bothering him. I've been avoiding the discussion for a long time. I don't want to say anything out loud; to make it real.

"We're friends!" I chuckle nervously. Somehow I let Luke get close. The same way I had let the rest of the runaways get close. But with Luke it was...different.

"Friends?" he scoffs. "Do you treat all your friends like this?"

The conversation is already exasperating. "Friendship isn't a zone I'm putting you in!" I scramble for words. "It's a standard. It means that no matter what happens between us, I will always have your back. And I hope that's the same for me."

The guilt pulls me from the memory, blasting me forward to when I'm saying goodbye. Sarge is trusting that I'll return because that's what I told him.

Before that guilt settles, a voice from behind me calls, "M!" It's Luke. "I love you."

And when I turn to tell him that I feel the same, "Doesn't love just suck?" is what comes out instead. Because the truth is, I'm not worthy of Luke's love. I'm a monster. He thinks he is, but little does he know what a terrible person I've been; what a failure I am. If I tell him how I feel, it will only hurt him more when I walk away. Because you have to end things before they end you.

And the guilt eats away at me. It tears at my soul until there's no light left and only darkness remains.

When the light floods into my eyes once more, I remember where I am. I'm in Omphalos. The train of depravity I got stuck on was not real, even though I felt every bit of it deep in my core. I'm a bit groggy, but I'm starting to understand what happened. It's easy to see how someone, especially a young child, could be swayed by this. If my memories were altered and I was forced to relive them over and over, I'd begin to question my reality, too.

The Reaver is sitting in the corner. I'm unable to classify the look on her face. I thought she'd be getting the ultimate enjoyment out of this, but it's almost as if something in my memories has upset *her*. I decide to use this to my advantage.

"I knew you liked to play mind games, I just didn't realize how sadistic you truly were," I play. I don't want her to see how shaken up I am. It's better to focus on her. My throat is dry and my voice is hoarse, but she hears me just fine.

"I do what needs to be done for the betterment of the flock." *Flock?* Oh—lions and sheep. Her eyes are studying me and, if I weren't so exhausted, I feel I would visibly shrink.

"I thought you wanted to get rid of all the lions so you'd have a bunch of sheep to exploit." I remember sitting by the fire with Mason over a year ago. He had told me that she didn't want any lions; no one that couldn't be cornered into a pen.

"I'm not weeding out the lions to take charge. I'm driving away the lions to *protect* the sheep." There's a slight pleading tone hidden in her voice. "Humanity is broken, and peace will only ever be temporary as long as both lion and sheep remain in the same enclosure. And who always wins in that war?"

It's becoming clear how she may have been able to convince enough people to believe in her cause. It makes sense now, what Giles had said on the way here. The Guardianship truly believes they are advancing Humanity.

"How did you decide that the lions were the threat?"

"A lion is a fighter. They will always be a fighter. Take away the sheep, and they will fight each other. Take away the lions, and the sheep will flourish."

She has an answer for everything, I'll give her that. But her screws are loose in a deep place. "Are you forgetting that sheep fight sometimes?" I'm vaguely remembering that males fight for breeding privileges. It's impossible to take away a social hierarchy. There will always be someone at the bottom.

"That's where I come in. The Shepherd. The one who has taken the responsibility of keeping the sheep safe from one another. Censoring the things that would make them different. This way they can all graze and be safe."

"And that's the cost? The reason Emma had to die?" Our first conversation plays back in my brain and the anger bubbles up through my veins. My face heats up. I lunge forward, attempting to sit up, but the harsh bite of the restraints stops me before I can extend fully. "You're telling me you killed my little sister, an innocent child, to try and pacify me?"

The Reaver's face shows a slight shocked expression. Maybe it's the sudden wrath, or maybe it's the mention of Emma, but something about her seems almost desperate as she speaks. "Everyone thinks it's about me, or the Guardianship. But it never was. It's always been about protecting those that cannot protect themselves. This job is not easy, but it is my duty."

This woman is severely twisted. It's obvious that she wants to do the right thing, but something in her brain is telling her that this is the way; that this is actually a good idea.

"Is that why you killed Senator Collins? Because he realized you're psycho?" I don't know why I bring him up. The whole conversation with Mason is playing back in my head. The power sharing, the killing. Does she really think I know nothing? With the remnants of the serum coursing through my veins, my memories are as sharp as ever.

"John Collins was a fool!" She shoots up out of the chair, causing it to skid backwards, and she slams her palm against the wall next to her. "He missed the overall picture. It takes a lion to drive out the rest of the lions, and he wanted me to be a sheep. We weren't going to get anywhere with that."

"So you killed him?" Clearly I've touched a nerve. "You killed the man that got you to where you are? Just like that?" I'm toying with her. She thinks she's the only one who can play games, but she's wrong.

"I drove out another lion to save the flock." Her eyes are dark, and I know I've burrowed deep under her skin.

"From where I'm standing, it's like you recruited all the lions and left the sheep defenseless." I grit my teeth. "Now what kind of shepherd would do that?" We stare into each other's eyes for a few minutes in silence. Her snake eyes to my grey pools.

There's something more about John Collins here, and I'm going to figure out what it is. Something tells me he holds a part in unlocking the Reaver's mind. But for every answer I get, twice as many questions take its place.

"I knew that you'd be hard to crack, but I was not expecting the Memory Actualization to send you in the opposite direction. We'll have to up your dosage next time." She leaves the room, clearly flustered.

I hadn't realized how sick she is. The Reaver truly believes this is the way to creating an enhanced Humanity. So why waste so much time on me? One *stupid commoner*, no more special than the next.

As I try and see any part of the Amity I thought I was in the mirror above me, my thoughts take off in all different directions. Perhaps it's never been about causing me suffering. Break me and she breaks Mason, the son of a prominent politician, and she breaks Luke, the officer that abandoned the Force and changed the way they do everything around here. Perhaps it's my connection to the real problem commoners that makes me a perfect candidate.

If this is true, I had been so focused on not giving her anymore leverage against me that I ended up walking myself right into her arms as the biggest leverage of all. Luke had been right.

What am I going to do?

CHAPTER FOURTEEN ○ AMITY

Emma is on my lap, her tears slowly soaking in my jeans. "Little M," I say, "do you know the story of Life and Death?"

She shakes her tiny head, rubbing against my stomach.

"It's a love story," I start. "You see, Life and Death love each other very much. They've loved each other since the beginning of time." She sits up now, allowing me to wipe the tears from her cheeks. Her small frown melts my heart. "Life always sends gifts to Death to show their love, and Death holds on to them forever and ever."

It's a bit grim for a four year old, but the harshness of life can't be withheld. "Momma was a gift to Death, and she'll be held safe forever and ever until Life sends us to be with her, too." I look deep into Emma's bright blue eyes. "It's going to be okay."

I jolt out of the memory drenched in sweat. This was the story that started it all. The MAP saw the ending, the true crux of my guilt; but it skipped over the beginning. I had told Emma that our mother was a gift to Death. Now she's there with her despite my promise.

"You okay, Miss Thorne?" Charlie's voice startles me all over again. It must finally be morning. I've been having severely vivid dreams all night as a reaction to the serum. Scenes that I buried and forgot about were suddenly galivanting through my mind, unwelcome.

"I told Emma that she wasn't going to die and that I'd always be there for her." My voice is small, but Charlie hears me. Of all the wicked memories that invaded my mind, the story of Life and Death has hit me the hardest. I'd almost completely forgotten about it until the Reaver had to drag it back out. It makes Emma's death all the more upsetting, if that's even possible.

"You did your best," is what Charlie replies. It's such a dad answer.

"My best wasn't good enough," I scoff lightly, mad at myself, at Charlie, at no one in particular, at everyone.

"That's always the fear, isn't it?" He chuckles softly. "You felt responsible for her and as you were moving along, you were probably wondering if you were doing the right thing. If you were doing enough."

Charlie is definitely hitting the nail on the head here. But he must be talking about his daughter. "You joined to save her?" I ask. We were interrupted yesterday and I didn't get his full answer. But it's earlier in the morning now, so no one should really be out to bother us.

"She was going to die without medical treatment." Charlie's answer catches me off guard. "It was either this or lose her. And this was the lesser of two evils."

It's silent while I get dragged down a memory lane set in Horrorville. This time I'm reliving saying goodbye to Zach. The squeeze of my hands, the last breath from his lungs. The intensity of the memory leaves me breathless. But I push the thoughts away momentarily to ask, "Is she okay now?"

"She's healthy," he starts. "She's not stuck in a commoner's school." Charlie sounds sad, like he knows that things suck no matter which way you look at them. "She will hopefully live to see a new world." He turns his face to look at me, the gleam in his eye vaguely familiar. *Is that hope?*

"You're a good father," I tell him, making me wonder about my own. I've tried to bury the feelings of guilt that surround my departure from him. The truth is that the serum doesn't let me bury anymore. It makes me dig up, unearth, excavate all of my guilt, and it makes me relive it. Right now my mind is stuck in a war, and the guilty side is prevailing.

I haven't seen my father in over a year. I don't know if he's alive, or where he is. I haven't even allowed myself to think about him. What a terrible daughter I am. After all he's done. After all he's had to endure just for a measly chance that Emma and I would see a better world.

"Amity?" Charlie breaks me from the curse of the serum. "You okay?" The way he's looking at me is everything I've always hated. But I remember Zach helping me come to terms with it. I lift my hand, gently wiping the tears sliding down my cheek.

"Sorry," I utter. "Do you feel you made the right choice?" My head is pounding, my thoughts are all over the place. There are a lot of decisions I've made in the past that I wonder about. Would Emma still be alive if I hadn't tried to save her? I know Zach would be. Will Sarge ever forgive me for leaving him? Was my father better off without me?

"One can only hope," he sighs, leaving me with a feeling of discontent.

○ ○ ○

"Isn't this jacket pretty?" I'm remembering my childhood friend, Grace, but her smile doesn't quite reach her eyes. She's trying to hide how hungry she is. She's trying to hide how utterly sad she's feeling.

"Yeah," I smile back. "You're always so beautiful." I have to be careful what I say. If I say I wish I had the stuff that she does, a cloud of depression settles over her. She doesn't realize I know what her family is doing. She doesn't think I know she has to choose between that coat or a meal.

Her family is humble. They don't like handouts. I've tried. But I ask her, "Are you hungry?" anyway, because I'm hoping that just once she'll tell me how dire it is. Then I could give her some bread from my bag.

"Only a little," she replies. "Like everyone else."

I snap out of my memory as Giles closes the door of the MAP lab behind me. The Reaver is standing near the MAP machine, already waiting. Nicole nervously takes charge, gently locking me in place. I'm feeling a bit irritable from the lack of sleep and the memory of Grace, the kind soul that had to starve to Death in order to not be singled out in the streets. This combination of restlessness leads me to ask a question that's been bothering me for quite some time.

"What's the point of giving the commoners nothing?" It always amazed me how she could claim she's protecting people when she's the root cause of most of their issues.

The Reaver dodges the question. "Starting with the attitude already?" She's smug. It makes me sick.

"Answer me," I demand. I'm much too tired to care how this will affect me later. I want someone to give me a good reason for why Grace had to die. For why they all had to die.

"You remind me of myself, when I was younger," the Reaver shifts direction. "Stubborn, tenacious. But with age came wisdom. You do not see that Humanity is too flawed to thrive without intervention."

"Killing people is the correct intervention?" Why I argue with her is lost on me. I know it won't get me anywhere. But hope lingers somewhere inside me, begging for some insight somehow. Some valid excuse for all this Death.

"Miss Thorne, please," the Reaver implores, but the tone subsides quickly. It's replaced with an indignant one. "Here's a life lesson for you," she starts. "If you give someone an inch, they'll take a mile. If you take away everything, they'll be grateful for what little you give them." She pushes the button to the machine, and that's the last thing I remember before my memories start swallowing me up.

My mother, Emma, my father. My attacker, the photograph. Trixie, Mason, Sarge, Zach. Emma again, Sarge again. Luke.

I emerge from the MAP completely spent. The same torturous Hell I went through yesterday was waiting for me again today, only this time it was tenfold. From start to finish, it felt so real I could believe it was time travel.

The Reaver demanded my dosage be upped, and boy do I feel it. The only reason I'm able to differentiate between reality and fabrication is because Luke's voice is ingrained in my subconscious, calmly explaining and keeping me grounded. My body and mind are so exhausted that even the thought of arguing with the Reaver leaves me weak. The memories were sharper, more in-depth. It didn't just target the crux of my guilt this time, it made me dig up more context.

A glance around the room shows that only Nicole is here with me. The Reaver must be bored already. "Was I that boring?" I ask, for no reason in particular.

"It was a...difficult session," Nicole settles on, uncomfortably. Something in my memories must *really* affect the Reaver. But what is it?

"Well forgive me. I didn't realize sitting and watching someone you're purposefully hurting could be so difficult," I mock.

Before Nicole has the chance to respond, the Reaver barges in, speaking first. "That's enough out of you," she scolds me.

Nicole shakes like a leaf while she helps me sit up. "Did I somehow disappoint you?" My voice is hoarse. How I still have the energy to talk back is beyond me.

"Truthfully, you disgust me," the Reaver seethes.

"Aw," I goad, "And I thought we had a real moment earlier."

"You are nothing more than a fascinating experiment," she sneers, clearly happy with her choice of words. "The wrapper that gets thrown away once the stuff inside is used up."

"So, I still remind you of your younger self, then?"

This sets the Reaver off. The veins in her forehead and neck bulge as she tries to keep herself contained. "Throw her back in, Miss Haddler."

"Headmistress?" Nicole questions.

"I said throw her back in!"

"It's not really recommended that you…" Nicole cowers as she's cut off.

"I make the rules around here, and I say you send her back in!"

"You a bit of a masochist, *Madame*?" I toy, smug that I'm able to get under her skin like this. It might be suicide, but at this rate, who cares. *Maybe I can take her down from the inside out after all.*

"Shut your mouth, you vile girl." The Reaver slams her fist down, smashing the button for the serum herself. It's not long before my memories begin to unfold.

It starts with yelling at my sick mother until my throat is raspy. Then I tell Emma the story of Life and Death and promise her she won't be a gift. After I run from my father, the memories seem to halt. The first two times, they played like a fast forwarded movie; strung together like reels of film. This time it's playing slow. I'm waiting by the guard rail. I know what's about to happen but I can't stop it.

The smell wafts into my nose first. My throat closes. I gag and choke as my lungs beg for air. It's completely dark, but then I feel them. Those damn hands.

It's been a while since I've lived through this nightmare; since it has haunted me in this capacity.

But this isn't a dream. This is Hell. The dirty nails, the iron grip. I sputter and gasp for air. Why is this happening to me? I struggle to pull away. *I deserve this, don't I?* It should be over soon. It feels like it will never be over. Why isn't Sarge rescuing me?

Sarge! Where is he? This is real, it has to be. *Is this how I die?* Sarge isn't here. Why isn't he here? *He's with Luke, Amity.* No! He was by the guardrail. Then it clicks.

Suddenly the pressure on my throat releases and my lungs fill with air. My mind unlocked the escape. They can't hurt me. This isn't real. If it was, Sarge would rescue me. He was there with me, which means he wouldn't let me die. Our love is too strong.

This time, my eyes open and I'm stuck halfway between subconscious and reality. There are muffled voices around me, but they aren't clear enough for me to catch anything. The tones, however, are angry.

"Figure this out," is all I catch from the Reaver as she slams the door behind her, reality hitting me full force. Nicole eyes me nervously before tapping away at her computer. Luke must have kept this trick to himself. *But how did he find out about it?* If I hadn't gotten out of that, what would have happened to me? Did the Reaver want to kill me in my own mind?

My head pounds with all of the unanswered questions bouncing around inside of it. There are too many moving parts in this machine to figure it out. I need a hint, a clue. I need something more to put me ahead. I guess I'll have to continue to dig under the Reaver's skin.

CHAPTER FIFTEEN ○ LUKE

It's been three weeks without Amity. The guilt of her inevitable torture eats away at me every day. Should I have kidnapped her? Should I have held her against her will until we made it to Creyke Point together? Deep down I know that she would have grown to resent me if I had done that. It's selfish, but that would have been even worse to deal with.

Some days I feel like shouting. My voice has been locked away for a long time to keep us all safe. Days where I'm extra irritable are the worst. It leaves me feeling pissed off at Sam even though Ren is the cause.

We're not too far from Aberdeen—maybe a week more at the pace we've been going. Being so close, but so far, has been yet another Hell I've had to combat. Overall, though, the journey has been fairly smooth, and for that I'm thankful. Nothing too crazy since the gang incident. But as I think the words, we stumble upon a large southern style mansion in the middle of the woods. The map doesn't show any buildings here. There's a large radius around the house that's an open field, but the sun doesn't make it in much. Somehow the canopy of trees extends, keeping the house hidden from a bird's eye view. I wonder if it's Force related? If it's not on the map though...

Wait here, Sam, I sign. He nods. I look to Sarge. Normally he sticks to Sam like glue, but right now he's pressed against my side, keeping his golden eyes on my face, waiting to follow. I guess that means something is off about the house.

Sarge and I move out into the open, leaving Sam relatively safe in the cover of the tree line. My hand is resting cautiously on my gun as we approach the wrap-around porch. Hopefully I'm wrong about a Force presence. Hopefully the house is empty and we get to stay here for the night. Giving Sam the luxury of a roof over his head and a nice bed to sleep on would be good for him.

Getting closer, it's hard to miss the blinds in one of the windows moving. It's clear that my hope for an empty house was poor judgement. I should've known it would be occupied, but what threat lies behind the closed door?

Sarge's hackles are raised as we creep onto the porch, the old splintering wood creaking beneath us. My gun is now out, by my side, while I knock on the thick mahogany door. Before knowing M, and before holding Sam's shaking body, I would've blasted through without giving it any thought. For some reason—today, right now—I've decided that whoever is behind the door gets a chance to come forward.

When the seconds become minutes and no one opens the door, I take one last look toward the forest to locate Sam. I know he's there, but he's sufficiently hidden enough that I don't immediately find him. Keeping my eye on him is a priority, but I don't want him to see what I'm about to do. I nod and he hides himself away, then I turn, blasting my foot into the door. It doesn't budge. Fuck that hurt.

I give it another attempt, this time bashing my shoulder into the wood, hoping my full weight will be enough. When it's not, the rage tears through me. My fist slams into the door repeatedly, and I ignore the fact that Sarge looks on with worried eyes.

"I know you're in there," I seethe, hoping I'm not loud enough to set Sam's tracker off. "Open the fucking door!"

This rage is volatile. This rage is not how I want to be defined, but damn does it feel good to let it out. Guilt spikes through me for a second, my fist rubbed raw already, but I don't care. The guilt is pushed aside. Screw whoever this is living here in this cushy house. Screw it all!

Just as my rage hits its peak, a deadbolt clicks from the other side. My gun is instantly in my hands, trained in the direction of the noise. Sarge is in defensive stance.

But I never get to pull the trigger. Sarge never attacks. An old woman with dark skin answers the door. She's in a small apron and her eyes are sweet. She reminds me of Josephine, which then reminds me that M would be disappointed in me. I put my gun away, the guilt instantly slamming deeper into my chest. Damn this rage. I do an Amity style eye roll in my head.

"Who d'ya think you are swingin' that gun up in my face?" The old woman is fiery. I imagine this is how Lacy will be in her old age. "You should be ashamed of yerself." Oh, believe me, lady. I am.

"I'm sorry, ma'am," I say. "I didn't mean to be rude."

"Don't be ma'amin' me, young man," she says. "I'm Mama June." I glance at Sarge. His eyes are laughing at me. What is happening here?

"Mama June," I nod. "I'm Luke, and this is Sarge." She barely even looks in his direction. Her beady eyes are locked on me. "I'm sorry to have gotten off on the wrong foot." My father would be pissed at me if he knew my first impression from this woman. He'd tell me he raised me better, more respectful. I'm trying, but can anyone blame me for being a bit wary?

"What'dya want?" She questions. I think, deep down, Mama June is in survival mode, too.

"We're travelling west, and hoping for a place to stay for the night." Mama June squints her eyes at me, focusing quickly on the gun still peeking out of my waistband.

"I'm a bit low on space right now," she says, "but yer more than welcome to come in fer a few to rest. I hope'ya understand." Her words are inviting, but her eyes and tone of voice are not. She doesn't want me in this house. She doesn't want me anywhere near here.

"Sure," I say. "That would be nice."

Mama June wearily opens the door. There's a grand staircase in front of us as we enter, with a small rounded foyer at the base to the right. On our left is a grand dining room with a table for a whole party. Further right is a skinny hallway leading to somewhere I can't see, and a room with a closed door. Just from this small view, it's clear this house is huge.

"You have no space in this whole mansion?" I raise my eyebrows.

"No." Mama June is quick with her response. It's rigid. "Keep yer dog close and have a seat in the dinin' room." Something isn't right here.

Sarge is sniffing the air beside me. Instead of having him stay near me, I walk toward the dining room and let him do his thing. He sticks his nose to the ground, tracking, until he's standing in the middle of a rug in the foyer at the base of the stairs. He stops to look at me.

"Hey!" Mama June cries when she turns to see Sarge isn't following. "What kind of..."

"What is it?" I interrupt. She didn't want Sarge sniffing around in here because she's hiding something. Now she can't get away without telling the truth.

"It's nothin' but an old family heirloom," scoffs Mama June, but I was talking to Sarge. "Yer dog has even worse manners than yerself."

Sarge starts to paw at the rug before transitioning into a full on dig. "Doesn't seem like nothing," I whisper under my breath.

"Stop it!" Mama June scolds. "Get away from there!" She grabs an old broom by the door, but before she can even raise it to hit Sarge, the handle is already gripped tightly in my hand.

"Oh, no you don't!"

"Let...go!" Mama June is flustered, and I feel a bit like an ass. But this woman is hiding something, and now I want to know what it is. "You no good..."

She's cut off when Sarge barks. I'd been too focused on Mama June that I hadn't noticed when Sarge pulled the rug away from its place. There's a large trap door in the middle of the spot. My eyes travel to the old woman's. There's defeat in her pupils.

"What is it?" I repeat.

"Don't hurt 'em," she says. "Don't take 'em back with you."

I walk over to the trap door, gently curling my fingers under the latch. Sarge steps off and waits patiently at my side. What, or who, does this refer to? Is she a crazy cat lady with millions of cats? Does she keep people locked in her dungeon so she's less alone out here?

The latch lifts and my muscles tense to pull the tough door from its hold. When I do, Sarge lets out a quick bark at what's inside. A dozen pairs of eyes stare back at me, and when the light finally breaks through the darkness, there's at least twelve young children ranging from what looks to be five all the way up to Sam's age standing in the musty space. They are all missing their right arms.

CHAPTER SIXTEEN ○ LUKE

I'VE CHECKED ON SAM TO MAKE SURE HE'S SAFE. HE IS. I TOLD him I'd come out and get him very soon. Sarge is laying on the ground, rolled onto his back for all of the one-armed children to pet him. His large tongue is flapped out onto the floor, keeping the children giggly. Mama June and I are in the dining room off to the side of the foyer. She's serving me some hot tea as she goes over what the hell is going on here.

Mama June is not a doctor. But her father was. She learned everything from him. If she were a doctor, right now she'd be serving the Guardianship's every need. She would not be operating on the small group of tainted children that her son in the Force brings her. She would not be here to give them a second chance.

"This house has been in my family fer generations," she explains. "Passed down time and time again, so my great great grandfather's legacy could be carried out." The man she's referring to had escaped the south during the first Civil War with the help of the Underground Railroad at the age of ten. After he was able to move west, he built this house with a secret bunker, so that he would be able to repay the favor if a second civil war broke out.

By cutting off the children's arms, Mama June effectively fools the Guardianship and the trackers. Her son, Tony, brings the children to one of the many predetermined locations that have special markings leading them to the house. When they arrive, Mama June operates right away, and walks miles into the woods around here to make it seem like the child is still moving. She teaches them how to utilize their left hands, and to cope in life without two arms.

Part of me is in awe at her commitment to these kids. But the other part thinks she's a dumbass. The Brain keeps track of all the children's pathing. I'm sure it's already picked up on the pattern. These kids all pass through the same spot and then stop moving shortly after, so if Ren is searching for something out of the ordinary, then she's bound to find it eventually.

"The land around this house used to be a farm." Mama June breaks me from my thoughts. "It was to help sustain the bodies that my family would shelter. But as the war decimated the land, I lost most of my crops. Tony steals what he can, but it's not much. These kids don't deserve to starve."

I told Mama June about Sam. She's not taken in a tainted child in a while because of the lack of resources and recent changes in the Force. Still, though, she's considering helping Sam. I'm not sure how to feel. This isn't a territory I'm used to. I'm trying to think about what M would do, but I'm drawing a blank.

As for the changes she's referring to, I'm definitely in the dark. Her son is her gateway into the Force, and right now I'm blind. She believed I was a Force officer myself, because of my gun. She recognized the style from having Tony around. But apparently he stopped by and said he wouldn't be able to come back much anymore. They've been rationing ever since.

Sam could very easily come with me after his operation, too, effectively keeping him away from this area and safe with me. But that would put me behind schedule. It seems selfish, but M has always been my reason. I promised her that I'd be at the rendezvous point and I'm not about to break that. Especially now that I'm learning about the Force changes. What else has Ren changed since I've been gone?

"What'reya doin' out in these parts anyway?" Mama June switches gears. Now that she knows I'm not an officer, she must be curious. I'm sure her motherly instincts are picking up on my trepidations as well.

"I'm heading to Aberdeen. Hoping to meet someone before heading off to Creyke Point."

"Creyke Point? And how d'ya plan on gettin' all the way out there?"

The rapid fire questions start to piss me off, but I bite back the attitude and answer as calm and collected as always. "The Human Protective Service. They are helping funnel people to safety."

Mama June stares at me in disbelief for a few moments before her eyes light up. "The clue!" she exclaims.

Okay, lady, let's not go completely batshit on me now. "Excuse me?"

"My son had found an old piece of paper, some sort of poem. It was crumpled in the dirt." She shoots out of the chair, scrambling around, rummaging in the China cabinet drawers. "It's hidden in the shadows."

"What?" Hidden in the shadows.

The phrase knocks me back a few years to my Force days. I'm the Master Sergeant overseeing the interrogation of a commoner guilty of treason in the eyes of Ren; a young man with a stubborn vengeance about him. Only those with information too valuable to lose make it into this room, but I'm not sure what this kid knows. He's about my age at the time, but I'm ready to please, so I don't care. I've learned to separate myself from the job, to pretend that this human being is trash that needs taking out, or a box that needs breaking down. It's depraved, I know. But it's what has to be done.

Ren's crackling voice filters through the earpiece. "Ask him again."

"Where are they going?" My voice is menacing, but the kid looks up at me with a black and blue face and blood-covered teeth. He smiles.

"Shadows," he giggles, madly. He spent a week in the White Room. No color, no sound, no stimulation. He said he was ready to talk. I wasn't so convinced. But Ren is desperate.

"Where?" I repeat, this time grabbing him by the collar. He's a bag of bones in my hands.

"It's hidden," he cackles, his body shuddering uncontrollably. "Hidden in the shadows!"

"Hit him," the voice in my ear cracks. There's barely a second before my fist is connecting to his face, blood spattering from his nose.

"You're for the wrong side," he cries. "It's hidden! You'll never find it!"

"Found it!" Mama June exclaims after rifling through another drawer. The slamming of the wood tears me from the vision of my past. In her hand is a tiny, crinkled up piece of paper. "I kept it just in case." She smooths it out over her chest before handing it to me.

> The search for salvation
> is closer than you think;
> 20 miles and an Angel's Port
> to satisfy your drink.
> Hidden in the shadows,
> where the Murdocks cry and creak.
> Calling you to shore again
> to find the Angel's Fleet.

"I think this might be the ramblings of a crazy person." I say the words, but something deep within me begs to be hopeful.

It makes sense how it adds up. The Human Protective Service, or H.P.S, has a connection near Port Angeles. Mason told me that much. This means that the poem is directions to their boat. The young man I'd tortured all those years ago must have been a part of it somehow.

"Pfft," Mama June scoffs. "Pull out yer map, boy."

I reach into my back pocket to grab the Relay. Apparently I don't do it fast enough because, before I'm able to open it, Mama June yanks it from my fingers and starts fiddling with it herself. She is ecstatic that she's figured it out. It's quite heartwarming, actually.

"If you follow Murdock creek, you'll land on a small beach. That must be where the Human Protective Service has their boat, or the *Angel's Fleet* in this case. Look." She hands the Relay back to me. It's situated over the beach.

When I first went on the run, it was already decided that I'd head North. It didn't matter what I would find, but I wanted to know if the whisperings I'd heard around were of any substance, or just the idle ramblings of the hopeless. It's clear now that there was truth to their words.

Now I know exactly where to go when M and I meet up again. That's only a small weight lifted off my shoulders, though. What happens if she never makes it to me? What about Sam? What do I do with him?

Staying here with Mama June may be his only chance. If M and I are to make it to Creyke Point, then Sam's tracker poses a threat. We may be able to stay quiet, but there are too many other variables along the way that could mess up the whole H.P.S and their system if the Force came for him. I guess I know what needs to be done.

"Will you take Sam?" I'm practically begging and it tastes foreign in my mouth. I never beg. But something deep in my gut is telling me that this is the way things have to go. "I give my word that I will send help the moment I can." Then, I add, "I'll leave you will all of my food."

A few seconds pass before Mama June nods her head. My shoulders dip as I relax a bit. I call to Sarge, interrupting the pile of children around him. They all moan and groan when I tell Sarge to retrieve Sam. Mama June orders the kids to their rooms and to stay silent, warning them not to come out until she gets them.

As the children scatter, I must have gone someplace else in my mind because a voice brings me back to reality. "It's alright to be scared." Mama June cuts into my thoughts. "In fact, it's good."

Scared? Pfft. I'm not scared. I've never been scared of anything. Not even Death itself. "What makes you think I'm scared?"

"I seen that look in yer eyes, boy," Mama June states. "Those the eyes of a scared man." I'm not scared. I'm not. Until M is involved, and now Sam. You know it's true, Warin. Fuck!

"Am I making the right choice?" Is leaving Sam really the best thing for him? Or is it the best thing for me? I've never really cared before, I just did what had to be done and justified it as I went. But I can't help but think how M would feel if I told her. Would she finally believe I was a monster?

"Yer the only one to know," is Mama June's answer.

"What did you mean when you said it was good?" I ask. That's the part that didn't make sense to me. Growing up, my father taught me that fear was useless; that it would only hold you back. So why does this woman think it's good? Is it a sign of her weakness?

Mama June takes a moment to stare deep into my soul. "It means you still have somethin' to lose."

Just then, the door slowly creaks open and I instinctively put my hand to my gun, but Mama June's palm rests on it, stopping me. Sarge and Sam walk in slowly. I motion for them both to come over, pulling out the Relay at the same time.

I quickly introduce Sam to Mama June. Then I tell him how he's going to be able to play with other children soon, but he'd have to be okay with losing his arm. The look on his face breaks my heart as he swiftly dips to hug me. I'm almost afraid I'll lose my strength.

"I need to give you one last hug while I still have both my arms," he whispers into my ear.

Sarge joins us shortly after, but then I pull away. I need to go. If I stay any longer, I'm afraid I'll push off my plans to meet M in order to help Sam recover. I can't, though. I made a promise to M that I would be in Aberdeen every day to wait for her. There's no time to push it off.

The Relay trembles in my hands as I type my goodbye. I make sure to let Sam know that I will send for him the second I can. A tear escapes his eye, but he nods in understanding. I remind him of how strong he is, then pull him in for one last hug before heading to the door.

At first I'm worried that Sarge won't understand and I'd have to fight him to come, but he follows me to the door after licking his goodbye. Sam and Mama June come after to see us out.

As Sarge and I walk away, I turn to look back at Sam. Mama June has her hands on his shoulders, and he raises his hand to wave at me. Something about the scene settles my worries, and deep down I know this is the right thing. I wave back. Sarge lets out a lone bark.

"He's gonna be alright," I say, staring into Sarge's golden eyes. "Now let's get to M."

CHAPTER SEVENTEEN ○ AMITY

Luke and I are in the tent, our labored breaths muddled together as we share a sweet embrace. This will hurt people, but in the moment I don't care. It isn't until Sarge growls, taking off from beside us, that panic starts to root itself in my chest.

I stumble out of the tent onto a war scene. "Him?" Mason cries. "You chose him?"

"Mason..." I call. "I'm sorry! I'm so sorry!" My knees hit the ground, my face hides in my palms. Suddenly, there's a hand trailing up and down my back, gently, softly, slowly.

"I know how you'll make it up to me." It's Mason.

"What do you mean? How?" I look into his round, benevolent face. His blue pools call to somewhere deep within me.

"It's time for a change," he starts. "You should listen to the Headmistress."

"Why are you saying this?" It's not like Mason. Yet, maybe it is. He *did* want me to give up on Emma. So maybe he's trying a different angle.

"M, it's too late for me, but not for you. Besides, you owe me for the heartache. You need to give up. Throw in the towel. Stop resisting."

"Mason, I..." Wait. *Did he call me M?* "I...think this might be a trick." I'm not sure how, or why, but something about this isn't right.

"I would never trick you, Amity. You know that." His voice sounds so real, his eyes staring into my soul so warm. This is all very confusing. My head pounds. Mason doesn't call me M; he doesn't use nicknames at all. Hell, I'm not sure he even *knows* it's my nickname.

"Yes," I agree.

"Then stop talking craziness," Mason chides. His tone is sweet, though. It almost leads to me second guessing myself. But no. This isn't Mason. It can't be.

"You wouldn't trick me," I start, "but I know who would."

The second I make my declaration, the walls fall away and I jolt awake. I'm stuck in the in-between, not quite conscious but not quite out either. The frustration in the Reaver's voice is palpable as I slowly come to.

"I thought we took care of this before?" Her hushed tone would still be heard from miles away.

Nicole is at a loss for words. Instead, she shrugs her shoulders. This act does not sit well with the Reaver.

Next thing I know, Nicole is being held up by her throat. She's gasping for air, squirming about, but the Reaver makes her look weightless. This is one more layer of Ren Keres I've never seen.

"What am I keeping you alive for if you're going to be useless?" the Reaver seethes.

"Madame," Nicole chokes out. "Please." She's gripping onto the Reaver's hand, helpless to make it easier to breathe. After a few seconds, she scoffs, dropping Nicole to the ground, disdainfully.

"Get Miss Thorne back to her room." She walks out without looking back.

Once the door shuts, adrenaline pumps through my veins. I somehow break out of my restraints, quickly running to Nicole's side. She blanches as I get close, quietly begging for me to spare her life.

"It's okay," I reassure. "I won't hurt you." Nicole looks up at me with tear-stained eyes. "I know how it feels to be strangled. Not fun." I chuckle in an attempt to lighten the mood.

I've never studied Nicole closely before. I guess I've never really had the chance lately. Her face is no longer smooth like it was when I first saw her. It's as if she's aged ten years in this short amount of time. The small gleam of light that I'd caught in her eyes before is clearly missing. Perhaps I can plant the seed here.

"Why do you put up with that?" This is a dumb question, I realize. I'm asking as if she really has a choice. "Let me rephrase. Do you believe in the Headmistress's plan?" The name tastes bitter in my mouth. I much prefer the moniker of *Reaver*.

"I used to look up to her," Nicole rasps. "I want to believe that this is all for the better." I sympathize with Nicole. She's confused. She's trying to find herself in all the mess. She truly wants to make a difference.

"And what if it's not?"

o o o

It's been a strange morning. I asked Charlie if he would be able to check in on Nicole. He said he would do his best. She had divulged sensitive information to me, helping with some of my unanswered questions, and for that, I can never repay her.

On the day of my stress test, the Reaver had surprised Nicole with a manual override code. Being the leader, Madame Keres comes equipped with hi-tech gear that others are not privy to. For me, she had used such technology to render my body useless in real life, which then translated into the construct. All the while, she put in a code for Giles to take control of the other girl, ensuring she shot herself and not me. Nicole said this was the first she'd ever known of such a thing.

The other unknown Nicole had been able to help with was which of my memories sends the Reaver into a crazy spell. Spoiler: It's anything to do with Luke. Luke saying he loves me, sleeping with him, anything.

I can't say that this knowledge has helped clear up any questions. It's does confirm what's been bothering me, though. This information leads me to believe that Luke plays a bigger role in my new reality here. *Maybe he made* you *the target, Amity*. No. I can't think about that now. At least he and Sarge are safe from her evil clutches. *Just move on.*

For the most part, the afternoon has been quiet, but occasionally I find myself being sucked down a rabbit hole of memories. The side effects of the MAP are usually just as bad as the MAP itself. In between the horrors, I keep apprehensively trying to solve the mysteries of my case. *Do you* really *want to know, Amity?*

Sometime after lunch, a group of kids—ranging anywhere from five all the way to late teens—starts walking down the hallway. Typically I wouldn't pay attention to traffic outside of my room, but this is a group larger than normal, and they all slow down as they pass the door. Charlie doesn't have the force field up, and his body tenses with worry when they stop in front of him.

All of them simultaneously thump their balled fists—the sign for A—to their chest twice, and raise them up above their head. A girl in the front of the group, probably a year or two younger than me, steps forward, demanding Charlie let me out.

"Please be on your way and I won't contact the Headmistress about this," Charlie answers.

"Now," demands the girl. "Or we'll hurt you."

I feel for Charlie. I know he doesn't want to hurt the children, but if he doesn't do anything, then his ass is the one to get beat. At this point I'm right behind him, shaking my head at the leader of the reckless kids. I'm careful in staying quiet to keep our secret safe.

But the girl screams, lunging at Charlie. Her mindless subjects follow. They pummel him to the cold tile and start kicking. One of the kids rushes past him to get to me.

"I need back up in the two hundred section of the student wing," Charlie calls, to anyone, or no one in particular. He sounds winded.

"Come out, Amity," the kid says, "you're free. We've got to hurry!"

Charlie is sputtering on the ground so, instead of escaping, I dive into the pile of bodies, screaming, begging for them to leave him be. "Stop," I cry, pushing my way to Charlie.

"Amity, we need to leave!"

Several officers round the corner at the same time. Some of the kids dart off, but none of them make it. The leader has stopped her assault on Charlie. "Run, Amity," she says. "Go!"

"Get away from him," I beg. "Why are you doing this?"

An officer sneaks up behind her, yanking her away from Charlie at the same time an officer grips me. She's being pulled, kicking and screaming. "Justice for Amity!" she chants.

"Justice for Emma!" the rest of the kids answer. *They're doing this for Emma?*

The officer gripping the girl forces her down on her knees. *No!* Another officer holds her steady. My legs become gelatin as a gun is positioned right between her eyes.

"No," I cry. "Don't hurt her!" At this point, the guard clutching my arm is the only thing keeping me upright. My legs completely give out when the other officer pulls the trigger. The girl slumps to the ground. I never even knew her name.

My quiet whimpers fill the air as Charlie, the leader, and all the kids are carted out of the hallways. "What should I do with the girl?" asks the officer holding me. I'm not sure who he's talking to, and I don't think I care.

After a few seconds, he answers the response of a voice I didn't get to hear. Then I'm getting dragged through the hallways until we're outside a room I don't recognize. Giles appears, taking me from the other nameless officer. We make our way through the door and I'm brought face to face with the Reaver.

"What am I doing here?" I rasp, my voice hoarse from my cries and screams. Giles steps back, letting the Reaver take over.

"Clearly the Memory Actualization Process isn't working on you," she says, "so we'll have to step it up."

"What is this?" I ask, changing the focus of the conversation. We're in a room with large capsules. It's a grid system; four by five. Each row is marked with a different color. Red, brown, blue, silver. She leads me down the row of blue ones.

"Elemental pods," she says. Each color represents a different element. Red is the fog that simulates being burned, brown is the earth that makes you feel like you're being buried alive. Silver is air, and simulates being shot at over and over. Finally, blue signifies water, and when you're in that pod, you feel like you're drowning. "Get in," she orders.

The third blue pod from the front is open and ready for me. Some of the pods have yellow lights on them, some have green, others have red. It makes me wonder how many of these are currently occupied.

I step up to the pod and get in. The only way to describe the feeling would be coffin-like. Straps shoot out from under me, looping across my body, holding me tight. "What's the point of this?" I know the point. Luke told me. I'm just stalling. Anything to prolong the inevitable drowning that's about to occur. First, she makes me drown mentally, now she's going to make me drown physically.

"The mere sight of you has incited riots in my facility."

"You're blaming me for being here?" This shoots anger into my chest. "You choose to kill these people, you demand I be here for the betterment of society, and then you blame me for their deaths?"

"If we're going to advance as a society, the human race must be modified. We can create weapons, technology, medicine, but nothing will advance us to our full potential if we do not change the inner most faults of Humanity."

"What does this have to do with me?" My voice sounds desperate. I don't like it.

"Something about you incites unrest in others."

"Just kill me! You're the monster who kills!" The rage is uncontrollable. My body tenses against the restraints. "Emma, that girl in the hallway. Trixie, all the tainted children. Josephine, John Collins. What's one more?"

Her eyes are alight with disgust and contempt. "You don't know what you're talking about."

"You say you're doing this for the greater good...but you're just a murderer."

The vein in her neck pops, but then she takes a deep breath. It couldn't have been more than five seconds and she's calm again; the switch of her moods instantaneous. *Wait.* Five seconds? *Could it be?* "If the bigger picture isn't clear to you, then you're not as smart as I hoped you were."

The Reaver closes the pod, and the air instantly leaves my lungs as fluid takes its place. The pods torture you, then you're asked questions to see how you've changed. If the Brain doesn't like what you input into its algorithm, then the torture begins again. I don't want any of this. The Reaver wants to break me. She wants to cut me down so she can replace all of the pieces with a newer version. But this doesn't change who I am fundamentally. If I were to have kids, genetically they wouldn't be any more agreeable than I am. I guess if she can change my thought patterns, though, then I can help raise the next generation of compliant sheep. She wants to break me just to prove that she can.

But I'm a lion. She could've killed me. Multiple times. But she chose to kill Emma in the end instead, despite how great of a candidate she was. Ren Keres is a sick, sadistic bitch that likes to watch people tremble with fear and drown in their pain and suffering. All the while, she's hiding behind a false sense of morality.

She knew that if she killed me, Emma might find out and she'd be soiled. But if she killed her? Well that would cause me the most pain of all. She said it before, that I remind her of a young version of herself. And so maybe she's not trying to break me, but she's trying to punish her own soul. What a demented way to do that.

CHAPTER EIGHTEEN ○ AMITY

CHARLIE'S BEEN M.I.A FOR ABOUT A WEEK. IT'S MADE THE TIME go by even slower, if such a thing were possible. I'm still shaken up about the reckless kids. Who were they and what was their purpose? That young girl lost her life for Emma—for me—and I want to know why.

The crotchety woman at my door opens the force field when the cart with my lunch turns the corner. She grumpily grabs the tray and lazily drops it to the floor. Whatever the slop of the day is bounces out, splashing over the edges. She then kicks the tray along the tile toward the middle of the room causing more to spill out of the sides. *It's okay, I didn't feel hungry anyway.*

After lunch time is over, Giles comes to fetch me like normal. He's repulsed by the mess of the room. So far I've been drowned four times, shot at two, and burned once. All that's left is getting buried alive. In between that, the Reaver's had me in the M.A.P. room for a constant torture cycle, to check my progress with losing myself. Each time I refuse to break. Each time, her anger level is raised to a new high.

Giles silently leads me to the pod room. Although I've seen him almost every day since getting here, I've not talked with him since the beginning. At first it seemed like he took pity on me. *Oh, the poor girl that doesn't understand.* Now it's like he's disgusted with having to share the same air. *Repulsive is the girl that doesn't learn.*

We make it to the row of brown pods and my heart pounds. Somehow, being buried alive seems like the worst of them. *Does everyone feel this way or is it just me?* My knees buckle, causing me to stumble, but Giles tightens his grip and angrily pulls me along.

There's a pod open already, and I know that it's waiting for me, but something else is holding my attention. By the door is a small table. On it, a cake adorned with ten little candles. If it was hard to breathe before, it's now damn near impossible. Giles shoves me toward the table and I smack into it, causing the fire from the candles to dance wickedly. No. Please no. *How could I have forgotten? How could I...*

"Blow out the candles, Miss Thorne," Giles presses. "You wouldn't want to miss your sister's birthday."

My limbs are shaking leaves blowing in a storm. I'd lost all track of time. I'd lost all sense of everything. It's Emma's birthday. She would be ten. My little M. Ten.

The onset of the panic attack is fast. My legs give out and everything around me goes dark. When I come to, the cake is knocked over, the table is sideways. Giles has his hand around the nape of my neck, lifting me off the ground, his mouth close to my ear. But before he can say anything, someone jumps from behind us, tackling Giles. He recovers and lands on his knees, not letting the assailant take him down the whole way. I, however, get thrown to the ground in the process and once I turn around, there are a few other kids pounding at the pods, trying to release the prisoners inside.

"Get off of me," Giles coughs while the young man on his back grips his throat. "Code Red."

I recognize the crazed look in the kid's eyes. I've seen it before, the look of utter fear and pure survival instinct. My body is immobile as I watch the scene unfold around me. "Run, Amity," the kid's voice is strained. He's tensing his thick arms to keep Giles in a chokehold.

Before my mind can process that he's talking to me, a dozen guards enter the pod room and take control of the unruly. One by one, each resister is put onto their knees, and the barrel of a gun is pressed to their heads. Even Giles gains the upper hand, throwing the kid diagonally over his shoulder, slamming the accoster onto his back.

When each of the newly tainted are targeted, Giles spits on the one that attacked him. "You all disgust me." He pulls his trigger. His subordinate officers follow. I struggle to keep the bile from rising into my throat. So much death. So much destruction. What is the point? Is it all for Emma? For me?

My stomach lurches, my body retches, but nothing actually comes out. It's been a while since I've eaten. Giles kicks the body of the kid out of the walkway and I retch harder.

What just happened? These kids are standing up and taking charge, only to be shot down. I realize that the resistance isn't going to start with me, because it's clear that it has already begun. This is the rise of the runaways. My body shudders with a million different emotions taking over. *All I cause is death and destruction...*

Giles finally yanks me up. My body is too weak to stand on its own; I'm basically floating. My head bobs as Giles subtly shakes me. "You and your sister are *nothing* alike," he spits. "She deserved better."

He throws me to the ground and I wrap my arms around my knees, pulling them toward my chest. He doesn't even bother grabbing me, just leaves me to my own devices while he orders his men to clean up the mess. A single tear escapes my eye while my body tenses in agony. This is how they get you to give up.

I don't know how much time passes, but I'm moved only after the bodies of the other kids are taken care of. A part of me wishes I were dead like them. Whoever picks me up holds me like a groom carries his new bride. It feels too tender to be Giles. The suit is white, anyway.

The soldier carrying me walks down hallway after hallway. The sweet physical contact reminds me of Luke, and I shed another tear. I'm taken into an elevator. I don't dare peek at myself in all the mirrors surrounding us. I don't want to see the forlorn eyes that would stare back. We go down three more hallways before Giles's voice filters into my ears. "She's here, Madame."

We turn the corner and the soldier's grasp loosens. My mind strains, attempting to prepare my legs for becoming solid instead of the gelatin that they are now. When I'm set down, my body doesn't cooperate. I fall to my hands and knees in front of Giles.

"Get up," he spits, slamming his thick boot into my side. When I don't move, he kicks me harder with a harsher demand.

"Marcus," the Reaver warns. It's an odd feeling to have her on my side; to hear such tenderness from her voice. Perhaps she's not as bad as I thought? *No! That's just your tired, hurt brain, Amity.*

"Why do you even care about this filth? We have what we need." Giles is unhinged. I've never heard such utter hatred spew from his lips before. Any hope that I harbored for Giles to turn around and change is wiped away. He's too far gone. "This one is nothing like Emma."

The mention of my sister throws the Reaver off balance. But it's not long before her calm voice speaks. "Don't you ever question my actions here, Mr. Giles, or you'll be spending your time with the filth you despise so much." I peek under my arm, finding her leaning into Giles. "And it won't be as a First Sergeant."

Giles swallows harshly and says, "Yes, Headmistress. I apologize," before he's dismissed and walks away.

After he's gone, the Reaver leans down to help me up. It's kind and gentle, matching none of her actions thus far. What game is she playing? I'm brought into a small room directly to our right. It's dark at first, but then the light pops on and I'm left even more confused.

There's a two way mirror of sorts. The Reaver places me directly in front of it. The image flickers on from the room through the glass. There's a man tied to a singular chair in the middle of the floor. He looks nearly zombified. An officer in a white uniform is standing near him, in his hand a cattle prod, or something similar. There's a nurse in the back, tapping away at a computer. They seem to be monitoring the man's health. The only other person in the room is an officer in a black uniform. At first, I think it might be Giles, but then I realize it's a random Master Sergeant. My body trembles. The Reaver's hand is draped on my shoulder, holding me steady.

"Oh, dear. Don't check out on me already. This is only the beginning." Her voice is evil. A direct contrast to her earlier tone. I want to close my eyes. *Was this her game?* Get me to somewhat relax only to knock me off my feet? Suddenly, a speaker kicks on above me, the voices from the other room filtering through.

"I told you I don't know where he is," the man says. His voice is tough, and he's fairly calm despite the situation around him. Perhaps he's too exhausted to be scared. The officer in white shocks him again and his whole body tenses.

"Do you know who this is?" the Reaver questions me as I watch on in horror. I scan my memories, trying to put an identity to this person, but I come up blank. Besides, his face is so pounded in, I'm not sure I'd be able to recognize him if he were my own reflection. But when he unclenches his eyes, a familiar feeling settles in my stomach. "This is Mr. Warin's father."

I shudder, pressing my hand against the glass, hoping he can somehow see through the mirror. "There has to be a better way."

"Pardon?" The Reaver is curious.

"Why don't you read his memories like everyone else?"

Luke's father is questioned again, this time on the whereabouts of his wife and daughter. He gives nothing away, getting shocked once more.

"Please..." I whisper.

"Speak up, Miss Thorne." The Reaver jostles me beneath her fingertips.

"Why are you doing this?" The pain in my voice is clear.

"His memories gave us nothing. But Lucas is smart. He knows the potential blind spots to keep his father in the dark. So this," she gestures toward the torturous scene in front of us, "is what happens when you're stuck in Limbo; when the information you hold is too important to let you die."

"This is a waste of manpower and space; keeping him alive even though you can't stand him." I share my observation aloud. *What information about Luke could she possibly need that's so important?* I turn my eye to her, trying to get a read.

It's clear that Luke's father annoys her, but I don't understand why. She doesn't want him dead in the same way she doesn't want to give up on me. What type of information could I possibly have? The only thing this has me believing is that Luke had always been the target. But it's as if the torture is what makes this satisfying to her, even if she knows she'll get nothing.

"I haven't seen him since he went AWOL," Luke's father spits at the officer.

Between my questions and the responses from Luke's father, the Reaver tenses, growing increasingly irritated. "You LIE!" She slams her hand on the button in front of us, her voice screeching through the room.

Luke's father turns his tired gaze toward the mirror with a smirk that shows me just where Luke got his from. "Hello, Ren."

"Where did he plan to meet you, Paul?" she seethes through the microphone. The use of his first name surprises me. I've realized that the Reaver doesn't use first names often. This is a sign that this man is of some importance to her.

"Like you've heard me say plenty of times before...no...where." His words are staccato as they exit his mouth, perfectly enunciating each word for extra emphasis. "He said we'd never see him again. Thanks to you." When he says the word *you,* it drips with disdain.

"I know how tough you are. But it's only a matter of time before you break. I'll see to it." This is all very perplexing. There's an animosity here that I can't quite put my finger on.

"You've seen inside my head, Ren. You can't punish anyone you think is like John without punishing yourself. You're more like him than anyone else," is what Luke's father says before he's shocked with a higher voltage. *Is he referring to John Collins?* "This is your own doing."

The Senator keeps coming up. He's just another piece of this puzzle that I'm confused about. Each time he's mentioned, the Reaver becomes almost unhinged. She turns to me after five seconds with a gleam in her eye that shoots fear straight through me. "This may not work on him, but you?" She presses the button again. "Atkins, come retrieve Miss Thorne." The Reaver releases the button, turning to me once more. "What a great way to celebrate. Welcome to Limbo."

My knees buckle beneath me as Atkins, the Master Sergeant overseeing Mr. Warin's torture, drags me into the room. Luke's father is being uncuffed from the chair and removed to make room for me. Luke's hazel eyes are a direct copy of his father's and, for a second, I'm brought face to face with Luke in my mind. I should've told him how I felt. If I die here, he'll never have heard the words he so desperately wanted to hear.

"Why do you want to know where Luke is?" I speak up, earning myself a slap in the face from Atkins. It only stops me momentarily. Why hasn't she asked me where he is? "Why not Mason Baines? Or my father?" I'm blatantly ignoring the cry to give up calling from the back of my mind.

"Enough, foolish girl!" Atkins smacks me again, this time causing the taste of blood to pool in my mouth. I must've bitten my tongue. But I don't stop. The Reaver can't win. If she's going to torture me, I'm not going to make it easy. I'm going to fight. If for no one else, than for Emma. *Happy Birthday, my sweet girl.*

"Why is Luke so important to you? And what does the Senator have to do with it?" At this, Atkins wraps his thick hand around my throat, causing me to sputter. I guess I can't keep talking if I can't breathe.

I'm trying to keep myself calm, but the severe gagging happens involuntarily. The panic that sets in is a direct line from the first time I was strangled by the side of the road. I thought I'd dealt with the trauma, but this is one hell of a trigger.

I'm brought to the brink of Death before Atkins lets go. My lungs burn as they struggle to pull air in.

"Have you learned your lesson?" The Reaver's snake voice slithers through the speakers. But the truth is, I haven't. Anger is what's coursing through my veins right now, not fear. Hell, I'm furious.

I lift my face and glare straight through the two way mirror. "You're a coward!" I say to her, but honestly I'm looking straight into my own soul in the reflection.

Before I recognize what's happening, a thick fist connects to my cheekbone and that's the last thing I sense before everything goes black.

CHAPTER NINETEEN ○ LUKE

12:05 PM. I'VE BEEN IN ABERDEEN FOR A WEEK NOW. STILL NO sign of M. This has been the worst personal Hell. Not only am I missing Sam—something I never pictured myself dealing with—but I have no idea what condition M is in, leaving me on edge since we got here. Sarge has had to deal with most of the wrath, and it makes guilt climb into my chest every time. He doesn't deserve the harsh treatment. I know M would be disappointed in me.

But the fact of the matter is that I'm not sure if M is alive, and I can't handle the emotions that are bottling up inside of me. The only inclination I have that M is still breathing is that I know how strong she is. Ren's too messed up in the head to just kill her. She obviously wants something from her, and M's strength and stubbornness will be her greatest weapon. Even *if* Ren has dissected her weakness. I peer down at Sarge to find sad eyes staring at me. Back to the Relay. 12:07 pm. Damn.

The next hour passes slowly. The last seven days have come and gone, and absolutely nothing has changed. I'm about ready to accept another day in Hell when the Guardianship Update music breaks the silence. Sarge jumps up out of his sleep, running to my side to catch a glimpse.

When the mark of the Guardianship disappears, something horrid takes its place. My heart sinks and floats all at once as I find myself staring at M. Her eyes are sunken in, she looks like she's a zombie. Sarge whimpers next to me, lifting his paw, trying to reach his owner through the screen. I wrap my arm around him, pretending it's for his comfort when really it's as much for me as it is for him.

The background isn't familiar to me. She's in a dark room. Her hands are conveniently off screen which means she's most likely restrained. Nothing in my brain will give me an answer on what Ren is planning to do. I've got a pretty good idea of what she's already done, though, and that hurts me enough.

"Go ahead, Miss Thorne," Ren says, off screen. At her words, M focuses on the camera in front of her, her eyes staring straight through me.

"People of Western America." Her voice is raspy, and only then do I notice the redness around her throat. "I beg of you to do the right thing." If I didn't know any better, I'd think Ren succeeded in breaking M. But that can't be right? M is playing her game. She has to be. "The riots need to stop. Emma wouldn't want this, and we don't need more chaos. The Headmistress just wants to rebuild." Her voice slices into my heart. The person speaking is not the M I know. This is a new M. An M I'm not quite sure can save herself. "Today is my sister's birthday, and for her I ask that you honor the plan," she starts again. "Please get someplace safe, and listen for the officers. They are coming. They don't want to hurt you, but they will do everything necessary to safeguard the true meaning of the Guardianship."

The screen goes black before I'm able to trace M's face in my mind. I'd been too focused on what she was saying. I hadn't realized today is Emma's birthday. It weighs on me that I'm not there to comfort her. But something about her words doesn't sit right in my head. Dropping all other thoughts, I immediately transcribe them on the Relay, reading it over and over again. Were these the words of Ren, or a key from Amity?

My eyes keep landing on the word "for". If the goal was to stop people's worries, why would she say listen *for* the officers instead of listen *to*? It's almost like it's a warning. But for whom?

Maybe I'm allowing myself to fill up with useless hope. Maybe I'm reaching. But I have to believe that the M I know is still in there. And that means I have to believe that she was sending a warning. But was it for me?

I'm going to treat this like a code. It's always better to be prepared, anyway. So I'll listen for the officers. Perhaps they found out about Aberdeen and this was her subtle way of telling me. They don't want to hurt me...does that mean they want to kill?

There's no time to waste. I start by setting up booby traps around the meeting spot that M and I discussed together. Some carefully placed foot traps with leftover rope, a nicely covered hole that Sarge had dug in no time. All of my trapping knowledge goes into this. As the sun begins to set, I wipe the sweat from my face and smile at a job well done.

The last thing I do is drape one of our blankets over a pile of leaves in the shape of a person. Sarge and I step carefully as we trek away from the masterpiece of traps and head North. If anyone is coming for us, they've got something completely different coming to them.

Once we're out of sight, we make a small camp in the brush of the forest. If this wasn't a warning, then I don't want to get too far away from the rendezvous point. If it is, well, I'm not sure what I'll be forced to do then.

I stare up at the lonely moon through the trees, attempting to force myself to sleep. Maybe I feel like punishing myself tonight, because the nightmares seem like a welcome distraction from reality. How messed up is that? I truly am a monster.

Next thing I know I'm walking down the halls of Omphalos in my mind. Ren has invited me into her special office to speak of a highly sensitive mission. For some reason, she likes me. That means she wants to make me Sergeant Major; her right hand man.

The door opens into a pristine white room with light grey furniture. I'm more of an earthy tones kind of guy, and all the clinical appearances around here tend to make me sick. Ren says it's important for purity and whatnot. Who am I to say otherwise, right?

Ren Keres is sitting stoically at her desk, her face down in whatever paperwork it is she has to do. She lifts her head and meets my eye, instantly smiling. There's something sinister about it, but I'm here for the protection this job gives my family—and the money—so who cares if she's evil? You gotta do what you gotta do.

Her hand is outstretched, signaling for me to sit on the long grey sofa perpendicular to her desk. I do. "Mr. Warin," she starts, casually getting up from her chair and circling around to sit beside me on the scratchy sofa. "You've been here for quite some time now, yes?" Her eyes are constantly studying you, reading your body language as if she were a human lie detector.

"Yes, ma'am," I state. I'd been in the Force since the very beginning, definitely not the only one, but definitely her favorite. My father raised me to be a fearless leader, and with Ren's help, I could now channel my anger into new projects. It was Ren that suggested I become Sergeant Major, and the further up I climbed, the better I felt. It didn't matter that my father had urged me not to. In fact, that was part of the thrill.

"You're a fantastic First Sergeant, but don't you think it's time to move up?" There's a suggestive tone in her voice. The truth is, I do want to move up. I've been a First Sergeant for almost three years now. But Ren's words are stuck in my head: "You must be willing to risk it all for the cause."

I've wanted a normal life. I've even wanted love. I'm not sure I'd be willing to risk it all for a cause I'm not 100% sure of yet. So I've been pushing it off. But Ren is not a patient woman. She is also the one person that could take away my benefits, so if she's telling me I need to move up, then I guess I have no other choice.

I nod to her.

"Very good," she praises, visibly relaxing. I hadn't noticed how tense she was before. "Then on to your assignment." She pauses, as if looking for the right words to say. "In order to move up in rank, you're going to have to prove your loyalty. To me, to the cause." She's eyeing me up, trying to gauge my reactions. I stay calm. "You'll have to pay the ultimate price to show the Guardianship you would do anything necessary."

She's stalling and it's pissing me off. "What do I have to do, Ren?" I sigh, exasperated. The vein in her forehead pokes out slightly at my attitude. She hates being called Ren.

After a few seconds, she takes a breath and begins anew. "You must kill your father." What? I don't let her see my confusion. I joined for the protection of my family, and now she's asking me to kill my own flesh and blood?

"That's it?" I'm speaking calmly. If she notices any apprehension, it's all of our heads on a platter.

She sneers, evil and full of pride. "Do so in front of your stepmother and her daughter," she says the words with slight disdain. Sorry I asked. What is her game here? After a few silent seconds, she speaks again. "I need to know that you'd do anything for the cause, and that there will be nothing—and no one—to get in your way." Her eyes darken as she places her hand on me. "You can do this, Lucas."

"Do Janet and Lily get protection still?" If I tell this woman I won't do it, then everyone dies. But if I ask my father to sacrifice himself, then he would do so to protect his family. That's the type of man he is.

Ren tilts her head curiously, then smiles. "Of course." Her eyes are dead.

Fast forward and I'm in a Force car, headed to my father's old town house in Parker, Arizona. Am I really going to kill my father? I spend the ride agonizing, justifying the horrid actions somehow. He didn't care to help my real mother. He was a respectable father, but not necessarily a loving one; especially as I got older. Ren has been more caring to me as my work superior. Maybe it wouldn't be so bad. He'd give me no trouble if I explained the situation, but Ren will be watching through my body cam at some point. I'd have to hurt Lily, also, and that's a thought almost too much to bear.

The car slows. I walk up to the door, gently knocking. My father answers after a few seconds with his usual fatherly sideways grin until he clocks the expression on my face. Once his mouth droops to ask what's wrong, I pull out my gun, grip his neck, and press the metal to his forehead.

My father is smart, and strong. He could get out of this if he wanted, and a part of me wishes he would. Instead he puts his hands up in surrender and slowly drops to his knees.

Janet comes running into the room, curious about the shuffle and screams at the sight. "It's okay," my father assures through the choke, never taking his eyes from mine. Lily finds her way to the scene eventually, her tiny cries slicing me.

"Luke..." she whispers, her hand to her mouth, smothering her small sobs. She's the only one who calls me Luke, and it momentarily makes the rage subside.

But then I do what Ren taught me. I channel all the red hot anger back, and I press the gun harder into my father's forehead.

"I have to," I whisper after an eternity passes, a single tear falling from my eye.

"It's okay, son," my father says, calmly. "Do what you have to do."

I shoot up off the terrain, covered in dirt and sweat. Back to reality, a noise in the distance ripped me from the torrent of sleep. Sarge is pressing all his weight against me, now licking my face to keep me grounded. Man, do I hate my nightmares. Out of everything I'm forced to relive, the day I was going to kill my own father is one of the worst.

I attempt to reorient my mind, reminding myself that it was just a dream and that I'm passed that point in my life. It's hard to do when reality hits and I remember that my family is probably dead anyway. The thing that kills me the most about that dream is that I'm not sure which I feel more guilty of: actually planning to kill my father, or not going through with it.

Another noise a short distance away sends all other thoughts out of my skull. Something, or someone, is near, and my survivalist brain is turned on full scale now, not letting anything cloud it up. I guess it does have its benefits sometimes. I glance at Sarge whose snout is in the air, silently finding the direction of the commotion.

It isn't until a loud scream and the snap of branches cuts through the dark that I understand what sound is barreling into my eardrums. The traps. Sarge and I crawl through the dirt ever so slowly until we come into view of the rendezvous point. It's there we see a group of confused Force officers. One is in the hole, clenching their leg. It wasn't deep, but I knew that it would at least sprain an ankle. Another one says they're going to search the area, but doesn't get far before he trips over a rope and gets knocked out by a blunt rock. The other three officers are left scratching their heads.

I can't help but laugh at the stupidity. Then I mentally punch myself for my own. The whispered cackles were too loud and I've drawn attention to myself. Damn it, Warin!

"You hear that?"

"I did"

"Sounded like it came from over there." This one points in my general location.

"I'll go check it out," says another.

"Step lightly," warns the last.

Shit. What am I going to do now? I could shoot at them from hiding. Maybe scare them off. My only other option is to send Sarge, but I won't risk his life because of my own ridiculousness. I take a moment to thank the stars that Sam isn't with us.

I slowly pull the gun from my waistband, careful to not make any noise. Then I take my other gun in my left. They need to believe there are multiple ambushers. I've got maybe seven total bullets between the two guns. That leaves me with only one gun for food if I use these up. I have to be smart.

As the officer gets closer, I ready my shot. Then, when he's just ten feet away, I send a bullet straight through his right shoulder. "Ah!" he cries, tumbling to the ground from the force. "It's an ambush!" he shouts, taking his gun into his left hand to shoot into the woods. The two other officers that aren't hurt come running. I don't let them get close before I put bullets in each of their shoulders as well. They both cry out in unison. Then I send another bullet into the first guy's left shoulder, rendering him useless.

"We gotta fall back," he says as the others shower the woods with bullets. Sarge and I back away as fast as we can, narrowly avoiding the shower of metal as it hurricanes through the forest. Luckily, we make it behind a thick tree trunk, but not before a bullet grazes my thigh.

"Ahhh," I quietly seethe through my teeth. Four bullets used is enough. Now they have to believe I've escaped, or I'm dead.

The bullets stop after a minute. Then, I quiet my breathing to hear what they have to say.

"You okay, Jake?" someone asks.

"Both my arms are limp!" he answers, clearly agitated.

"This was definitely a trap," the last one says. I peek out from behind the tree to see the officer with two bullets in him being helped up. "The Headmistress is going to have our heads."

These soldiers aren't smart. But they do make a good point. Do I think this will cause Ren to kill M? No. She wouldn't go through all this trouble just to kill her. But I am worried that she will torture her even worse. I'm already worried that M is in too deep to make it out alive.

Did I make a mistake? Maybe I need to accept that I should find some help. Our best bet would be Mason Baines, the annoyingly perfect politician's son from our runaway group. As much as I want to profusely vomit at the thought of needing Mason for anything, I can't deny that his connections to the H.P.S might serve M well.

This means that I have to walk away. This means I break my vow to her. I told her I wasn't going anywhere—that I'd be in Aberdeen every day, twice a day—but now I'm thinking of leaving. It causes my gut to wrench, doing flips inside my abdomen. But then the thought of my father pops into my head, uninvited. He would've told me to go. He would've said that sometimes it's bigger than any one person and you have to think quickly and concisely before your window of opportunity shatters into a million pieces.

I know what must be done. I have to break my vow to M in order to save her. She'd forgive me if she knew. She'd have to, right? She wanted me to go anyway.

Sarge catches my eye and there's an unspoken understanding. He makes me feel closer to M. "Time to find the boat."

CHAPTER TWENTY ○ LUKE

I̲t̲ t̲a̲k̲e̲s̲ a̲ d̲a̲y̲ o̲r̲ s̲o̲, b̲u̲t̲ s̲a̲r̲g̲e̲ a̲n̲d̲ i̲ f̲i̲n̲a̲l̲l̲y̲ f̲i̲n̲d̲ s̲o̲m̲e̲-thing. A beach in the distance. The light color of the sand can vaguely be seen through the dense forest. We followed the old Murdock Creek until now and if we continue on, it will lead us straight into the beach.

For some reason, though, Sarge stops dead in his tracks, refusing to walk on. The forest in front of us looks vast, yet empty. But maybe there's an enemy nearby. I question him. "What's up?"

He lets out a quiet, lone bark and firmly plants himself into a sit. He doesn't seem worried; his body language is relaxed. Is he being stubborn? Is he finally realizing we're leaving M behind?

"What?" I sigh. "There's nothing around!" But Sarge stares at me with his big, golden eyes. It's hard to keep the anger from rooting itself into my chest. Being this close means I'm growing impatient for the roadblocks that keep popping up. It's already taken too long because of this stupid limp. Damn graze wounds. "Whatever." I roll my eyes. "I'll go without you." I turn away from him and walk, creating a gap between us. Sarge lets out another bark, but it doesn't stop me. Instead, I glance behind me with a self-assured look and say, "Come on, then, if..."

The breath is knocked from my lungs as I smack into something hard. Fucking hell. Did I really run into a tree? I press my palm to my head and look forward again. There's not a tree immediately in front of me. What the?

My arm extends, reaching out until my fingers touch a solid surface where there should otherwise be nothing. Sarge then runs up beside me, jumping up and licking at my face. His eyes are smug when I meet them, as if to say, *I tried to tell you.* "Okay, okay. Next time I'll listen to you."

The barrier continues, and we cautiously follow along for almost a mile before having to slow at the sight of a person. We dip low, hiding in the brush. He seems a tad suspicious as we maneuver through the thick bushes and leaves to get a closer look, but we're able to keep ourselves hidden.

The man has a simple sailor suit on, with a small insignia on his chest. It looks like a winged individual inside a red circle. Could this be the Angel's Fleet? I decide that we won't immediately make ourselves known. He may not look like a Force officer, but this could still be a trap.

After a substantial amount of time passes, someone else hobbles down the path and the guard stands at attention, resting a hand on his hip—rather a hidden gun—as the young woman approaches.

"Can you help me?" she croaks. Her body is dirty like her clothes. Her hair is matted, her shoes are falling apart, and she looks like a bag of bones. She's obviously been having a rough time.

"What can I do for you, ma'am?" the guard answers. His voice is instantly kind.

"I'm trying to find the Service?" she whispers, glancing around nervously. "Do you know where to go? You have that symbol." She points to the insignia on his chest. Perhaps there's a whole underground operation to help people find this place.

"State your name," the guard says. After the woman answers shyly, he presses something on his belt and a small opening appears, giving a clear view into the secret beach behind the cloaked wall.

This is it! This is the place!

I lead Sarge to the guard moments after the door closes behind him. "Hello," I say once we're closer. The man rests his hand on his gun like he had for the woman. "Got any openings for Creyke Point?" I try my best smile, but honestly I have no idea how this works. Do I have to point out the insignia? My impatience has made us look suspicious. Damn it, Warin, get your head out of your ass.

"There are no animals allowed." He's stoic, not at all the kind voice he'd offered up to the woman before. "But you are more than welcome to pass on your own." This makes me angry.

"This isn't just *any* animal." My voice is growing tense with anger as I keep my teeth clenched.

"I'm sorry, sir, but that animal cannot come on the ship," he repeats, this time harsher. So, you want to play it that way?

I chuckle lightly, casually leaning toward him before my face turns serious and I thrust my fist at his collar, grabbing his stupid shirt. "Oh, he's coming," I threaten. The anger comes out like the flip of a switch, and the adrenaline it causes helps me lift the man as if he weighs two pounds.

He's scared, like he's going to piss his pants, and I do feel a slight pang of guilt. But I need to get to Mason and there's no way I'm breaking my promise to M after already breaking my vow. The man is trying to reach his gun to subdue me, but I won't let that happen. I grip him tighter, thrusting him harder into the wall.

"I'm...I'm sorry," he stutters. "I wish..."

"Shut your hole," I cut him off. "I need to see Mason Baines and the dog comes with. End of discussion." I drop the man, his shirt all bunched around his neck now. The door pops open, and at first I think I've won, but then another seaman steps toward us, gun in hand.

"What seems to be the prob..." he stops as Sarge enters his view.

So now I'll have to fight two assholes. Whatever. But I'm taken off guard when the new guy turns to the one I've manhandled, dropping his weapon. "D, don't you know who this is?" The man is practically giddy.

Bunched shirt shakes his head with wide eyes.

"This is the admirable Sergeant!"

I breathe out a laugh. "Well I wouldn't really say I'm admirable, but..."

This time it's their turn to interrupt me. "Not you!" The man steps aside. "The dog!" I roll my hazels and Sarge smiles up at me with smug eyes. "Right this way, sir."

The door opens again and the second man leads us through. He introduces himself as Admiral Blade. He's the head of operations for the Shadow Service connection, and he's excited to finally meet Sarge. Forget me, I guess.

"You must be Mr. Warin, then?" Blade asks. I nod my head. "We had all but given up hope!"

The beach isn't large, but it is beautiful. It's broken up into quadrants. One area is a large, communal showering space. There are a bunch of curtains hanging around. Another is a small cafeteria for stuffing your face. A couple tables, some food trays. Then there are a few rows of beds which must be sleeping quarters for the workers in the Service. Finally, there's a row of three small rescue boats along the water's edge.

"Would you like to get cleaned up before we head out?" Blade offers. "Or maybe you are hungry?" At the sound of the h-word, Sarge lets out a swift whine.

"I guess that means you'd like to eat?" I say to Sarge. He answers me with a lick of his lips and we follow Admiral Blade into the small café. I'm not a fan of fabricated meals, so I only gather what Sarge wants, placing it on the table for him to chow down.

"How do you guys protect yourself from infiltrators?" I'm curious as to how they remain off of the Guardianship's radar.

"We constantly scan bodies for hidden cameras. If a camera is detected, we knock them out, cover the camera, and move them to a new location far away. They are none the wiser when they wake up. If they don't have a camera, we trust that they are citizens in need of help. If we find out they are not, then we promptly imprison them.

His answer is straight to the point. It makes sense. All Force personnel are equipped with body cams. Most commoners wouldn't even have the funds to cover a broken camera, let alone a fully operational one. "How did you know who we were?" I ask.

"Mr. Baines had requested that we keep an eye out for a Miss Thorne, a Mr. Warin, and the admirable Sergeant. When we saw Miss Thorne on the Update, we had lost our hope." His eyes actually hold sadness in them for a moment. "But Mr. Baines will be happy to know that you are on your way."

"I highly doubt that," I mutter to myself.

CHAPTER TWENTY-ONE ○ LUKE

It hadn't taken all that long to get to Creyke Point. General Blade escorted us a few miles offshore where we entered into a submarine. Then, the submarine carried us the rest of the way, until we made it into the basement of H.P.S Headquarters. We haven't been waiting all that long before Mason Baines makes his way toward us.

"Warin." Mason nods to me as he walks up. "How did Am..." his voice fades as the look on my face seemingly answers his unfinished question. His eyes cast downward, his lips do a bit of a twitch. He thinks M has been captured.

"She went willingly," I clarify. He glances up at me with a sharp glare.

"She what?"

"Ren got into her head. She turned herself in." The nonchalance of my tone is waning as calm and collected Luke struggles to keep his cool. The words I'm saying rehash old feelings, putting me in a sour mood.

"Why in God's name didn't you stop her?" Mason thinks he knows the situation, as per usual.

"I tried to talk her out of it," I scoff. How dumb of him to think I wouldn't.

"Oh, you tried to *talk?*" His snarky tone reminds me how much I despise him, but he's of some importance to M which means punching his face is off-limits.

"She's a grown woman. She can make her own decisions." My words are rational, but in the context of our conversation, they're ridiculous. I wouldn't ever admit that to Mason, though.

Something about what I've said sends me spiraling into a memory. Lucas Warin at thirteen is a spitfire menace. His father is yelling at him, asking where he's been. War has ravaged his little town, and the streets are typically bare except for maybe a dead body or two.

"Out," Lucas spits back. He'd been in the woods. He wasn't looking for trouble, but he wasn't counting on staying out of it.

"Son, it's too dangerous out there," his father chides.

"You go out every day!" Lucas is tired of the same old fight. His father taught him to be fearless, so *what* out there could be so bad?

"It's my job, Lucas," he sighs. "And I was trained for war." Lucas's father isn't exactly humble about being a Marine. He claims he's on the side of justice, but Lucas thinks he's full of shit. "Why do you have to defy me?"

"Why don't you ask mom why she tried to get away from you, maybe that would answer your question."

The look on his father's face is horror mixed with shock. It's the same every time Lucas mentions his dead mother. "I've told you before that she's a grown woman. She made her decision. You don't get to make one until you're grown as well."

"Well it was a terrible decision! How dare…" Mason shouts, ripping me from the past. His expression is a mix of disgust and contempt.

I cut him off. "She would've never forgiven me if I held her back!" I shout in his face.

"She could be dead right now!" Mason is losing his composure quickly. Sarge stands up, putting himself in between me and Mason. It's a sign that all of the runaways have come to learn, and it feels good knowing Sarge has taken my side. Mason stops, takes a deep breath, then continues. "You don't think she would've forgiven you eventually?"

I rub my thumb and forefinger in between my eyebrows to squash the growing headache Mason is causing. "Where's the rest of us?" I ask, attempting to change the subject before Angry Luke comes out.

Mason's jaw ticks, making him appear deadly. "Lacy has been off enjoying Creyke Point, and as for Abigail, well…" There's a huge pit forming in the bottom of my stomach. It's the feeling a soldier gets when he's about to learn that one of his own didn't make it.

"I'm sorry." I stop him, placing my hand on his shoulder. While I may not officially know that my sister is dead along with the rest of my family, I've been assuming so for two and a half years now. I know how it feels to lose the person that you felt it was your duty to protect. And now I've done it again losing M…

"Lucas Warin!" a voice calls from behind me, interrupting my moment of silence for Abby. I turn to find Lacy moving toward me with outstretched arms.

As if a switch is flicked, I push past my solemn sorrow, burying it deep in my chest. "Elise Barnett," I smirk back, allowing her to wrap her arms around me. The contact feels strange, causing me to tense.

"I told you that name in confidence!" she cries, playfully smacking me. "Where's Amity?" she asks as she pulls away. I don't have to answer. Her face morphs into a frown. I thought my expression had been kept plain, but it seems I've let my eyes give away the pain. "No…" she shakes her head. "No! Not her, too!" Tiny droplets of water pool on her dark lashes.

A lightbulb goes off in my head as realization dawns. "No," I assure her. "She's not dead." Then I think better of saying something I don't exactly know to be true. "At least, I hope not."

"What the hell is going on here?" Ah, there's the fiery Lacy I know.

"Lacy, I'll fill you in, come on." Mason holds out his arm for her to hook hers onto. "I'm about to show Luke around."

All of H.P.S Headquarters is underground. Where the Guardianship built into the sky for Force operations, the Service decided to burrow down to stay hidden and be better equipped for protection against potential air raids. Smart.

Before we make it out of the basement, something catches my eye. "What is this?" There's a large screen with dozens of video feeds.

"It's surveillance." Mason's eyes are alight like a kid in a candy store. I scan the wall until a video of a group of young adults catches my attention. They're marching down the street of an old Slum, blocked by Ren's executive order to condense everyone. All of them line up, pounding their fists to their chests twice before raising them in the air. The guards standing at the perimeter meet them with raised guns. Then, the rioters take off to attack the guards. Most are shot before ever making it, but the ones that do are gone within minutes.

My breathing picks up as I struggle to keep myself calm. Don't show how affected you are, Warin. "Why are we just sitting here?" I yell. "Why are we watching this?" I slam my fist against the screen and a small part of it goes dark. The guards around us lift their weapons toward me, like the ones in the video did to those innocents. I've probably ruined thousands of dollars' worth of equipment for these guys—and let them see my emotion—but fuck it. Whatever is going on here is sickening.

"Woah, hey." Mason raises his hands to diffuse the situation. Lacy looks at me with terror in her eyes; like I'm crazy. "Let's step away, I'll explain."

My jaw is locked and ticking, and my fists are clenched at my sides. I scan the room. Everyone serves to piss me off more. It isn't until my eyes meet Sarge's that I find the will power to count down from five. I nod to Mason after a century, letting him lead me away.

Into the elevator, up a floor or two, out into a small, circular hangout spot inverted into the floor. It's one of many in this room. We sit, Lacy cuddled to Sarge on my right and Mason directly across from me. "They call themselves Amiteers," he starts.

"What the hell are you talking about?" Of all the bullshit dumb fuckery that could come out of his mouth, this takes the cake.

Mason inhales, taking a deep breath, clearly struggling to keep calm. "I thought you and Amity were goners," Mason begins. "So I was using the Thorne's story as a way to rally the people."

Something about this instantly sets me off. M's story wasn't his to use. Sarge lifts his head from Lacy's lap to watch me. Okay, Warin, take a deep breath. "Why not use Abby?" He never exactly told me what happened but that doesn't matter. He could've shared the Baines's story, rather than the one that wasn't his.

"Abigail was a hero and a sad loss. But Emma's death was a tragedy—a senseless murder. I figured the people would respond to her more. And losing Amity, too?" His eyes are begging me to understand, but really they are begging to be gouged out. I don't understand what it is about Mason that pisses me off, but I'm afraid I'm very close to beating him up. His senselessness is what played M's guilt, and it's his lack of regard for his role in it that tips me over the edge.

"What happened to her?" I need to stop talking about Emma and M. I need Mason to be the sad shell of an older brother so that the rage will stop building inside of me.

"Infection," he spits, quick and heartless.

Oh, yes. The bullet wound. She courageously dove in front of a gun to save Lacy's life, and this is what she's reduced to? Despicable.

"Anyway," Mason averts the conversation. "Now that I know Amity isn't dead, it makes sense."

My eyebrows tuck in, creating a hood over my eyes. What does he mean by this? And why doesn't he want to talk about Abby? The look on my face must ask the question because he continues without the need for me to open my mouth.

"I must have royally ticked off the Headmistress," he admits. Suddenly the events of Emma's one-year deathiversary make sense. Ren thought M was the one to turn her sister into a martyr. "My contacts searched all over for you guys, but found nothing. When the Headmistress called Amity out over the Update, I got word about it right away. I hoped, even prayed, that this meant you were on your way. I made sure that each of the Admirals knew who you were, and that you were to be brought to me straight away."

I know Mason thinks he's the good guy here. And maybe deep down, the reason I hate him is because I know this to actually be true. But my wrath is the only thing that comes out. "So you're the reason she's in there," I grit. Sarge sits up completely now, turning his body toward me. Mason thought he was doing the right thing, but I firmly believe that if he had used his own damn sister as a martyr, then M and I would still be together.

"As far as I'm concerned, *you're* the reason she's in there," Mason snaps.

Before my brain processes its own actions, I'm on my feet and moving at Mason with a murderous glare. I don't make it the full way, though, because Sarge grabbed my shirt in between his teeth and is yanking me back. All it takes is a second and I can force myself to count down from five. Unfortunately, that's all it takes to set me off as well.

I back up, sitting down and ignoring the waves of uncomfortability flowing from Lacy. "What does this have to do with the video?" My voice is calm now. It's clear it throws Mason off balance. My ability to shift effortless between moods has always been somewhat of a surprise to most people. My parents never really turned their heads to it much, but everyone else has. Everyone except Ren Keres. She's the one who helped me channel it.

"Those individuals standing up to the guards were Amiteers." Mason clarifies. "People who identify with Amity and want justice for Emma and everyone like her. Our sources show them all over. The Resistance is spreading."

CHAPTER TWENTY-TWO ○ LUKE

I'M WAITING FOR MASON IN MY ROOM. IT'S A SMALL, CIRCULAR pod in the middle of thousands. It has a bed and a desk. That's it. There's barely any room for me and Sarge. Mason had a separate *suite* set aside for Sarge, but there was no way in Hell I was going to let him out of my sight. Thankfully, Sarge agreed.

The Service leader, General Olivier Favager, has requested to meet me. Mason said it was in regards to maps of the Guardianship's facilities. I made it clear that he's shit out of luck; I don't have any maps. The General is expecting me anyway.

When the tiny clock reads 3:45, Mason knocks on my door before sliding it open. Sarge sits up quickly, looking back at me. I nod. He runs to Mason and subjects him to an onslaught of sloppy dog kisses.

"Alright, Sarge," I say after a few minutes. I stand, almost banging my head against the ceiling of the pod. "Let's do this."

Mason walks us through the maze of pod rooms and out of the resident area of the facility. The people who get to live in H.P.S Headquarters are those of importance. Most everyone else lives in Compound One, the underwater housing bunker off the shore of Creyke Point. That's apparently where Lacy has chosen to stay. They have slightly bigger rooms over there, with the option for roommates. They are welcome to submarine ferry over to the mainland at any time to enjoy the amenities provided. Seems like a pretty sweet gig in comparison to living in Western America.

The doors are nonexistent here. Instead, there are grids of sensors that everyone must pass through. The system is able to identify who you are and if you have permission to access.

Mason steps through the first grid and the screen on the perpendicular wall lights up with his information. The see-through body outline on the screen shows a red spot on his lower back and a dim red spot on his right shoulder. I guess they couldn't take the bullet out. At least they made his arm usable again. Pity. He has a high security clearance, which means he has access to basically everything at H.P.S Headquarters.

I pause for a second before stepping through. Sarge is waiting on my lead. "Don't be scared," Mason goads, "it doesn't hurt." If M had any sort of indifference to Mason the way I do, I'd dive through the grid and knock his teeth in.

But instead I roll my eyes—a habit I've come to realize I picked up from M—and step through the grid. Sarge follows close to my side.

Both of us are shown on the screen simultaneously. Sarge's body outline is clear and his security clearance is the same as Mason's. My outline blinks red in three spots, signifying the three guns I have on me. Next to my clearance status it says "NTK". It means Need to Know.

"Why the hell does the dog have a higher clearance than me?"

"Everyone loves the dog," Mason shoots back quickly.

The deeper we go, the more rigorous the grids become. As long as I follow behind Mason and enter within five seconds, my presence is allowed because of his. Then we enter a room deep within the facility that's guarded by a live officer. He opens the door for us and we're greeted by a man with silver hair and a serious face.

"General." Mason nods at him.

"Mr. Baines," Olivier answers back. "Mr. Warin."

There's a map of Western America on the giant monitor to our right and a large flat table in the center of the room. I give a half-assed nod in the General's direction. My sour mood is unexplainable, but I've given up trying to decipher it.

"Mr. Warin has agreed to exchange information," Mason says. I've agreed? As if I had a choice. Pfft. It pisses me off even more that he addresses me as Mr. Warin.

"Yes, thank you, Mr...." I cut Olivier off before I hear Mr. Warin yet again.

"General, you should know there's a house here," I walk over, pointing to the map on the screen. "Roughly, anyway. It's full of one-armed tainted children. You should send someone to get them and someone to wait around for more."

"More?" Mason questions. "One-armed?"

"The woman there, Mama June, has an operation with her son in the Force. He brings her tainted children and she removes their arms to save them from the tracker."

"Jesus," Mason utters to himself, shaking his head.

"We will do our best, Mr. Warin," the General speaks. "We want to help every child possible, but our spaces are limited. Our resources are running too low to needlessly create new limbs for these children. We're trying to figure out something for the trackers, and our second underwater bunker is nearly complete." The smugness of this guy irritates me. Does he even want to help?

"Keep me updated," is all I say before turning to walk away.

"This is not why we summoned you in here, Mr. Warin," the General calls to me before I can leave. I turn back. "We need a map of their facilities."

My mood is not conducive to dealing with people right now. Especially *these* people. The irritation is bubbling up inside of me;

the emotions that Ren taught me to harness and turn me into a ruthless authoritarian. "Like I told Mason already, I don't..."

The General holds his finger up to silence me. Then, he brings it to his temple and taps twice.

A confused look settles on my face. It multiplies tenfold when Mason hands me a small electrode device. The wire is connected to the control panel under the large monitor with the map. I hesitantly place it on my temple. The second I do, a blue grid hologram plane immediately appears on the table in front of us.

Mason is smiling a shit-eating grin, and the General is back to his serious disposition. A woman walks in with a shimmering liquid. She hands it to me. "Drink," she commands. Unease creeps into my chest. It's not that I'm scared to drink it, it's more that I demand answers.

"What is it?" I ask as it presses to my lips. The liquid sloshes into my mouth. It tastes chalky.

"Memory enhancer," the nameless woman says before she turns and exits.

"All you have to do is think," Olivier states. "Today we want Omphalos. Close your eyes and picture yourself walking through the halls, into special rooms, past secret doors. The more you recall, the sharper the blueprints will be."

I glance at Mason. His face holds an excited expression. This must be something he's been dying to watch. Sarge's golden pools meet mine while he sits beside me, and that's the last thing I see before my eyes close and I'm lost in Omphalos.

I step off the O-train, crossing the barren landscape and pulling my ID card out to slide it through the lock of the back entrance. Through one set of doors, then the next, and I funnel out into the long, white hallway. Most of it looks the same, but as I pass each intersection, corner, turn, I clearly picture what each of the rooms are, and how many feet apart each one is.

This memory enhancer is doing most of the work. It's not like a simulation. It's not allowing me to picture walking through the facility, it's drudging up a specific memory and forcing me to relive it. So when I suddenly dip down a hallway I would never go, I know which nightmare this serum has dropped me into.

Not long before this memory, I stumbled upon a blueprint of Omphalos. I didn't think much of it, sitting on Ren's desk, but when she looked away, I studied it. She had just told me to kill my father, so I think I was looking for something, anything to utilize. Turns out there was a secret hallway, hidden door and all, in the middle of the facility. It was the spot that held the Brain.

I'd warned M about the Brain. It's a smart AI that's always watching and listening. I needed to see what it knew. The problem with the Brain is that it's a tattle tale, and its loyalties lie with its Headmistress. So I knew that unless I could bargain with a droid, I'd have to run away.

Ren had trusted me. She wanted me by her side through it all. But when I got to my father's house, held that gun to his head, I couldn't do it. He wasn't mad, or scared. No. His tired hazel eyes met mine and he said, "It's okay, son, do what you have to do," instead.

Something in me changed the day I'm now reliving in a hi-tech office in H.P.S Headquarters. The day I often relive in my sleep. I no longer wanted to be the man on top, I wanted to be the honorable man my father was. That wouldn't be possible if I stayed in the Force.

So I warned them to hide, to get out, that they'd most likely never see me again, and I marched straight to the Brain to see what it knew, and to wreak havoc on whatever I could before leaving.

I'm not sure why the serum enhanced this memory. Maybe it's the one that was the most prevalent in my head. But it's more than that. The memory itself isn't just enhanced. So are the emotions.

I'm angry, frustrated, tense, yet cool, calculating, collected. Even my body is physically reacting. By the time I get to the Brain, my body is hot and my breathing is ragged. It isn't until Mason's hands grab at me from reality and pull me away that I open my eyes. He looks at me with a confused expression.

Sarge is pressing into my side, hoping to calm me down. The blue grid plane that had been in front of me before is now a small scale 3D rendering of Mt. Diablo, the location of Omphalos. Inside each room is even the correct placement for machines. It's not complete, though. There are spots that remain without a grid; spots of black that have nothing to them.

"Is that all you need?" I ask. "It looks incomplete."

"For now, yes," Olivier answers me.

"Those holes are blanks in your memory. The scanner couldn't find anything for those areas." Mason fills me in. I nod, but my confusion is still present.

"The H.P.S is indebted to you for this information," the General thanks me. "We'll require you for multiple sessions to gain more insight."

"My..." I hesitate before I say *girlfriend* and readjust. "My friend, Amity, is stuck in there. Now that you have a modeled map, could we get some sort of extraction?"

"That is the goal, in due time," he answers.

"I was expecting something more finite, and soon." Staying calm is proving to be harder and harder as the minutes pass.

"Mr. Warin, it would be an unnecessary risk to our men to attempt such a thing this early, especially for one individual." The rage shoots into every fiber of my being within seconds.

"Your face is an unnecessary risk," I snap back at the leader, rolling my eyes.

"Luke!" Mason chides. "Are you five?"

"No, I'm pissed!" I'm struggling to keep the anger at bay, but what else is new. This whole thing is stupid. What the hell are they doing here if they can't get some one-armed kids and break M out of a measly little facility?

Mason glances toward the General, sending him off with a look. Despite my attitude, Olivier isn't fazed. It's a few seconds before Mason and I are alone.

"Look," he sighs, "I know Amity means a lot to you. She means a lot to me, too." His eyes are troubled as he speaks. It makes me want to punch his round head in. If he cared about M at all, he'd be doing everything he could to get to her. Instead, he's standing back like a coward, using *her* story. Sarge interrupts my wayward thoughts by nudging my balled up fist. It helps bring the anger down a notch or two. "We can't force the risk that we had taken last year on anyone. They won't let us through this time. Besides, look how it turned out for us."

"Loss is a byproduct of war," I spit. "It's what has to be done."

"Is that how you were able to justify being in the American Liberation Force, Mr. First Sergeant? I saw your badge, I saw your rank. Have you forgotten that *you* are the one that pulled the trigger on innocents? Quit making me out to be the bad guy here."

My anger goes from manageable to completely unhinged within a matter of seconds. There isn't enough time for Sarge to attempt to calm me down before I race toward Mason. My fist is about to connect to his face as my other one grips at the collar of his shirt, but something in his expression tells me this is exactly what he wants. It halts me.

I pause. "You want me to hit you," I realize aloud, letting him out of my grasp, backing away. He doesn't say anything. "Why?"

Silence persists for a few moments. Then, "Because you were right," he sighs. "I should be punished for Amity being in that facility." So he finally admits fault. Too little, too late. He's not going to get what he wants. He doesn't deserve that.

"You're such a coward," is what claws its way out of my mouth before my wavering filter can stop me.

"Luke, stop acting like you're the only one who has lost something!" Mason shouts, his face turning red. The sad, sorry tone his voice had taken earlier is now long gone.

"Yeah, well I lost my *every*thing." Sarge follows me out of the room, leaving Mason behind without another word. "He doesn't get it," I say, sighing as I look down into Sarge's golden eyes.

I never truly understood when M said Sarge made her feel less alone. I always thought she meant physically. But I get it now. Sarge is the only one who knows how I'm feeling because he lost his everything, too.

CHAPTER TWENTY-THREE ◦ AMITY

I ASK WHERE CHARLIE IS EVEN THOUGH I'LL GET NO ANSWER. I'm beginning to really worry about him. Those kids did him in pretty good.

The guard kicks my food tray toward me. Thankfully it's a sandwich, so nothing spills. "Infirmary."

Well, it's not good news, but it's not necessarily bad, either. At least the answer implies he's still alive.

The food looks plain and disgusting like any other day, and I choose to not eat again. I know I can't survive like this for much longer, but I'm struggling to decide if I care or not.

Being pushed through Limbo has doubled my guilt. I told the whole country that they should stop fighting because it's not what Emma would've wanted. I gave up Luke's plan for Aberdeen fairly easily to stop the pain, hoping that he actually listened to me and left me behind. Then, thinking that he would've actually left tears at me even more. I'm all over the place. The only redeemable thing I've done is give a last ditch effort of driving Luke away. The subtle warning that the officers were coming was all I could do. I don't think the Reaver picked up on it.

It bothers me that she's doing all this extra work with me. Just kill me. What is it that I could possibly help her with? I've come to the realization that it's Luke she wants. And there's nothing left for me to give her.

It's not long after lunch before I'm taken from my room by Atkins and strapped back into the Limbo chair. There's something different this time, though. There's a second chair, opposite me. Fear creeps up into my gut.

The speaker kicks on above me. "You led my men to an ambush," the Reaver spits through the microphone. "How did you sneak the lie through?" She had asked if Luke was expecting me. I told her yes. Then I was asked if he'd be alone. I answered the same.

"It wasn't a lie."

"Who is with him?" she demands. "Or was that even him?"

"You've been inside my head. You know exactly as much as I do." She's silent. I imagine her looking at me with a curious eye. The beep of the lie detector in the back isn't quiet at all, though. Atkins leans forward with his cattle prod and shocks me, causing my body to tense.

I know my answer to be false. She can't get me to reveal where he is or who he's with unless she finds the emotion surrounding it. I don't feel any guilt about Luke getting out of Aberdeen or even his plan of escape to Creyke Point, so unless I tell her outright, she's in the dark. That's the flaw with the MAP.

Learning that her officers stumbled onto some traps leaves me with a sense of optimism—something I thought I had to squander. This means that Luke had understood my warning and is, hopefully, safe.

"Don't make me ask again," the Reaver seethes.

"If he's not in Aberdeen, then I don't know where he is." The scanner in the back of the room screams at my lie once again. Damn it. I should've said that he could be anywhere; with anyone. My knowledge of Creyke Point made my phrase a lie.

The shock is more intense this time. It causes my jaw to lock and my teeth to clamp down, grinding on each other.

"Where is he?" the Reaver bellows through the speakers. "Where is my son?" *Son?*

I wish I could see her face right now. I can't believe she'd be so deranged as to believe Luke is her son, and even more crazy to think I'd believe it as well. "You're not Luke's mother," I start, but my voice fades before I'm able to say anything else. Every muscle in my body is exhausted.

The voice that filters into the room is the complete opposite of the tone that had shouted before. This response is calm; the switch almost instantaneous. "You've always thought yourself so clever, Miss Thorne. Always ahead of the game. But you're as dumb as every other commoner. You're nothing special." The Reaver steps through the door after a few seconds, making her way over to me. She puts her palms on either side of my body, leaning down so I catch a glimpse of her dark eyes.

"Luke's mother is dead," I challenge, keeping my voice as steady as possible. He told me the woman from the photo I'd seen last year wasn't his birth mom. His real mother had left him behind and was killed during the Undoing.

A playful look settles in the Reaver's eyes as she says, "Oh, but is she really?" A mischievous smile spreads across her face and, for a second, I believe her, because it's a spirit I've seen before. *No. This can't be.* Can it?

My mind races to all the signs. The pain she dealt with during my MAP, the countdown from five, the instantaneous switch of moods, the animosity towards Luke's father. Luke is her crux. *Luke is her son!*

"No," I say out loud, realization dawning on me. "No!"

It all smacks into me at once. I see clearly now that the bits of evil he fought so hard to get rid of is the same evil that resides in the monster in front of me. How could a mother cause all of this heartache for other children? How broken do you have to be?

"Tough pill to swallow?" she goads. "Didn't realize I was your mother-in-law?" Her voice is scratchy with wit; her tone utterly evil.

"Does he know?" My throat is dry. He would've told me if he knew, right? Or maybe he wouldn't. Maybe he told me his mother was dead to make it easier. He felt he was unworthy of my love; maybe it's because of some deep-seated mommy issues. I think I might be sick.

My question seems to throw the Reaver off her game. "No," she sighs.

This is the closest I've gotten to understanding her. I knew Luke was the reason I'm here, but I had gotten the why wrong. It's not Force related, or revenge. It's maternal.

"So, what?" I joke, pushing past the anxiety. "You want to study me, to see why your son loves me, so you can try and have that for yourself?"

"You never truly think before you speak, do you, vile girl?" she snaps. Yanking the prod from Atkins, she sends a sharp voltage through my skin. It stops me only for a second.

"There's something else you want from me, then?" I sneer, the taste of blood clinging to my teeth.

The Reaver stays quiet. I've got her hooked.

"Why spend so much time on me?" I finally ask, breaking the silence. What information could I possibly have that she doesn't have yet? She must have seen it all in my mind somehow.

"Among other things, Miss Thorne, you're a bug," the Reaver answers. "No matter what I've thrown at you, you've stayed true to who you are. You're a flaw in my system. I need to see what makes you tick. I need to make sure that whatever is going on inside of you can never happen inside of anyone else."

"So I'm a means to an end?" Clearly Luke plays more of a part in this than she's letting on, but I'll play into her game if it will give me answers.

"Nothing happens overnight. This is only the beginning," she reveals. "Galivanting through the streets, selecting random people to entrust with the future of Humanity, is reckless. You need to find the Exceptional and cultivate them. Even one tainted individual could ruin the whole bunch. But I try to exhaust everything I have before choosing to give up on a commoner. You must believe me."

"I can't."

The more I talk to this woman, the more puzzled I find myself. Piecing together her psyche is proving to be the greatest challenge yet. All I'm doing is sending myself further down the rabbit hole.

She lets out an exasperated sigh. "As much as I despise you, I think you might be the key. To Humanity. To Luke. To my Legacy." This woman is delusional. Nothing she's been saying has made any sense at all. "Now tell me where my son is."

I laugh a deep, hearty laugh for reasons unknown to me. "You really think he's going to love and accept you?" My words are harsh, and the strength they possess is clear as her face morphs into an expression of pain. "You asked him to kill his father. The man you can't even kill yourself. You're nothing more than a puppeteer, having these people do your dirty work. Your own *son*."

"Fine," she speaks after five seconds. "Go fetch Mr. Warin." The icy chill of her tongue leaves goosebumps to spread across my body. *Oh, no, what have I done?*

Giles enters the room quicker than anticipated, holding Luke's father by the arm. His hazel eyes lift and pass over mine before settling on the Reaver. "Ren, what a lovely surprise." His tone is dry, emotionless.

"I will give you one last chance to tell me where my son is, or you're going to die. Right here, right now." Panic flashes in my eyes, but Mr. Warin's stay calm.

"He doesn't know anything!" I cry, earning a swift shock from Atkins. My words divert his attention from his ex.

"And who is this?" he asks her.

"Oh," she sighs. "Our son's latest."

Mr. Warin's eyes grow wide at this news. He focuses back on the Reaver. "What the hell is going on here, Ren?" He's angry, now.

"Someone is going to tell me where my son is, or you die, Paul." She pulls a small gun out from her back. It was completely hidden. She turns to me, slightly. "I make no one do my dirty work." She pulls the trigger.

Despite the hyper silencer, the sound reverberates off the walls, slamming into my skull. *I got Luke's father killed. He's dead. He's dead because of me.* The hyperventilation that follows the incident is painful. It can't be stopped as Luke's father slinks to the floor like a sack of potatoes. My breath is nearly uncatchable while Giles and another officer pull him out of the room.

"Ready to talk?"

What's the point? Why should I talk? She should just kill me. I'm the cause of this. If I ever make it back to Luke, I'll have to tell him I killed his father. I'll have to tell him. I'll have to...

"Perhaps this will sway your decision."

Just as the Reaver finishes her sentence, a new Master Sergeant walks through the door, leading a young girl behind her.

At first, my eyebrows pull in with confusion and I'm momentarily left without answers. Is she going to kill a new person every time I refuse to talk? Why not kill me? But then my expression changes as recognition settles in my pupils.

"Aha. You know her, then?" There's smugness in the Reaver's voice that sends chills straight down my spine.

I'm now beginning to realize what the second chair is for. Luke's father was never the plan to derail me. This was.

The young girl is lead, scared and trembling, to the seat where she's locked in like I am. I know what this is. It's leverage. I'd miscalculated with my confidence. I never expected the Reaver would kill Luke's father; her ex. But now that she's knocked the wind out of me, she's going to do her worst. She knows my weakness. She knows I'll give her everything if she plays on my guilt. And what better way to do that than to kill the father of someone I love and use the girl that I fear I may have orphaned.

She's much older now, maybe fifteen, but the face is still the same as the happy, smiling, young girl from the crinkled old photograph. Her eyes are wide with fear, but she's holding her head high.

"Don't ruin this girl's chance at being exceptional." My voice is barely a whisper.

"This girl," the Reaver spits, "is one of the rebels from the first riot. One of those wenches that took down your poor Charlie." Her head is tilted like a dog ready to play, and the smile on her face suggests she's got something up her sleeve. Perhaps always asking about Charlie was a bad idea. *Damn it, Amity!* "She's an Amiteer." She says the word with disgust, cutting my thoughts out.

My face settles back into a look of confusion. *What's an Amiteer?* Is that what those kids are calling themselves?

"Do you think she'd still stand by you if she knew what kind of monster you are? What terrible things you've done?"

This time it's the girl's turn to be confused. She doesn't know I found her picture. She doesn't know I left someone important to her to die. She doesn't know about Trixie, or Zach, or Luke's father. The Reaver is right. If she knew, she wouldn't have risked her life for me.

"What does this have to do with Luke?" I ask. If I can keep the Reaver off her game, then perhaps I can save this girl from whatever plans are in store for her. Perhaps I can save her the way I couldn't save Luke's father.

"You're going to tell me where Lucas is, or you're going to watch this girl get tortured. Do you want the guilt of Paul's death *and* this girl's pain on your conscience?" The Reaver leans in close for only me to hear now. "Although, it would be rather satisfying to make you relive it over and over and over."

My mouth pops open in shock, but the girl doesn't miss a beat before crying, "Don't do it, Amity. I can take it!"

In the same breath, Atkins takes the prod and zaps the girl. Her eyes roll up into the back of her head for a few seconds, then her body relaxes as the prod is removed. "No," I silently cry.

"I promise," the girl breathes. "I'm fine."

Atkins grips her hair at the base of her neck, yanking her head back so she's staring up at him. Her cries of agony shoot pain into my chest. She's been here for a long time. She had to be exceptional enough to stay in Omphalos. So why did she falter? What caused her to believe in the rebels?

"Stop!" I cry.

"No!" the girl screams and is answered with a shock to her chest. Her head is still cocked back. She's suffered enough being here, going through Omphalos. She shouldn't have to suffer any more because of me.

"I'll tell you!"

"Amity, don't!" Atkins releases her hair and rears his arm back, slapping her across the face. I wince at the sound. How can he do this to a child?

"Come on, Miss Thorne," the Reaver pushes. "You're going to let this girl's blood drip on your hands?"

I don't take my eyes from the girl. She's begging me with hers to stay strong. And I want to. For her, for all the kids like her. For

Luke's father who did the same until he paid for it with his life. But as Atkins puts the prod to her skin again, I find myself unable to justify this chaos. The marks left on the girl's flesh will be constant reminders to her of this trauma. How could I live with myself knowing that I'm causing this girl irreparable damage?

"It's oh..." the girl starts, but doesn't get to finish before the prod is against her skin again.

"First you kill this girl's uncle, her only living relative; the one who raised her. Then you get your boyfriend's father killed. Now you're going to watch the poor sap get tortured?" The Reaver enunciates each sentence perfectly, making sure the girl hears exactly what she's saying.

"What?" the girl cries. The broken look in her eyes sends a single tear to drip down my cheek. I don't even know this girl's name. I don't know why she's here. But I hurt her uncle, and she's fighting for my cause despite me being the reason for so much death. Atkins shocks her again, leaving barely any time for the emotional pain to settle.

"I'm sorry," I choke out. It doesn't matter that her uncle attacked me. It doesn't matter that I have no idea if he's actually dead. It doesn't matter that I didn't pull the trigger on Luke's father, or hold the prod that shocked this girl. The only thing that matters now is that I've caused this girl, and so many others, to suffer.

Atkins shocks her again. And again. And again. There's no time in between for her to rest. Her winces, her cries, her shudders. They kill me.

"Stop!" I beg. "Please!" But Atkins doesn't stop.

"Will you cooperate?" the Reaver questions, no doubt enjoying the scene that's unfolding. "No more attitude. You'll do as I say?"

"Yes!" I cry. "Yes!" A steady flow of tears trail down my face now.

The Reaver holds her hand up to Atkins and he stops the

onslaught of shocks. The girl's body is covered in red burn marks, her eyelids are too heavy to keep her eyes open very wide.

I want to apologize to this girl for everything she's ever had to endure. I want to ease all of the pain I may have inadvertently caused. But no words come out of my throat. They get stuck inside until I feel I might choke on them.

"You're afraid," the Reaver whispers in my ear.

"What do I have to be afraid of?" My voice finally makes an appearance.

"That everyone will leave because they'll finally see how terrible you are. Like this girl has."

I don't respond. I'm not even sure what I'd say if I wanted to.

"I understand," she continues. "The only difference between me and you is that I've done all of this *for* them. Especially Lucas. You're a selfish little girl deep down, claiming to do the right thing when you're only stopping your own anguish. All you ever cause is chaos and destruction. Pain."

Her words cut into me. I don't want to believe her, but I'm exhausted and she's very convincing. She's right, though, isn't she? I'd do anything to stop the guilt that floods my chest and drowns me. Everything I've done up until this point has just led to more death, more disorder, more guilt.

The Reaver doesn't stop her onslaught of painful words. "Lucas will see what a monster you are, and you'll be as *undeserving* of him in his eyes as you think I am."

CHAPTER TWENTY-FOUR ○ LUKE

The air is fresh in my lungs. We've travelled above headquarters for a moment because it was beginning to feel stagnant below ground. Besides, what kind of life would a dog have if he didn't get to run outside?

Sarge is galivanting through the freshly cut field and loving every moment of it. I know the only thing that would make him happier would be to have M here, too. The same feeling plagues me as well.

The Service offers amenities a few miles away. They call it the Complex. Families can leave the compound at any time and enjoy parks, walking, swimming, hiking, sports, nature. The Complex is like the Community Clubhouse—the go-to. Bars, restaurants, events. They've been able to offer these things because they utilize underwater for housing. It's safer that way. There's a gym and some play areas in the bunker, too, but nothing beats breathing in the fresh air which is the major selling point with the Complex. It keeps you from going stir crazy.

It's something I've checked out before, with Lacy and her girlfriend, Sonya. Sonya being the ex-girlfriend of Zach, Amity's friend that sacrificed himself to save her from crazy cannibals in the forest over a year ago. I wish I could take that hurt from M, but some things are too painfully deep.

I was a bit surprised that Sonya swings both ways, but honestly Lacy and Sonya are good for each other. M will be happy to finally meet her after all Zach had told her. She still holds onto the notion that Sonya will help her process the grief. I hope for her sake that she will. Sonya and Lacy sure bonded over it.

I'm not one for socializing like they are, though, so Sarge and I meander our way through the woods instead. It's still fresh air and space from the dank underground that is H.P.S Headquarters. We don't get anywhere far before a loud, wailing siren sounds off. My body proves to stay calm, but suddenly my mind is all over the place. "Sarge!" I call. He's on the far edge of the field. He'll be over here in no time.

My brain is so focused on Sarge, making sure he gets back to me in one piece, that it doesn't process my name being called. When I feel the slight touch of someone behind me, my soldier survivalist switch is flipped, forcing me to whirl around, grabbing the person by the throat and instantly pointing my gun into their skull. Mason's blue puppy dog eyes stare terrified, yet annoyed, at me.

When reality finally clicks, I release him. By this point, Sarge is next to me, awaiting the next command. "What's happening?" I ask Mason, completely ignoring the fact that I almost blew his brains out.

"Looks like fighter jets?" Mason's not all that sure. He rubs his neck subconsciously from the pain. "We need to get to Headquarters, now."

"Are Lacy and Sonya safe?"

"If they're not in Compound One, they should be safe at the Complex."

I nod, following Mason to cross half of the large field back to the entrance. Once we're stepping into the hidden cave that leads to the elevator, tiny shouts fill my ears from a distance—barely heard above the wailing siren.

I turn around to see jets—Western American—roaring

through the sky. There's a large group of individuals running for their lives off in the distance. They are trying to make it back from the Complex.

"I thought you said the Complex was safe?" A metal door descends from the mouth of the cave, to protect the opening from any potential bombs or attacks. But at the rate it's going, the people running aren't going to make it.

"Everything shuts down and locks up. They could've been on the trails or in the shuttle." His eyebrows pull in, but he doesn't seem too concerned otherwise.

"We have to help them!" I shout, but before I get anywhere, Mason lunges to hold me back. "Let go!" I shove him away. Sarge takes off to do the same.

"Grab the dog!"

Mason and some other Service guards are grabbing at me now, pulling me into the cave and out of harm's way. "What if Lacy and Sonya are out there?"

Sarge is yelping, but I honestly have no idea why. Is it because he's being held back, too? I don't care. I want...no, I *need* to help these people.

"Let it go, Luke." Mason speaks through clenched teeth.

If my question about the girls has affected him in any way, he's not showing it. Three guys are struggling to hold me back, and probably double that to hold Sarge, and as the anger pushes the adrenaline further, their grip on me starts to slip.

But then the shots from a fighter jet spray the opening of the cave, causing me to stumble back. The jet circles around for the people. The innocents. No!

The door is practically closed now. The first line of victims are scrambling toward it, and I watch the looks of horror as their faces disappear behind the metal. One of them is a kid Sam's age.

Probably felt like life was finally picking up, only to watch it all be torn away again.

"Open the damn door!" I shout. Through the metal, the muffled bangs and screams filter into my ears. The anger claws its way back into my heart, completely taking over. "How could you leave those innocents to die like that?" My voice is raspy with rage.

"You and Sarge would've been killed!" He's not understanding the problem here. "Thanks for saving my life, Mason," he mocks, scoffing. I don't ever remember him having such an attitude.

"They needed help! And what did you do? You hid in the safety of this prison!" My body is radiating heat. Normally, Sarge would attempt to calm me down, but I think even he knows how volatile I'm becoming.

"They knew the risks of leaving the Compound. They can't be protected out in the open," Mason attempts to reason. Fuck this guy for trying to justify the cowardice of this place.

The rage boils until suddenly it can no longer be contained. This time, no one dares hold me back as I tackle Mason to the hard concrete. My fists connect to his face, but there's not an ounce of remorse to be found. The only thing that pulls me out of the mood is the sound of bombs rattling the base. The earth around us shakes. The screams outside are silenced.

I fall back onto the ground away from Mason. Two Service guards immediately run to help him up. Sarge nudges himself onto my lap.

"I stopped you from doing something stupid," Mason rasps. He spits blood tinged saliva out onto the floor. "This is what you should've done for Amity." There's a moment of silence before he scoffs. "You'll forgive me eventually."

He walks away without another word.

○   ○   ○

SARGE AND I have been holed up in our room. The tiny screams, the muffled bangs, the horrified looks, they won't stop invading my mind. I know that war is unfair. I know that sometimes sacrifice must be made. But this place is beginning to feel more like Western America every day that I'm stuck here with no help for M or Sam, or the innocents like them. Thankfully, Lacy and Sonya were safe in Compound One. That's the only thing that gives me solace through the night.

It isn't until the next morning that we're disturbed. My eyes are sandy and raw, and I don't remove my dead gaze from the ceiling. Sarge lifts his head from the bed, his tail beating hesitantly.

After a few moments of awkward silence, I turn my head to see Mason standing here. His lip is swollen, his left eye is red and busted. Shit. I really did a number on him. He stares at me with an incredulous look on his face. "If I'm able to get out of bed, you should be able to as well."

My eyes tumble in my skull. It makes me feel closer to M in some way. Then I slowly sit up, leaning my palms on the bed, pushing my chest forward. My voice still doesn't care to come forward, though. I can't help the anger that's present.

"You're still upset?" His good eyebrow shoots up before he scoffs. "It's a byproduct of war," he quotes my phrase from what feels like eons ago. When I don't reply, he sighs again. "Why is this any different than what you did to that girl in the woods?"

Sometimes I wonder if Mason Baines has a death wish. My body tenses as I tighten my grip on the edge of the bed. The mention of Trixie has my anger doubling by the second. Thankfully, Sarge gets to me first and stretches his head across my lap. "That was out of mercy." I say. My teeth are as tight as the rest of my body. There's no way he could justify the slaughter from yesterday as a mercy kill.

"No," he replies. "You did it to save the group and to help Amity." He may be partially correct. About M anyway. But killing Trixie is something that eats at me. I try not to think about it all that much because the memory often sucks me in, trapping me for hours.

"So you did it to save me? Pfft," I scoff.

"I did it for Amity," he states, matter-of-factly. This piques my interest. The questioning look on my face clues him in on my curiosity. "I got word of a possible extraction right before the sirens."

My throat closes a bit from shock, leaving me speechless. An extraction? Could this be true?

Mason shakes his head with disdain. "Is that justification enough?"

The truth is that my mind has moved on from the deaths. Just like that, I've moved on. I know that makes me a monster, but if it means I get to save M, then so be it. I'm going to Hell already, anyway. "Mason, look..."

"Save it," he cuts me off, slightly irritated. "This morning they confirmed it. More than ever, the H.P.S wants retribution for the attack. There's even a group of missionaries that agreed to go in for an extraction attempt." Sarge lifts his head from my lap, staring at Mason with the same intensity that I am.

"When?"

"A few days, maybe," he shares. "We've got to scout out the damage first." Silence. Then, "They are going to try and extract as many children as possible."

"What changed?" I'm keeping myself stoic, still unsure if this is all a sick joke. Besides the attack from yesterday, there's nothing else I can think of.

"The completion of Compound Two for starters. But Cateline found a way to cloak our men like all of the other equipment." Cateline Pierre is the brains behind the tech of the Service. She found a way to make humans appear invisible to those not wearing a special device. "We can be there in no time, and disappear all the same. They won't even know what's happening."

Hope shoots into my chest, but my face remains impassive. Sarge's tail beats wildly against the bed now. We could save M!

"What are the plans for getting inside once we're there?" I ask. I have to keep a clear head. The Force teaches you to lose all emotion; to forget about your old self and push past feelings. I blamed Ren for a long time for taking away my ability to love. But I realize that's not the case. Like M, I too felt that love was a weakness, that it only made it hurt worse when they left, and I wanted to go far. So I kept pushing. And the further up the ladder I climbed, the more Humanity I had to lose. Ren asked me to kill my father because she needed a cold-blooded right hand man leading the Force. Someone like her. But it's a good thing I came to my senses when I did. Now I'll use the love I feel to fight harder than ever before.

"That's your department." Mason breaks me out of my thoughts. "General Favager put you in charge of the team that goes in first." His neck tenses slightly as he speaks, alerting me to his disdain for the General's choice.

"Are you on the team?" I smirk at Mason, throwing him off balance with the switch of my mood.

"Yes and no." He's smug, but slightly irritated. "Follow me."

Mason leads as Sarge and I follow. We're headed toward the tech division. We go through an insane amount of checkpoints before eventually getting to the final barrier. It's a real set of doors, not a grid like most of the others. Mason scans his iris on the retinal scanner, and the doors slide open to reveal a ginormous room filled with hovercrafts, weapons, and small tech. The space is vast and very little of it isn't being used.

"I won't be with you physically," Mason says as he walks us deeper into the maze. "But you'll have these." He stops quickly, spinning to grab something off of a table to our right. It's a small case with two tiny dots in it.

"What is this?"

"WICS. Wirelessly Integrated Communication Systems." He peels one of the dots off and places it directly behind his earlobe. The second he pulls his finger away, the device disappears.

"Where did it go?" I don't want some technology seeping into me somehow. I don't want to ever give the Service the ability to make me into a mindless droid. Ren had talked about that before, and it seems pretty clear that the Service would have that capability as well.

"Nowhere!" He seems genuinely excited about the idea. His smile doesn't stretch as far as usual because of the beating. "It's Chameleon Tech. Perfectly color matching and, as far as we know, undetectable under current A.L.F standards. Cateline will be putting it into everything."

I reach out, picking up the other tab from the case. Then, I slowly place it behind my ear and look in the small mirror on the table. Nothing. I know it's there, but I can't see it. "How close do you have to be?"

"It's unlimited range!" Mason's eyes are alight with excitement. Or, the one not swollen closed is.

I get it. I was a broke kid from the slums of Parker, Arizona. I remember the feeling when seeing all of the Force technology for the first time. That stuff is nothing in comparison.

I nod at him and he peels off the device, returning it to its natural grey color. I do the same. "What about weapons?" I ask. The Guardianship may be behind on all this other crap, but the weapons they've developed are pretty decent. I watched M blast out the back of a dude's skull with only a sliver of target space and no formal training. That's pretty good. And who knows what they have now.

"Cateline is working on some special gear as we speak." Mason places the case back on the table. "But there will be time for that in the coming days. Come. Let's go meet your team."

Sarge and I follow Mason out of the room, through the long protective hallways of the tech division, and toward the residential division. Instead of going to the resident hangout, we go to the cafeteria. It's a casual spot for the most part, for friendly gatherings and informal meetings. It's a large, flat room with circular tables recessed into the floor. It's like the residential hangout spot, only these have a continuous plush booth surrounding each one and there are servers that come around to bring you food and drinks.

"Your team is over there." Mason points toward a group of four individuals sitting in one of the tables.

"Only four?" Not that I'm complaining. The less idiots I have to be in charge of, the better. But I find it hard to believe that the five of us—six with Mason in the background—will be able to pull off a heist this big.

"There will be more to get as many kids as possible, including the ones from the house you informed the General about, but those four will be going with you to open up Omphalos and rescue Amity," Mason clarifies.

I nod. Okay, that makes sense. I fail to keep my heartrate calm at the thought of Sam. Both M and Sam will be here soon. There will be time for emotions then.

"You should know it was volunteer only, so go easy on them." Mason raises his brow slightly. "They are doing this for you."

"Well, I…"

He interrupts me. "Not you," he interjects, a shit-eating grin on his face. "Sarge." He reaches out his hand, patting Sarge on the head. He then turns, walking away without another word. Jackass.

Sarge is sitting next to me, watching Mason as he leaves. I glance down and he catches my eye with a smile of his own kind. "Yeah, yeah, I get it. You're the favorite," I huff. His eyes soften at my words. "We'll see her soon," I assure him, placing my hand on his head. It's almost as if he nods at my words. "Now let's go meet the team."

CHAPTER TWENTY-FIVE ○ LUKE

The group quiets their conversations once Sarge and I walk up. There are three men and one woman. One of the guys instantly starts gushing over Sarge, and the others look up at me uncomfortably, waiting for their comrade to settle.

"Oh, my goodness, it's Sarge! He's so cute," the man says. "Isn't he just the cu..." He turns toward the woman to see the look of embarrassment on her face. He winces slightly as he flips his gaze to me. "Oh...sorry boss."

"What's your name?" He's the youngest here, probably a fresh adult. His hair holds the Baines' quality goldish blonde, but his eyes are a dark brown instead of an intense variation of blue. He's thin, unkempt, weak-looking, probably doesn't follow directions, basically a terrible choice for a soldier...STOP, Warin. You're being too harsh, start over.

"Axom Hoover," the kid says. Axom? So help me. I refrain from rolling my eyes. "First year H.P.S." So I was correct. Terrible choice for such an intense plan.

"First year Hoover," I nod slightly. "What are you trying to prove?" Clearly someone who volunteers for a dangerous mission right out of training to save someone they don't even know has something to prove. Axom looks at me with a sense of bewilderment and slight discomfort.

"Sir?" Axom speaks. Respectful, I'll give him that.

"What exactly are you trying to prove by being here?" I repeat, this time a bit harsher.

The others refuse to meet my eye, but Axom refuses to look away. There's something about him I like, but also that I despise. Hopefully his answer doesn't push us into a rocky start.

"Mr. Warin," he starts, standing. "My family was in the Complex during yesterday's events. Mason told us that his friend Amity might be the key we need to finally take down the Guardianship. And I'll do anything to make that happen."

Chills cover every inch of my body as Axom speaks, the memories of yesterday circling around in my head like a tornado. Sarge nudges his snout into my hand subtly, leaning his weight into my thigh. I nod, unable to rouse any words from within. Axom sits back down and the rest of the group reaches out to show that they are with him.

It is at this moment that my eyes are opened. These people have suffered and lost at the daggered hands of the Guardianship like so many others. They are willing to risk their life to help get M, but it's neither for me, nor for her…it's for them.

After a moment of silence, the other three team members make their introductions. The last two men are brothers. Trevor and Thomas are twenty-five and twenty-three respectively. After their mother got sick, their father paid good money to a coyote with contacts in the Slum trading world to lead them to safety. The coyote was an undercover member of the Service that gave her life for the boys. They were shy of adulthood by the time they made it to Creyke Point, but they pledged loyalty to the Service that so graciously saved them.

Charlotte is the brave woman who stepped forward when Olivier's Admirals recruited volunteers. Out of the whole team, she's the only non-Western American. She's also the only one that doesn't have some tragic backstory that's driving her. Charlotte is

M's age and she empathizes with the cause. She only hoped that someone would volunteer for her if she were in a similar position. I told her that M would in a heartbeat.

Once initial introductions are done, I give them my officer spiel. This includes my own short introduction and my training experience. I conveniently leave out being a part of the Force, blurring the lines to avoid any potential animosity. As I leader, I need them to trust and respect me. If I tell them about the Force, I'll lose everything right away.

When I'm done, I question them on their training. They lead me and Sarge through the bowels of the already deep underground Headquarters into a vast training gym of sorts. There's a large mat in the center for hand to hand combat, a shooting range off to the left, and an obstacle course to the right.

As we enter, there's a basket full of small dots or something that each of the team members take. They place them on their temples and the dot disappears.

"What's that?" I question. Is it WICS? I could see how they'd need that for team cooperative training, but anything else? Not so much.

They look at me as if I've somehow sprouted three heads. "It's the STARS equipment that all Service members wear?" Charlotte says it like a question, clearly wondering if I know anything.

"Oh, right, the STARS," I smirk, glancing down at Sarge to chuckle. Then I look up, my face growing serious in an instant. "What the fuck does that mean?"

Charlotte cowers slightly at my sudden shift of mood. Axom steps forward, speaking. "It stands for Stabilizing Target and Range Simulator," he clarifies. "It analyzes movement around us and controls our muscles to do what we're asking of them, even if our execution is less than ideal. It also allows us to see Chameleon Tech."

"Excuse me?" I stare at them in disbelief.

"Sir," Axom starts again, "it helps us…"

I hold my hand up to stop him. "I heard you. I'm wondering if any of you truly know how to fight?" The group stares at me silently, then Trevor steps forward.

"The STARS is a defensive advantage, but you still have to know offensive maneuvers, sir." Still, I'll take that as a no. They've only ever relied on technology to do their bidding. But they don't know anything about a true fight.

"Alright, toss them in the basket." At first, everyone is hesitant, trying to gauge if I'm truly being serious. Then they all slowly pick the STARS off, walking them back to the basket. "My father was a Marine," I say as they shuffle around me. "He taught me to rely on my wits, *not* technology. Because what happens when technology fails?"

A new voice comes from behind me. A soft, sweet sounding one. "I assure you, my technology never fails."

I turn to see a woman with deep blue eyes and dark hair pulled into a bun behind her head. She wears a long white lab coat with the name "Pierre" embroidered on the left flap. This must be Cateline. She's a lot younger than I'd anticipated for such a woman of excellence. For all that she's accomplished, I'd have guessed she was at least late thirties.

I return her playful smile with a smirk. "Sounds like a challenge to me."

Cateline tilts her head in question, but never loses her smile, as if to say, *this should be good*. "What did you have in mind?" Her tone is suggestive.

"Axom," I call. "Grab a STARS and meet me on the mat." The tingle of the impending fight has my adrenaline pumping already. Something about it makes excitement shoot through my veins.

"Sarge, you stay here and watch."

Axom and I meet in the center of the mat. "What are we doing, boss?" He's a bit nervous which only drives my confidence higher.

I project my voice outward so that everyone will hear it. "If I can keep up with Mr. Hoover here without any augmentation, then we do this my way." My eyes catch Cateline's, and they're the only ones in awe. Everyone else looks shocked. Except for Sarge. He's watching me with happy goldens.

"Sir," Axom starts, "I don't think you realize..."

"Axom," I interrupt him. "There is much for you to learn." I smirk. "Now shut up and fight me."

My father was a smart man. He taught me well. Technology is algorithms, patterns, cold contact with no emotion. There's no forced adrenaline—no drive for survival—when every move isn't truly your own. I learned to outsmart the MAPing machines, and I bargained with a droid. There's always a flaw somewhere and if you find it, you unlock a whole world where nothing can stop you. I just have to focus and figure out the door to this one. Although... I think I already have.

"Wait," I stop, backing out of my focus on Axom.

"What, you come to your senses already?" he goads.

"You wish," I answer. "I want to confirm that everyone in the Service wears these?" My mind instantly travels back to my first instance with the Service. That gentlemen outside of the wall in Shadow. I was able to get him into a position where I was in charge. He was never given a chance to think. So my theory is that the advantage is only as good as the person it's attached to. They may be able to move in a way they'd not be able to without it, but they have to have a sharp mind, and quick mental reflexes.

"Yeah," Charlotte answers. "Now let's see some ass-kicking!"

"My pleasure," I grin.

I'm light on my feet, bouncing back and forth on my toes. With my limited understanding, I can only assume how the STARS works. It must send a signal to the brain when it senses a threat, and in that same millisecond, the wearer has to tell it how it wants to respond. If you don't give the wearer enough time to think, they can't use it to their advantage.

First I start with a swift right hook at half power only to be expertly dodged. I'm slow, gaining a sense of the type of fighter that Axom is. His control of the STARS is impeccable. He waits until the last second to move his face out of the way. Axom steps back, hardly in a position to defend himself. Why would he worry if the STARS will do all the moving anyway?

I go in for a few more right hooks. Each time, Axom's head dips to the left at the last second. He's a very patterned fighter. He doesn't try to fight back. He's the type that lets his opponent get weak and sloppy before he'll step in.

The others are beginning to look at me as if I'm going crazy. But they don't realize I'm sizing up my opponent. The thing about fighting is to learn their weaknesses. My father taught me that long before Ren helped me perfect it. So this time, when I go in for the right hook, I stop short and send a quick left hook out of nowhere as the STARS leans Axom's head to dodge. Axom's mental reflex is quicker than I thought, and he jolts his head away, but not before I clip his left ear with my fist.

Axom gapes at me with surprise as he steps back this time. "I think that's the first time someone's got me." His astonishment leaves me dumbfounded. It's clear he's too comfortable. He was expecting the right hook over and over and got lazy.

So this time I go for the left and he's expecting it. I do a left, then a right. Then another right and a left. He expertly dodges each time, switching up his leans. He even tries to fight back, and the adrenaline pumping in my veins exhilarates me. Then I offer a left hook and attempt an uppercut with my right fist. He catches me, blocking my knuckles with his arm. His face holds a cocky smile.

"Nice try," he jokes. He thinks he has me. He thinks he's smarter.

I offer him my finest smirk before expertly flipping my hand around his wrist and grabbing his forearm with all my strength. I have him right where I want him. He can't escape, he's getting flustered. I pull down quickly, and jam my knee into his face. The STARS tenses his muscles as he tries to escape, but my grip is too strong. He doesn't know what to tell it, he doesn't have the survivalist knowledge that he needs.

Before he's able to process what's happening after the blow, I circle around, still holding him and place him in a chokehold. I'm sure the STARS is screaming in his head, telling him that a threat lurks nearby. "Tap out," I whisper. "Go ahead."

He does.

I release my hold on Axom, then raise my hands above my head in victory. He slams to his knees, holding his throat to catch his breath.

"I didn't want to take out my boss on the first day," he coughs. I chuckle, slapping him playfully, respectfully, on the back. Then I walk over to Cateline.

"Well done, Mr. Warin," she praises, her beaming smile almost blinding. Nothing like I'd be if I had been proven wrong. "You must work with me some time. Perhaps we could improve my designs." Her eyes hold a titillating gaze.

"Please, call me Luke," I insist. Mr. Warin drudges up terrible memories. "I'd be happy to, once this mission is over."

She nods. "Please let me know if there is anything I can do to help in the meantime."

"Actually," I say, after a few moments. "I've got some ideas."

CHAPTER TWENTY-SIX ○ LUKE

"You ready?" Mason peeks his head in the door to my residential pod.

My head bobs sternly. Sarge and I follow him to the tech division. Today is the day. I'll pick my weapons, get outfitted in the Chameleon Tech suit, and my team and I will go in and break M out.

Sarge is staying here with Mason. He doesn't know yet, and I have no idea how he'll react, but I won't put him in harm's way when we're this close. If shit goes south, I need him to be okay. My heart is already achy with stress about M and all the shit she's had to overcome. I won't add the potential loss of Sarge to her already gigantic list.

Once we're in the tech division, there's a massive spread of weapons laid out for me. Each weapon has to be registered to its user. It completely jams up if someone else tries to utilize it. So even if the enemy somehow finds it through the Chameleon Tech, they'd get absolutely nowhere with it. That's what we're doing now.

Cateline took my guns and made her own improvements, adding advanced safety features while staying true to their original wonder. She also put in a special order for a long range weapon of my choice. I'm giddy with anticipation.

Despite my taste for original hardware, there's only one gun I recognize on the table of a dozen or so. It's my father's 9mm

Beretta. I've been carrying it since I turned seventeen.

It's the gun he taught me how to shoot with. It's tight, accurate, reliable. With such precision machinery, it's well-built and meant to last a long time. Obviously.

It's great in all environments and conditions which is why it's perfect to have in every arsenal's collection. I can send a bullet through a body knowing it won't go too far beyond that because of its precise stopping power. This way, I know my bullets are only damaging who I want, and not the ones I don't. It's an all-around great short range weapon. And it's my fathers; probably the last piece of him I'll ever have.

It's restored now that Cateline has worked on it, but it still feels right and familiar when I hold it in my hand. I quickly register it to me and place it back in its normal spot in my waistband. An awful sense of unease is gone now that the gun is back with me.

Next up is the long range weapon I asked for: a Winchester .308. It's body is nothing like a normal one. This new design must be Cateline's doing. But still, the .308 is great for one hundred to two hundred yard shots all the way up to eight hundred or nine hundred if I really needed. I wanted an 1-6x24 scope for easier targeting. Longer mag? No thank you. A ten round mag is perfect. If you go any longer it tends to get in the way. Besides, I've never needed more rounds than that.

Then, the trigger. A feather trigger is best because you have less pull back when firing. I can hear my father drilling it into me now: Even a small amount of play can drastically change your trajectory.

Which leads me into rifling. The 1:7 rifling of the .308 gives way to perfect spiraling. Too much spin on a bullet over a long distance may offset your aim. Too little and it may lag. The .308 is the perfect choice for longer distances for this reason.

And finally, to improve it all that much more, a silencer.

Cateline's design of the silencer is ten times quieter than the hyper silencers that the Force has…and those are pretty damn quiet. You could use one of these guns right in front of someone and they'd never know unless they watched you pull the trigger. Which, coupled with Chameleon Tech, means that people will be dropping like flies and no one will know why. They won't even know which direction to search.

I register the gun to me and sling it over my shoulder. Mason suggests I pick another, new technologically advanced gun just in case. I know he's referring to when he lost control of his right arm last year, but I'm better than that. I have the ability to shoot with both, and if I lose both, well…there's nothing a gun will be able to do about that. I'll have to beat them with my limp arms.

But in order to keep the tension between us low, I select a simplistic pistol. It's basically a newer version of the Force weapons we encountered last year. Except this one has the better silencer, an on/off switch for Chameleon Tech, and even more precision when it comes to targeting.

The development of the memory serum in the Service paved the way to finding something for enhanced thoughts, and Cateline made it so each gun will secrete the correct amount to give your mind the boost it needs.

It's not a bad choice to have, especially in the event that someone from my team needs a gun. In that case, extra is always better, and it's perfect that it's fool-proof for them. Of course, that also means we'd have to complete a gun transfer. But in the grand scheme of things, the pros outweigh any con I can come up with about having it. Hell, even M may need something on the way out.

Once the weapons are picked and registered, Mason points me in the direction of the showers. Apparently the Service has a pre-mission ritual that helps performance. Cateline also believes the

Chameleon Tech fabric will work better if we're freshly clean with a closer shave of hair, so I'll be going through a complete makeover.

"Sarge," I address him, getting down on one knee so we're eye to eye. "You're going with Mason now." He regards me with curious golden eyes as I speak. His head tilts with confusion. "I'm getting her back," I put my hand on his head, petting him. He closes his eyes at the contact. "I'm going to get her, but you've gotta stay here. You've gotta trust me."

Sarge opens his eyes, and it's like a nod of understanding. I stand up. As I do, Sarge walks to Mason's side, sitting. The action makes me feel less guilty for leaving him behind. Especially since I'm breaking my promise to M.

I move in close to Mason, my lips basically touching his ear. "If anything happens to him," I warn, "I'll gut you."

"I'll keep him safe for *Amity*," he spits as I turn and walk away. I don't care that he won't take care of Sarge on my account. As long as he's safe, Mason can do it for any reason he wants; whatever helps him sleep at night.

Before I'm completely out of sight, Sarge lets out a solitary bark. I turn, and our eyes meet one last time. It's as if he's saying, *good luck,* or *get her back safe*. I nod to him.

Through the door is a sauna of sorts. It's all wood grain and steam. Much more my style compared to the bright, pristine whites of the Guardianship. I quickly strip down, leaving my clothes on a shelf by the door, and walk down the long corridor. With each step, I find myself feeling more and more relieved. By the time I'm at the end, my muscles are completely relaxed and my skin isn't as tight. This must be magical steam, scientifically enhanced somehow.

At the end of the hallway is a table with a mirror and a trimmer. I waste no time in shaving my head into a short buzzcut. Hopefully M will recognize me and not be too reminded of

Zach in the process. I don't want our reunion to be plagued with sadness.

The next step is into a small cubical. The door closes behind me, and shower heads come out of the walls and ceiling. Then, each one turns on, massaging my already relaxed muscles. There's a single giant square one above my head. It starts last and drips heavenly water down my body.

After a few minutes, the water turns white and I realize that it's automatically shooting soap out. My fingers fan through my hair and rub my scalp. Then the water turns clear again as it rinses me. The streams at my feet turn off first, then all of the heads begin turning off from bottom to top. The one above me is last to go.

The absence of water doesn't instantly chill my bones like I thought it would. Instead, my body is warm, refreshed, and relaxed. It's understandable why they have every Service member do this before a mission. I feel as though I could do anything.

When I step through the next door, there's a bunch of mechanical beams. They move like limbs; elbows, wrists, and hands with nimble fingers. Each holds something between their metal grips. I situate myself in the center of the room on a circle marked into the floor. Once I'm settled and still, the arms place spot-like devices strategically over my body. One on each foot, hip, hand, bicep. One at the base of my neck, one on my chest, and one directly on top of my head. It feels strange. Then, the arms back away.

I'm cleared to step through the next door to find an outfit of tight clothes folded neatly on a small table. Next to them is a full-body mirror. I'm careful not to disturb whatever the arms put on me as the shirt and pants are pulled on. The clothes have holes that match up with the placement of the devices. Everything sits flush against my skin as if nothing is even there. What's even more amazing is the fact that once the clothes are in place, the spots perfectly color match to the fabric; completely camouflaged.

As I head toward the mirror, something lights up on the glass. It's a sentence. *Touch the device on your chest.* Okay. My hand finds its way to the dot on my chest and when I touch it, somehow fabric rolls out of all the spots until I'm completely covered in it. At least, I think. I can't see a damn thing in the mirror anymore. I'm cloaked.

Another mechanical beam comes out of the floor and in its metal fingers it holds yet another device. This time, it places it on my right temple. As soon as the machine meets my skin, my body appears in the mirror again. The suit, now that I can see it, is tight, sleek, and looks like something a superhero would wear in a movie. It dons the H.P.S insignia in the middle of the chest, but everything else is plain except for the spots where the devices are. Now that I have the ability to see them, they stick out in stark black. The rest of the suit is deep blues, greens, and greys. Sort of shimmery with all the colors.

Once I'm done checking it out in the mirror, I step through the next door into the control room of Headquarters. We'll need to take the elevator up to the surface. So I do.

Suddenly my mind decides we're going to be in a sour mood. The last time I'd been in this area was when the massacre that plagued my ears went down.

Mason, Sarge, and the rest of the group are waiting for me by the opening. It's time to board the hovercraft and get on our way. No one else is cloaked right now so I touch the dot on my chest to make myself known.

We say our goodbyes, and then Mason hands me a STARS. "Take this for Amity," he says. "It's all we have."

I nod, then stick the STARS onto my other temple for safekeeping. Before leaving, I pat Sarge on the head one last time. The group and I board the hovercraft, but it takes entirely too long for them to settle into their seats. Then we're airborne. The adrenaline hits soon after we take off. I'm ready to see M again.

It's not long after we leave that we near our destination. "Remember to keep your Chameleon Tech on at all times," I address to the team. "The last edition of Force guns were produced to be idiot-proof. All the user had to do was think clearly about the target and the gun would do the rest. Who knows what new shit they have now. But they can't focus on you if they can't see you."

We're getting close now. Mt. Diablo can already be seen in the distance. This is it. M will be with us soon. Sarge is safe, back with Mason, and I hope she forgives me for leaving him behind. I didn't want to risk losing him.

We're about to touch down by the O-train when I share one last piece of advice. "Before we go," I start. "Please consider only killing for mercy." The team looks at me with slightly confused expressions. So, I elaborate. "I know it's hard to separate the Guardianship from the individual, but," I pause knowing I'm about to potentially lose the respect I need as a leader. Then, I speak anyway. "I was once a Force officer," I admit. The group is mostly shocked, but they haven't seemed to check out on me yet. "There are plenty of reasons people join, but it's almost never because they're a monster."

M had been the one that held this view. She believes that no one should be judged. I think I'm finally starting to believe that, too. I might have been made for battle, but that doesn't mean I have to hurt others. Maybe there's a way to be who I am without being a killer.

Everyone nods at me, but only Axom speaks up. "We're with you, boss."

CHAPTER TWENTY-SEVEN ○ AMITY

I PULL MYSELF OUT OF BED IN THE MORNING HOURS; CHECKING once again if Charlie is back. He's been gone for a few weeks now and I'm worried that they won't let him back...or worse.

But when my eyes adjust to the light, it's clear that Charlie's tall frame is standing in the doorway. Energy surges through me as I shoot out of bed to turn on the light. It's been way too long. I need to hear Charlie's voice.

His head tilts slightly once the light flickers on. The smile that spreads across my face is unstoppable when he subtly taps the button for the force field. "Charlie!"

"Miss Thorne," he wheezes, yet matches my smile. He must not be entirely fixed up yet. The thought instantly has me frowning, stopping me dead in my tracks. "What's wrong?" Charlie is concerned. Of course he is. He's a dad at heart. He doesn't care about his own feelings, he only cares about those around him.

But I'm a monster. Madame Keres was right. Charlie shouldn't care so much when I'm the reason he was hurt in the first place. "I didn't want to believe the Headmistress," I start. "But she's been right all along."

"Excuse me?" he questions. By now I've slowly lowered myself onto the ground. I'm hugging my knees to my chest. How can I explain to Charlie that I'm a monster?

My voice is strained as I speak. "I want to get rid of the parts

I hate, but I'm afraid there would be nothing left to love." I'm at fault for so many things that the weight is holding me completely immobile.

I stormed the facility and got Emma killed, which started with losing Zach, hurting Mason. I chose my blood over Trixie; I chose my life over Veronica's uncle—that's the name of the girl I watched get tortured. I got Luke's father killed, I left my own father, I left Sarge. I watched innocents die because of me. Charlie almost lost his life. The blood on my hands is dripping in waves.

Charlie's face holds a sad expression when he turns his head to the side, catching a glimpse of me. *Why'd you open up anyway, Amity? It's a waste of time.* "Miss Thorne, I may not be your father, but I imagine that wherever he is, he would be proud of you. I know I am." His voice is soft, reassuring. But the act of shocking, over and over, against my skin, against Veronica's, terrorizes my mind, sending the guilt deeper, internalizing, until it builds an impenetrable wall.

"Things don't actually get better, we just get used to the pain," I sigh. "And this body is a vessel for chaos."

"Miss Thorne!" Charlie chides. "There are plenty of people in this country, and even right here in this facility, that have your back. I know first-hand," he jokes, but the reminder of him being hurt is one more nail in the coffin for me. He clears his throat and begins again. This time, more serious. "The attack wasn't your fault."

"Of course you'd say that, Charlie. You're too nice. But I'm a monster," I cry. Charlie doesn't understand. He doesn't get that I'm at fault for all of it. For everything.

"Miss Thorne, listen to me." His voice gets quieter until I'm barely able to hear the hushed tones. "I knew they were coming."

What?

The look of confusion on my face must be apparent because

when Charlie tilts his head to the side to gauge my expression, he decides to clarify.

"There's resistance amongst the Force students here, and it was a plan to get you out. We couldn't tell you in case the Headmistress were to stumble upon it in your memories. I'm sorry you had to witness it, but they were only doing what they were told."

"Excuse me?" Suddenly I'm more alert. "You knew?"

"Yes," Charlie answers. "It was a diversion to hopefully help you escape." He chuckles lightly. This only mildly helps the guilt.

"Well, I'm sorry it was for nothing…" My voice fades.

"It's not for nothing, Amity. It's all for you," Charlie starts again. "I can't answer why you were the one they latched on to. I can't tell you why the Headmistress has decided you are the key. But what I can tell you is that there is so much more light in you than there is darkness. You just have to open the blinds."

Tears drip down my face while I sit in the middle of the floor, but I don't move. Charlie is a good man. And maybe he's right. There has to be an end in sight. The Reaver can break me down, toss me into darkness, and pray it leaves me blind, but the light will always shine through. A wise man once told me that love is not a weakness, and where the Reaver fights with hatred, I fight with love.

"Thank you," I tell him, and he turns his head to smile at me. Then, something changes. He lifts his hand to his ear, frowning. "What's wrong, Charlie?" I ask, sensing the shift in mood. My stomach instantly ties itself in knots.

"There's been a breach in the facility," he says. He turns around completely, abandoning his post. "I'm breaking you out." He's determined.

"What? No. What about your daughter?" I'm confused. I know he was a part of the plan before, but he still appeared as a loyal officer. He fooled me. But this? He can't come back from this.

"Miss Thorne, you need to promise me something." His voice is shaking. It makes me nervous. "Promise me that if things go south, you'll kill me."

"Charlie..." Tears well up in my eyes.

"I need you to promise me, Amity. They can't get me, or they'll use my daughter as a pawn."

The tears are fully dripping now, but I acquiesce. I've been in Limbo, I've felt what it's like to watch someone else get tortured, killed. I can't imagine how it would feel if that person was my own child. So I make a promise to Charlie that breaks my heart, but will help keep his whole.

"Good." He nods, handing me his gun. "Take this, and let's get out of here."

Charlie holds me by the arm as if I'm a prisoner being escorted. I wonder who has dared to come into Omphalos and tear it down. A small part of me—deep down—hopes it's Luke. What a bit of poetic justice for the Reaver to be burned by her own son. But another, more rational, part of me hopes Luke is as far away as possible, because if something were to happen to him, or Sarge, I don't know if I'd be able to come back from it.

We make it through two halls before sirens start blaring. By the third hallway, there are Force soldiers on the ground. The sight doesn't stop Charlie, and we trudge the never ending maze that is Omphalos.

"She's headed toward the exit!" It sounds like Giles. Charlie meets my eye, his pupils dilating with panic.

"Hurry!" It's the Reaver.

Before we're out of the hallway, the Reaver and Giles round one of the many corners. There are more officers coming from behind, so we can't turn around either. I won't let Charlie get hurt, and I don't want to kill him. Some quick thinking leaves me with a new plan.

"Let go of me, you A.L.F scum!" I shout, pulling against Charlie's grip. At first, he's confused and hurt, but then it seems to register once I shout again.

"Mr. Masters," the Reaver greets Charlie with a nod. "What do we have here?" Her eyes are dark as usual, but her flawless face is flushed; her perfect hair is out of place.

I'm still pulling against Charlie, but then he takes my arm, flopping me to the cold tiled floor face first. "Stop resisting, you good-for-nothing commoner!" he shouts.

Now I know why he looked so hurt. Even though it's all an act, hearing such a foul thing from Charlie's mouth cuts deep. He rests his foot on my back to keep me down.

"My apologies, Headmistress," Charlie says. "This troublesome whelp was trying to escape. I've retrieved her for you."

It's silent for a few seconds, and if I could see the Reaver's face, I'd bet her eyes are squinted with disbelief. She steps around me, circling behind Charlie's back. Her grey heels are the only thing in my view as she passes by. "Is that so?" she questions.

My body shudders beneath Charlie's boot at her tone. She doesn't believe him.

Suddenly, Charlie's seething groans fill my ears. His boot lifts off my back, allowing Giles to yank me from the floor. I'm left to see the Reaver holding Charlie by the base of the neck with her special device; the one that leaves a person immobile. My legs grow weak.

"Do you think I'm that dense, Mr. Masters?" She tightens her grip, making Charlie tense even worse at the pain. "There's no time to deal with you now." She nods to an officer behind her as she releases her hand from Charlie's neck. He's weak as she steps away from him. The other officer comes forward, rears back his fist, and slams his knuckles into Charlie's stomach.

"No!" I shout, jolting forward to help. Giles stops me before I get anywhere.

"Miss Thorne," Charlie huffs. "Promise." The officer continues his slow beating of Charlie as the Reaver rushes us away.

I dip quickly, attempting to remove myself from Giles's grasp. "Let me go!" I yank, making myself deadweight. My shoulder cries out in pain as Giles heaves me back up.

"Stand!" he booms.

Charlie's groans eat away at me, so I try harder. "No!" I shout. "Get off of me."

The Reaver stops and, this time, it's me who gets the device to the neck. I'm instantly limp and tense all at once. My shirt lifts, revealing a bit of skin. The cold air that rushes me is my clue.

"Oh?" she starts. "What do we have here?" The Reaver reaches into my waistband to pull out Charlie's gun. "Too bad your little plan didn't work." She releases her hold, dropping me to the ground with a hard thud. Giles then yanks my body up again, and we carry on as the Reaver tosses the weapon behind us.

"Charlie," I whisper as we turn the corner. I failed once again.

It's not long before we're running. I have a hard time keeping up. Everyone is tense. "Time is running out," Giles mentions to the Reaver once we stop. "They'll be on us any minute."

The Reaver shoots daggers at Giles while she clicks a tile in the wall. Suddenly, a keypad appears. *A hidden room?* She inputs a code and next thing I know, I'm being shuffled into an elevator.

Mere seconds pass and we're in a cushy office with stiff grey furniture. This must be the Reaver's domain. Giles shoves me onto one of the couches while the Reaver makes a beeline for a cabinet on the opposite side of the room. She pulls a glass bottle full of amber liquid from it, downing half its contents.

"Madame, we have to kill her," Giles implores.

The Reaver doesn't reply with words. Instead, she answers by slamming the heavy glass onto the small counter.

"You know why he's here," Giles pleads. "Killing her is the only option." *He?* Could it be Luke?

"No!" the Reaver shouts, not her usually-composed self. She swipes her arm angrily, sending the glass bottle flying before it shatters into a million pieces. "We can't."

"We can't wait them out!" he cries. "He won't leave without her and she can't get away again. People know her! It will be the Death of the Guardianship. All that we've worked for." Giles is nearly hysterical.

"That's exactly my point," the Reaver scoffs at Giles's lack of understanding. Her demeanor is calm all of sudden. She turns to walk toward him now. "We can't kill her, or we'll start a war. You know what happened the last time." Her voice is raw as she alludes to Emma's death.

I don't know what comes over me, but I cackle the most maniacally evil laugh. It cuts them off. "I hope you all burn in the Hell you've created," I say.

The Reaver's eyes darken, her frown creating harsh wrinkles on her face. Then she says, "There's one last thing to do." A look of determination settles upon her, and suddenly I'm chilled to the bone.

Giles looks shocked. "Do you mean...?"

"Yes, Marcus," she grins. "Drain her memories."

What?

CHAPTER TWENTY-EIGHT ○ LUKE

"We're going to need access to the control room," I say.

"You're going to need access to the whole facility," Mason retorts in my ear. Screw this guy. He's cushy in his little spot at Headquarters. Not like us here, the ones *actually* risking our lives for M. Being here drudges up so many unwanted memories. There's no need to be here longer than we have to.

The Chameleon Tech makes us invisible to the outside world, but unfortunately it's still possible to be heard. We're positioned by the base of the O-train steps, keeping our voices low to avoid alerting any patrols. Not that they could find us. "I'll have to use the door guard's credentials. I gave mine to Amity." Mine wouldn't have worked anyway, I'm sure.

We should be able to slip through no problem, but we'll need a code to match which means we either reveal ourselves and take it by force, or we wait around silently until the door guards switch. As leader, I decide on the former, because we don't have the kind of time needed for the latter and I'm much too impatient. Besides, we're the way in for the rest of the troops that are coming.

After some quick thinking, I settle on a plan. The team is going to silently knock out all of the patrols in the area while I make myself known to the guard at the door. A small part of me is worried that if Ren finds out we're coming, she'll put a Code Black on M the way she did to Emma last year; that she'd stage the same thing to happen to me as it did with her. I don't share this fear with the team.

Instead, when they tell me they're ready, I make my way over to the door guard. It feels strange walking straight through without anyone knowing I'm even here. As I pass by a seemingly lazy guard, I bump into him and stifle my laugh at his confused expression. Alright, no more games. I quiet my steps as I zero in on my target. He's staring straight out, his back to the deep hall that leads into the mountain. Sneaking around him, I position myself directly behind him.

"Wonderful weather we're having, aye?" The smirk can be heard in my voice while he jumps slightly, turning around to find a face to match the voice.

"Jesus, you snuck…" His face is devoid of color once he realizes that no one is behind him. "Hello?" His voice quivers. "Is someone there?"

"Yes," I respond. The guard jumps again, holding up his weapon. What he's aiming for isn't clear, though. I'm directly beside him. "Me."

As the word exits my mouth, I quickly tap on my chest, revealing myself. "What the…?" He tries to turn, to point his gun in my direction, but my hand is already blocking it as I deliver a sweet right hook to his face. The force causes him to loosen his grip, and I have no trouble yanking the gun away. I toss it behind me. Then, I quickly grab the guard, slap the Disengager onto his temple, and release him. I had asked Cateline for a special device that could jam all communication from a certain individual. Now he won't be able to alert anyone on the inside. "Hello?" he questions after his Code Red doesn't work.

"You have no one," my voice is sinister. "No one can hear you."

His eyes open with panic for a few moments, but then he turns to get help from the guards behind him. Only, my team has already knocked everyone out using a highly sedating shot from the Dreamroot that Nan had given M. I must admit that Cateline knows how to deliver.

Upon realization that he truly is alone, he spins toward me again, trembling in fear. "What are you?" he asks. "What do you want?"

"Your access to the facility," I say, moving closer.

Trevor and Thomas step forward, grabbing his arms, rendering him immobile. They kick the back of his legs out and he drops to his knees.

Of course, I believe he wets himself in the process because he can't see the men that hold him now. He thinks it's only me. I use this to my advantage and say, "You'll be able to help me with that, right?"

The man cowers as I move closer. He tilts his head away, silently begging for me to show mercy. He's shaking like a leaf, and I reach out to remove his ID. Joseph Seeger, three star Master Sergeant. Not bad. Axom and Charlotte are with us now; they watch with amusement.

"Thank you, Mr. Seeger," I do my best impression of Ren. "Now I'll be needing your code and then you'll be ready to take a nice nap."

"What?" He's full of fear again. He believes I'm going to kill him.

"Your code?" I repeat, stepping closer. Trevor and Thomas are doing a wonderful job of keeping him stuck. "Then I'll be long gone by the time you wake up." I choose not to be too torturous. His whole body relaxes once he realizes he won't actually be dying today.

"Six, five, seven, oh, nine, one," he states, speaking quickly. Gotcha.

"How do we know if he's telling the truth?" Axom asks, whispering quietly into my ear.

The smirk that spreads across my face is unstoppable. My team doesn't know the special orders I had asked Cateline to make. In my suit is a specialized lie detector. I had mentioned the ones that the Force uses and she was quickly able to develop something to implant into my outfit. There was no loud beep when he told me, so I know it's the truth. "Put him to sleep."

"Boss?" Axom asks again. But Thomas has the needle in his neck before I have to answer.

"Let's move." I tap the device on my chest, cloaking up once again. When we get to the door, I realize how much has been altered. This keypad is nothing like the original. The ID card presses gently against the pad, and a woman's voice fills the air.

"Seeger comma Joseph," it says. The image of the man unconscious behind us pops onto the screen. "Please enter your PIN." A pin pad appears, so I type the code. "Access denied," the robotic voice says. "Biometric measures unmatched."

Shit.

"He gave us the wrong number?" Charlotte asks, showing slight concern.

"I told you," Axom jumps in.

"No," I answer, seething. Suddenly I'm too angry to focus. "It was the wrong hand that typed it in." Ren must have added a third point of verification and here we are playing right into her game. If the Guardianship wasn't aware of our presence before, they are certainly being alerted by the Brain now. Fuck!

The rage is too much to bear. It needs to be let out; channeled into something that will help get us in. My eyes meet the guard sleeping soundly behind us and it's clear what must be done.

My legs carry me faster than I ever thought possible. The .308 is off my shoulder and in my hands in record time. My foot finds its way to Joseph's forearm while I click the secret button on my rifle to reveal a small stabbing knife. The butt of the instrument slams into his wrist with all of my rage as force behind it. Blood spurts everywhere. I grind the knife, then lift it to slam again. The cracking sound only drives me further as I repeatedly jam the gun, grind the knife, and pull, twisting with my foot. Until it finally snaps. I pick up the severed hand and make my way to the keypad, ignoring the worried expressions of those around me.

The PIN is entered again, this time with the correct fingerprints, and the light on the door blinks from red to green. Ha! Fuck you, Ren. Thankfully she didn't ask for it to be a living biometric reading. I open the door a crack, but before I let the rest of my team shuffle past me, I tell them they'll have to lead the way. The piece of flesh I now possess does not have Chameleon Tech capabilities and a floating hand is a way for people to locate us.

"I'll talk you through the way to the control room," Mason says to the whole group. They murmur their approvals and off we go. "Couldn't you have just taken his finger?" He directs his last words to me.

I place the device given to me by the H.P.S. in the door to keep it open for those coming after us, then settle into the back as my team takes the lead. Trevor, Thomas, Charlotte, Axom, then me. They make quick work of any guards that come in our path while Mason leads the way from his own control room. The pace at which we pass through the halls is astonishing, and it leaves me feeling hopeful that perhaps we haven't been compromised yet.

"The others are in now. They're about to start gathering children," Mason shares in my ear at the same time we make it to the control room. "Locate her and get her as fast as you can."

"No shit, Sherlock." The words come out before I'm able to stop myself. Joseph's hand is starting to get stiff by the time I need it for the PIN. I'm hoping Master Sergeants still have the privilege to access.

When the light goes from red to green, a sigh of relief escapes my lips. But I don't allow myself to get too hopeful. Deep down, it's hard to ignore the feeling that this is all some game.

The team takes out the guards and I immediately head to the panel. The action sends me back to when M and I were here last, and my heart beats wildly as a small modicum of fear creeps into my chest. Will M's file have a Code Black?

Just then, sirens sound throughout Omphalos. They are loud, making it hard to concentrate. On the maps along the walls, all of the marks that signify children are being rounded up. Somewhere in all this mess is M, and we have to get to her before someone else does.

An eternity passes before I find her file. Thankfully there's no official Code Black, but the whole place is on lockdown so it's doubtful they'd take the time to update it. I notice her room number. 204. Poor M.

Axom pulls out the Omniscient Circulation System (OCS), the Service's advanced form of the Relay, and it downloads her information. Then we race toward the location where the tracker places her. According to the map, it seems she's heading in our direction.

The adrenaline soars to new highs as we take off through the oh-so-familiar hallways. There are guards lying everywhere. Most, if not all, should be in a deep sleep, but some of these bodies are so mangled I find it hard to believe.

Mason says we'll be able to cut M off at the next turn. My legs move quicker, my heart beats faster. "Luke," Mason's voice filters through my mind again. I don't care enough to answer. But then:

"Boss?" Axom's voice pulls me from my running. I turn to find him stopped, a confused look plastered across his face.

"What?" I spit, harsher than intended. M is so close that I can feel it in my bones. Even this tiny delay is enough to surge anger through my body, and pity for the group that Sarge isn't here to at least try and keep me calm.

Mason sends the bad news to my head like a tidal wave of knives coming to stab at me. "Amity's location has changed."

CHAPTER TWENTY-NINE ○ LUKE

"Sir," Axom says as he pulls out the OCS. "It's true."

"Let me see that." I hold out my arm for the Relay, or OCS, whatever the hell it is. I'm too irate to care. Mason is right, Axom is right. We should've been able to cut her off by the end of the hallway, but now her tracker is showing her at the very top of the mountain.

The control I'd hoped to keep is lost, so as the device leaves my hand and smashes into the wall, I surprisingly don't feel bad. There's only one thing in the top of the mountain: Ren's office.

"Good thing they're basically indestructible." The sarcasm in Mason's voice is palpable, even through the WICS. It's not helping my anger any.

My mind is whirring. What are we going to do? There are entrances all over the place to get to her office, but I only know of one. The fact that M disappeared in this next hallway tells me there's one there as well. Even if we could somehow find it, you need a special code to start the elevator. Shit!

"What's the call, boss?" Charlotte's tender voice stands out against the blare of the sirens.

"Let me think!" I shout, pressing my palms to my forehead in hopes to push an idea from my skull somehow. Think, Warin, think! Fuck! Does it matter? Should we try my code anyway? Would it even still work?

"What's up there?" one of the brothers asks. Who knows which one is which when I'm seeing red.

Mason comes to the rescue, saying, "The Headmistress's office."

It's silent for a few moments before Axom speaks up. "She's gotta come down eventually, right?" His face holds a lopsided, hopeful smile and suddenly I feel like punching it off of him. But that won't serve any purpose other than to slow me down. Do I really care though? Shit, yes, you do, Warin.

Chaos shuffles all around us as officers come and go. Hopefully most of the kids are evacuated by now and are on their way to Compound Two. And better yet, hopefully the team in charge of Mama June's has gotten to them and Sam is already safe, waiting for me. It gives me a slight ease in anger, at least for a second.

"I've only been to her office once," I share with the group. "What are the odds that the code she gave me then still works?"

The group is silent, but Mason has no trouble answering. "They did last year," he reminds me.

Although he's correct, that was before they completely switched the systems. They use different cards now, and Ren doesn't give third chances so I doubt she'd have left it. Then it hits me. There's a window in her office. Ren always did enjoy a nice view. "Could we get up there from the outside?"

"What do you mean?" Mason questions.

"Her office has a window," I enlighten him. "It's a one way, so it'll take some time to locate, but maybe if half of us go that route, I can stay here with the other half and search for the hidden keypad."

Trevor speaks up now. "Thomas and I love climbing. The hovercraft should get us up there no problem. We'll search."

I nod to him, relieved. "It's bulletproof glass," I warn. "Once you actually find it, you'll have to tackle that challenge."

"Nothing is truly bulletproof unless the Service makes it."

Thomas smiles. "Let's go, brother."

They disappear around the corner. That leaves me, Axom, and Charlotte to scout the whole damn hallway for something hidden, something I'm not even sure will work anyway. This feels like a waste of time. It's hard to keep the helplessness from spreading through my chest. It won't get me anywhere, though, so it needs to be pushed out.

"What are we looking for, boss?" Axom wants to know. But I'm not quite sure how to answer it.

As far as I'm aware, each floor has two or three hidden elevators to get to Ren's office. This was a safety measure because that same elevator is the only one that travels directly to the O-train for a quick escape. This little tidbit of information is what leads me to believe that something terrible is going to happen. Ren could've gotten away. She could've taken M and left, faster than any of us would have been able to catch her. But she didn't. Why?

Either way, each entrance is completely hidden. Clicking a specific tile will reveal the keypad, then putting in a unique code with fingerprint verification is how the door opens. Only the Sergeant Major has access besides Ren. The Sergeant Major, and me.

"Well," I start. "Mason would you map out the duration to get to the nineteenth floor of the military wing?"

"Give me a second." I know where the hidden entrance is on that floor because it used to be my on-site suite. I'm not sure if it'll be faster than aimlessly searching this hallway, though. "Can you set the OCS down to scan? Hopefully it still works after its kiss with the wall."

"Axom," I order. He sets the OCS down, telling it to scan. After Mason receives it, he runs it through whatever software he needs to. "Well?" I'm impatient. We've already wasted too much time.

"Looks like power to the normal elevator is down and…" he

pauses, no doubt going through the information popping up for him. "The military wing seems to be blocked off. Unfortunately I think it'd be better to search for the door she went through."

"Spread out," I command. "Start pushing on all the tiles."

"All of them?" Axom groans.

"Yes." I shouldn't have to repeat myself, but so be it. There's no use arguing anyway. The hidden doors rarely have rhyme or reason when it comes to placement. Ren told me that sometimes they are low, and sometimes they are high. Some are at the end of a hall, but then others are in the middle. Before I ask the question on my mind, Charlotte asks for me.

"Do we have a last general location of the tracker?" She's smart. "It would help narrow things down."

"About a quarter of the way down?" Mason answers with a question.

The scoff that escapes my throat is unavoidable. We head to the general area of where we believe the elevator to be. It's still an enormous amount of tiles. "What's your problem with Mason?" Charlotte asks. Clearly she doesn't know how to mind her own damn business.

I think about answering. Mason would be none the wiser because of the way the WICS works. But instead, I end up completely ignoring her. "Get to work," I grumble before touching my fingertips to the cold tile. We're going to be here forever.

Time passes slowly as the three of us struggle to do anything of use. This all feels like a huge waste; like M is going to be upset that I'm not busting down every door to get to her. But my self-pity doesn't last for too long before one of the brothers sends good news into my brain. "We found the glass."

"How long until you think you could get in?" I ask, my voice desperate. Calm down, Warin. Keep a level head.

"Five minutes," one of them answers.

"Keep searching in the meantime," I order Axom and Charlotte. My mind is all over the place at the moment, so they'll have to pick up my slack for the next five minutes. This is it. M is so close. Once they get her, we can stop this and get to Creyke Point. We can…

"We're in, boss," Thomas says. Or Trevor. "But there's no one here."

No. That can't be. She's there. She has to be there! Suddenly, the rage is forming inside of me again, threatening to take control. I count down from five to keep my cool. It almost doesn't work. "What do you mean? Isn't her tracker there?"

"It looks like it," Axom answers.

"I'm sorry, Luke," says Charlotte. Her sad, sympathetic tone pisses me off. I don't want her to be sorry. But all the anger escapes me as a disturbing thought crosses my mind.

No. It can't be. "Is there…is there an arm laying anywhere?"

"Excuse me?"

"Just search the room for an arm! Maybe Ren misled us. Made us think Amity was still here even if she wasn't."

"Is it possible we got the wrong tracker?" Charlotte asks beside me.

"Trackers are linked to DNA," I share. "So, no. Each individual can only have one. This prevents people from playing the system. Her tracker is here." I pause. "She might not be with it, though."

"Wait!" Mason says, startling me. "She's below the mountain."

"There's nothing below the mountain," I argue. "Even the basement barely goes below ground."

"Take a look for yourself, jackass," he says. I hate his guts. "She is below the mountain, directly in line with where she was at the top. It's why I didn't catch it at first."

"Oh, for fucks sake." I frantically search the basement hallways for the secret keypad. It's hard when you can't tell which tiles you've tried and which ones you haven't. Everything looks the same.

"What good of a watchman are you if you can't keep watch?"

My head rolls back as I shout at the ceiling. The roar of my yell reverberates off the white walls. But then I see it. A small circle, barely noticeable on the perfect paint. It's definitely out of place, and a few paces to my left. It sits in the middle of the ceiling.

The mark brings me back to a conversation I'd had with Ren once. She was going on about the circle of life or something. How the circle is the most perfect shape and how it means Humanity should be perfect to prevent people from having shitty lives. It's not a coincidence that there's a random circle on the ceiling. This must be some sort of indication for the door.

It's in the middle of the ceiling, so does that tell me that it's in the middle of the wall? And which one? Left or right? Ugh! Damn you, Ren. "Charlotte," I get her attention, then point to the wall. "Try over there."

Charlotte takes one wall, I take the other. Only a minute passes before I hear, "Boss!"

I turn to find Charlotte with a beaming smile and a now exposed keypad. Yes! This is it. The last hope. I take a deep breath as I step toward it. Then my fingers tap the screen and I enter my code: My mom's birthday.

The tiles part and the elevator opens up. I should've known it would work. My mother and Ren share the same birthday, and she's too full of herself to remove the code.

Axom, Charlotte, and I step into the elevator. There's a small covered panel that I pry open. It houses a button with a brain on it. I push it, and we descend into the pits of Hell below us.

CHAPTER THIRTY ∘ AMITY

We enter the Reaver's private elevator once again, this time travelling below the basement, to a place I'm not sure is on any facility map. It's a dank, one room, prison-like cell with a single black pod in the middle. The scene looks like something straight out of a horror novel; ominous and eerie.

As we get closer, the floor opens up and a screen rises from the pits below us. This must be the controls. Knowing how the colors of the pods correspond to the torture on the inside, I hate to think how black matches with memory draining. *Is it painful?*

I chuckle to myself in the moment; a nervous laughter that's probably more of a survival response and less of an actual humor-based reaction. I'm about to lose all of my memories—everything that I've experienced in my life—and I'm questioning if it will be physically painful? What is wrong with me?

"Should I defend the office?" Giles asks. "It won't be long now before Golden Boy figures out his codes still work." There's a hint of disgust in his tone as he speaks. It must be Luke he's referring to. My heart does flips in my chest.

"Watch your attitude, Marcus," the Reaver seethes, shoving me forward as if I were the one that said it. "Strip, Miss Thorne."

"Excuse me?" I say at the same time Giles opens his mouth.

"Mistress, I've always had your back, but..." Giles fans his hands around. "How many times are we going to lose good men over your little pet?"

"Marcus," she warns through her teeth. "Strip!" she says back at me. She's getting irritated. Maybe I can use this to my advantage.

"He's betrayed you, but I haven't!" I've never seen Giles so desperate for attention or approval.

The Reaver turns away from me momentarily, pulling a small device from her pocket. Giles's eyes grow wide at the sight. "I will kill you right here, right now, if you say one more thing to undermine me. Is that clear?"

Giles feebly nods. *Is he shaking?*

"Good. Now get the O-train ready." Giles quickly leaves the way we came and the Reaver returns the device back into her pocket. When she sees I haven't taken my clothes off, her irritation nearly triples. "Don't make me cut the clothes off of you. You're going to want them in one piece."

What does she mean by that? My mind is circling, trying to make sense of the whole situation. *Is she expecting that I make it out of here?* Is that what she wants?

I strip down, slowly, until I'm completely bare. Then I'm pointed in the direction I'm supposed to be going.

This pod is different from the others. Instead of a tough bed, it has a pool of liquid. Black and murky, like a dirty swamp capable of concealing monsters. I hesitate slightly, but then place myself in. There's no wet feeling on my skin. It must be the same temperature as my body because it's like it's not even there.

Once I'm in the pod, the Reaver taps away at the monitor, and soon my legs are being held in place by some strange sensation coming from beneath them.

"Why did you leave him?" The goal is to work her up, stall her until Luke finds the way in. She's oddly calm for knowing he's coming. Besides, my curiosity has always gotten the better of me.

"What?"

"Why did you leave Luke behind? How can you claim to love him if you left him when he needed you?" My voice is raw with emotion. "He was a child!" I implore.

The Reaver ignores me now, still inputting information into the monitor.

"A child needs their mother!" I cry, and this time the tears flow from my eyes as if it's their job. I lost my mother. I know the sickness wasn't the most painful thing for her, it was leaving her children behind. Emma was young; she deserved to have her. I don't understand how any mother could just walk away from her own child. "You have no empathy!"

"It is *because* I am so empathetic that I am doing this. That I have done the things I've done," she screams in my face, quieting my drive to push her. "I know the darkest parts of Humanity. I have felt the deepest pits of despair because of Humanity's faults." I believe this is the closest I've seen into the Reaver's heart. Something, or someone, hurt her. She's been burned and for once, she wants to do the burning herself.

"Then why leave your son to feel the same?" The Reaver is silent for a few seconds. "You may as well tell me, since I'll lose it all anyway," I prod.

"My father left me as a young child." She opens up after what feels like an eternity. I'm shocked that my proposal worked. "I hated him for it. But then I realized it was my no good addict mother that was taking all the cash he left, and blowing it on whatever she could. He stopped coming around. She blamed me."

My heart actually splinters for a young Ren Keres. No child deserves to feel unwanted. Which still leaves me wondering why she would do the same for her own child. I don't dare speak up, though, for fear of stopping her.

"Could I blame the man for trying to build something of himself?" She turns away from me momentarily to wipe her eyes. "Why would such a prominent man want such a blemish on his record?" When she turns back, her eyes are glossed over. But it's only a few seconds before they dry up. "Their weaknesses made me strong," she says. "So after a while, I knew I needed to do the same for Lucas. No matter how much it hurt me." *What?* She softens.

"You left him because you wanted him to be strong?" I question. I can't say I fully understand. Luke is strong for many reasons, and I'd like to believe he'd still be strong if he didn't have to suffer such a loss. But even I know that losing a parent creates a tough outer shell; something that the Reaver believes is important.

"Precisely," she admits. "I had to suffer without my son, watch him grow up from a distance, all so that he would learn of the strength within himself. And now I want him by my side so that we can change Humanity together. It's all I wanted for me and my father, but he failed to see it."

"That's why you want him?" The Reaver always knows how to throw me off. "How do you know he wants the same?"

"He joined the cause, didn't he?" she argues. "We hit a bit of a misunderstanding, that's all."

"Why didn't you ask him to turn himself in? Why me?"

She ponders for a moment, then opens up once again. "He needs to make the choice on his own or it won't work. As for you? Well, you happened to have something I needed, plus a little extra." She smiles knowingly.

"You're sick!" is what slips out before I'm able stop myself.

"Is it so wrong for a mother to want her son to share the legacy she's creating? Parents should do everything they can to leave their children with a better world." The Reaver is begging me to understand. But then her features tighten up again as she snaps out of whatever fantasy land she was just in. "So even if they take your body, you'll be a shell. I won't let some stupid commoner that opened her legs for my son get in the way of my plans." She taps away at the monitor again, and suddenly my body is being pulled into place within the pod.

"Kill me!" I cry. "Why spend all this time?" I'm hyperventilating; downright hysterical.

"I wouldn't do that to Lucas," she says. "He'll have to leave you on his own. Hopefully you forgetting about him will speed up the process." She slams the lid of the pod down and the darkness swallows me up.

"No!" I cry into the void. "Just kill me! Just kill me, please!" Zach, Abby, Lacy, Mason, Luke, Sarge. They'll be gone. My family: My mother, father, Emma. All of them. It'll be like they never existed in my life.

"I told you before," the Reaver's voice swirls around me. "The Tainted can't be saved."

o o o

My body feels like it no longer exists. I'm floating into black nothingness. Sarge, Emma, Luke, Mason, the runaways. They're all here.

Time moves in slow motion backwards. At first, I'm able to remember why I'm in a pod at Omphalos, but then I'm just floating. The Reaver walks away from me instead of toward, the tracker is taken from my skin, and Giles leads me back to Burns. The commoners spit on me until I hide away in the forest.

My heart skips a beat as I'm walking with Sarge and Luke. Nan is here, alive, and then gone. Emma comes to life and so does Trixie. The pain is only momentary as the people I once knew and love are brought back only to be whisked away by force as if I've never known them at all.

One minute, Luke is in front of me, pressing his palm to my cheek, and the next he's just a whisper of a man I vaguely recognize. Who is this man in front of me now that walks away from our camp in the pitch black? Have I seen him before?

But then he's gone. Along with the rest of them. And it's just Sarge and I until I leave him in the woods behind my house to cry in my room over my dead mother. *I'm all alone*, I think. This is what it's like to be alone.

CHAPTER THIRTY-ONE ○ LUKE

I PULL M OUT OF THE POD, DISCONNECT THE TINY LEECH-LIKE synapses from in the water, and use my body as a shield for her naked form. "Here, put these on." I hand her the clothes she was wearing before; the god-awful plain grey outfit that everyone in the clutches of the Guardianship wears. I mentally kick myself for not kissing her or being more gentle, but that's war for you.

She's a doe-eyed beauty when she realizes she's naked, and nervously covers the parts of her she wishes to be concealed. It's almost as if she's embarrassed, like I've never seen her naked before. I'm not about to argue, though, because there are two others here with me now that she's currently unable to see.

Once she's dressed, I take the spare STARS, slowly attempting to press it on her temple. She jerks back as if I'm going to hurt her. My eyebrows pull in. "It's alright, M. I'm here now."

At the sound of her nickname, she looks up with a shocked expression. "I'm sorry, who are you?"

I chuckle, smirking at her. What a funny joke. It *has* felt like forever since I've last seen her. But her face never breaks out into a smile to match mine. Instead, it holds fear and distrust. "Amity, come on. Quit playing."

Her face crumples with confusion, her mouth is downturned. She looks around as if she's only now getting her bearings. "Where am I?" She appears genuinely puzzled. "Where's my father?

Where's Emma?" Her eyes connect with mine. They hold panic in the irises as her sister's name passes her lips. Oh, what did they do to you?

"Let's get you out of here," I repeat. My hand is held suspended in the air with the STARS sitting between my fingers. She's clearly terrified, but she's too stubborn to admit it.

"What is that?" she questions.

"M," but she cuts me off.

"Don't call me that." She rolls her eyes. Ouch, okay. Déjà vu?

"Amity," I start over, "we don't have a lot of time."

Axom speaks from behind me, startling M. "I thought you said she'd be leaping into your arms?"

"What was that?" M jumps, her eyes searching for the noise. Damn it, Axom.

"If you'd let me put this on you, you'd be able to see." I'm begging her with my gaze. This person is nothing like the Amity I've grown to love. This is someone different. This is someone that no longer sees me as an ally. If only I had the picture of Emma with me. Maybe then she would trust me.

An eternity passes before she gently nods, allowing me to put the STARS on her head. As my fingers brush her skin ever-so-lightly, her mouth parts, barely noticeable. It's a small action, but it helps keep me calm. Maybe the Amity I know is in there somewhere, hidden, covered; imprisoned.

"Woah," she says as her eyes focus on the two soldiers behind me. Axom waves like a dumbass, Charlotte smiles meagerly.

"What's taking so long, sir?" Thomas speaks from wherever in the facility he is now. Hopefully he and his brother are already out on the hovercraft.

Then, Mason cuts in. "Tell her you'll take her to Emma."

"Excuse me?" I say, clearly pissed at the idea.

"What?" M asks. I forgot that Mason's voice exists in my head only at the moment.

"Do it," Mason urges.

"Who's the leader of this team?" I seethe. M looks at me as if I've grown nine heads. Charlotte tells her I'm talking to someone else, then says we're wasting too much time and we need to go.

"What's happening here?" M finally shouts, stamping her foot like an errant toddler.

"Do it, Warin," Mason repeats.

I look into M's eyes and my heart explodes into a splintering mess. I've done a lot of bad things in my day. Terrible things, hurtful things. But lying to the woman I love about her dead sister seems like crossing a forbidden line.

Then my soldier brain kicks in, pushing all emotion aside. It loads the chamber, cocks the gun, and pulls the trigger. "We'll take you to Emma, but we have to hurry." The words taste awful in my mouth. They make me want to gag.

Her pupils dilate with fear, but she nods. We head toward the elevator, Axom and Charlotte in front, M, and then me trailing behind. Before we get there, M whirls around and says, "Just for the record, I don't trust you. But I'd do anything for Emma." My heart shatters again.

"I know," I choke out, willing her to understand.

She turns away and we load up the elevator. It's mere milliseconds before we're out into the basement. We're so close, so very close that the adrenaline picks up and flows through my bloodstream. The emotions are running wild in my head, so much is happening, that I fail to realize the trip sensor at the base of the exit before it's too late.

"Wait!"

Axom and Charlotte step out over the threshold of the door

and don't make it far before they're both crushed by falling rock; the STARS unable to send the warning fast enough. M screams as I lunge forward to grab her, but the pressure of the heavy earth crumbling is causing the walls to fall around us and we need to move. I have to forget my team. I have to push them out of my head and move on, like a soldier would.

"Mason," I say. "Find us a safe place."

I scoop M up into my arms and she clings to me as if I'll drop her. Mason gives directions in my ear. My lungs burn from the remnants of the fog still present and the dirt and dust swirling around us isn't helping. I'm trying to dodge falling tile and rock to make it back to the private elevator. I never thought I'd say this, but I thank everything that is holy that I'm wearing a STARS myself. It moves my tired muscles for me. But I can only keep this up for so long. We have to go below ground.

Once the elevator opens up, an explosion pushes us. Debris ricochets everywhere. "M!" I cry as we're shot forward into the cubicle. There's only enough time to see M completely limp against the walls before I lose consciousness.

CHAPTER THIRTY-TWO ○ LUKE

M is lying motionless in a stiff hospital bed. There are wires and tubes and beeps and tears. Sarge is resting his head on the mattress beside her, clearly upset that he can't be closer somehow. Lacy and Sonya are holding hands, doing some sort of prayer, on the visitor's love seat off to my left, and Mason is outside talking with the doctor.

Mason told me that Axom and Charlotte didn't make it. I figured as much, but the thought still kills me. They volunteered to help me and I failed them. I let my emotions get in the way. If I'd have been my usual, hard ass self, not distracted, I'd have seen the trap sooner. Maybe they'd still be alive.

Somehow I came out of this with only a few nasty scrapes along my back and a sprained wrist. Thankfully Sarge hadn't been with us. Mason alerted a rescue party to search the rubble and Sarge was their leader. They found both me and M unconscious. I recovered fairly quickly with the Service's help, but M's body is struggling.

My knuckles tense as I give the end of the bed a death grip, trying to keep my emotions in check. I'm a soldier; this stuff happens. We mourn quietly and move on, we bury it deep within us and we only dig it up once a year. But the truth is, if M dies, then nothing will be worth it for me anymore. She's my only family now. My emotions have already failed me. I don't need any more loss on my conscience.

If I had to choose, I'd have preferred her die a long time ago than be this close. Now I'm starting to empathize a bit more about how she felt getting so close to saving Emma. I wish we had the Service on our side when we attempted the first time. Maybe M wouldn't feel so broken if we'd been able to save her sister.

But I understand that wishful thinking isn't going to get me anywhere. So I clench my eyes shut and count to five. When I get to one, my muscles relax and I settle my gaze over M once more.

Who knows if she even feels the same way as me. When she didn't recognize me, it was like a harpoon shot straight into my gut. She said she didn't trust me. Ren must have tortured her mercilessly. There's no way she'd forget about me otherwise, right?

Mason sent scouts to look for Mark Thorne, the infamous propaganda writer and M's father. He's somewhere in the wilderness of Creyke Point. Apparently the guilt of his daughters' deaths weighed him down too far and he took off to be alone. They haven't found him since Mason learned that M was alive, and I sure as hell doubt Mark would want to see his daughter like this, but I could be wrong. Who knows if he even survived the bombs from a week ago.

M barely talked of her father, but I saw bits and pieces of his life while living in their house. She insisted we sleep in his room despite the fact that it was the worst location to be vulnerable in. This tells me more about her love for him than any story could. She'd occasionally sit outside Emma's bedroom door, her back to the old splintered wood, her face in her hands. It was hard for her to be around things of Emma's, but she wanted to be surrounded by things of her father's. It was her comfort.

I hope for M's sake that the scouts are able to find him soon. Alive. Because she *will* live, and she's going to need someone solid. If that someone can't be me for whatever reason, then her father sure as hell fits the bill better than anyone else.

A gentle hand on my back brings me into reality. I turn my eyes to meet Lacy's worried face. It's only then that I realize how tense and angry my whole body is. I release the bed, letting my arms hang limply at my sides.

"She's gonna be okay," Lacy comforts, but empty words mean nothing to me. What does she know? Instantly I'm angry, the rage tearing through my body, quickly tightening my muscles once more. Lacy must pick up on this because she says, "It's okay to feel scared. This is a safe space. Don't hold it in."

Scared? She thinks I'm scared? Pfft. I'm fucking terrified. I know M struggles with her guilt, but if she dies, my guilt will be stronger than ever. How selfish is it of me to want her to continue to suffer so that I could see her live and feel less of the guilt myself?

This thought loosens something inside of me, causing a single tear to break free and roll down my cheek. Damn it, Warin, you're weak!

I idly notice Sarge lift his head from the corner of my eye. He's torn between leaving M's side and ignoring this out of place emotion from his latest companion.

I swipe the tear from my face as Mason turns from the doctor, entering the room once again. Lacy gently rests her palm on my arm, below my shoulder, nodding to me with a soft smile, before Sonya takes her place beside her. We're all dripping with concern, nervous to hear Mason's recount.

The look on his round face leaves me apprehensive. I don't think she's going to die; I've seen that look on plenty of faces while soldiers lie in critical condition. No. This is something different. M isn't going to die...but something is terribly wrong.

"What did the doctor say?" Lacy jumps in first.

Mason's mouth pops open to speak, but then he closes it again.

His hand reaches behind his neck, a tell-tale sign he doesn't know what to say. My knuckles tense as fists ball up at my sides. "The... uh...report of her body showed heavy signs of torture, but they say she'll pull through."

Sonya and Lacy visibly relax beside me, pulling each other in for a sweet embrace. I, on the other hand, see straight through Mason. There's something he's having a hard time saying. "And?" I prompt.

The girls turn toward Mason quickly, immediately dropping their relief. Mason's eyes grow wide as he formulates the words in his head into a sentence spoken aloud. "The report of her brain, well..." His voice fades into the hums and beeps of the background.

Suddenly I'm hit with a realization. "Her memories were wiped." I don't know why I hadn't thought of it before. I guess I'd been caught up in the moment.

Mason nods uncomfortably.

There was one story about memory wiping. One. Ren used it on John Collins before she killed him. I'd almost completely forgotten about it. She told me that she had a plan for such a practice, but it needed to be perfected and should only be used as a last resort. John Collins was a simple case of trial gone wrong. Or so I thought at first.

The day I told my family they had to run, my father told me to find the files on John Collins. I thought it was out of place, but I held true to my promise. When I found the Brain, it gave me everything. The memory wiping report, the death certificate, there was even a playback of his memories hidden there, so anyone smart enough to find them could watch like a movie.

I downloaded everything I could find onto my Relay and I got the hell out of there as fast as I could. The following days on the run were full of discoveries.

John Collins had a gorgeous debutant wife and a beautifully perfect daughter. The most picture perfect life and family anyone could ask for. In the public's eye, he was a well-known family man.

Turns out, he wasn't so squeaky clean. John Collins had a daughter with a drug addict right before his career took off. This doesn't sit well with the perfect politician image, so he left. At first he would visit every so often, then he'd sent money. But eventually he stopped coming, and so did the cash.

His poor secret daughter grew up in poverty with a chip on her shoulder and a hatred for the flaws of Humanity. The flaws that cause you to abandon, to run, to lie, to cheat, to steal. That daughter was Ren.

I read her journals on how she felt, all attached to the reports, and it made sense as to why she wanted me to kill my father. It's because she killed her own.

But she tried everything she could to get him to love her. All in her own messed up way. The last attempt being to wipe his memories and rekindle the relationship from scratch. But she didn't foresee him losing everything and becoming a shell of a man. So when the rage took over, she killed him in front of his wife and daughter and sent them to live in a shithole for the rest of their miserable existences. It was this part of the report that made me realize how much Ren loves toying with the mind.

So what is it that Ren needed this time? She didn't kill M, which means her plan was foiled early, or it was never a part of the plan to begin with. And if the latter is the case, then what was she trying to hide? What is her game?

"Can't they bring them back?" Lacy's desperate question pulls me out of my messy memories. I know the answer to this, but I let Mason explain.

"Think of it like a hard drive. Those memories were transferred to another location. There is still a small inkling that they were there, but it's a wisp. The doctors injected her with a more potent serum than the one Luke's been witness to."

Lacy seems confused, but I understand perfectly. M is going to wake up and not be M. Or, at least, she'll be a different version than we're used to.

"So what's going to happen?" Sonya butts in, speaking for Lacy who, for once, is too stunned to say anything.

"She may have violent flashbacks from her past as a side effect, she may get all her memories back, she may only get pieces we'll have to help her connect. But in any case, it's the best they could do."

I want to hit him. For no other reason than to be a vessel that removes all of my anger. But punching Mason won't fix anything. I've got to take out the *precious* Headmistress.

"Could they see how far back she lost?" I ask. From the files I stole, I know that the process takes the most recent memories first. M was asking about Emma when I found her, but didn't remember me, which means she's lost anywhere between the last two to nine or ten years.

"The map of her brain seems to be processing trauma. Their best guess is six or so years, to just after her mother passed." Mason's voice sounds broken and it irks me. I don't have time to dwell on it long, though.

M's eyes flutter open. She looks around, confused. "Where am I? Where's my dad?" she asks, hoarsely. Her eyes grow wide. "Where's Emma?"

And so it begins.

ACKNOWLEDGEMENTS

A NEW BOOK MEANS A NEW SET OF ACKNOWLEDGEMENTS. Yet, having a small circle means that there will be plenty of the same people!

First, I want to thank my best friend Morgan. She worked her butt off to try and give me the feedback I was looking for even though she was exhausted more than half the time. I truly don't know what I would do without her. At this point it's become a ritual or superstition; something I must do before even considering a draft to be good. So, if you're reading it in this book and you think it's great, just know that someone out there named Morgan agrees with you.

I want to thank Jameson, always. He's been gone two years now (at the time of writing this) but he is still very much present in every word on every page.

I'm thankful for Matthew, for listening to me drone on and on. I tend to talk a lot about my book to anyone who will listen, and because he can't really get away from me, he's the (un)lucky individual that gets to hear it all. Though, I'm thankful that he wants to be a part of it.

A big thanks to Jess, for putting up with constant questions about word choice. I'm so glad she puts up with me and my continuous snapchat messages!

Thanks to my online friend, Squee (Randy), for helping me shape the synopsis, all while I forced him into the dark of not knowing what was to come. Once I finally allowed him to read it, he was such a massive help to the editing process. He's been a very big supporter and I'm so lucky to have him!

I'm thankful for my online friend, Jghost (Jamie), for giving me little bits of help with anything and everything I sent him. Most of the time it's out of the blue with no context, but he takes it like a champ and gives me exactly the types of advice I'm looking for.

Thanks to my enthusiastic editors, Clare, Stephanie, and Annelle. They've helped transform this book into a truly wonderful, polished work of art. I'm so blessed to have them in my corner!

I'm thankful for my grandmother, Lori, who tells me all the time that I should spend my life writing. It really does help to hear such a thing. I hope to do as she says, obviously. Besides, who wouldn't take grandma's advice?

A huge thank you to my mother, Amy, for her constant support and for being my biggest saleswoman! She really knows how to sling the books! Hopefully she does good work on this one as well. I've no doubt she'll shower her support twice as hard this time. Her kind words and love are what complete my soul.

Thanks to my dad, Marty, for always allowing me the time to focus on my writing even when I have obligations elsewhere! It was through him that I found my love of writing and I wouldn't be where I am now without him.

A massive thank you to my sister, Stephanie, who once again designed a perfect book. She knows the perfect banter to help me when I'm feeling stuck, and is the perfect amount of different to give me the fresh view I need. She's always been there for me every step of the way and I couldn't ask for a better lifetime friend.

And last, but certainly not least, I'd like to thank GetCovers and the wonderful team that has yet again delivered such a perfect cover design for the second book of this series!

A MILLION TIMES, THANK YOU TO ALL!